the Reluctant Muslim

INTRIGUE, MURDER AND ROMANCE
IN MARSEILLE

ALEXANDER LOGAN

Best Wishes

Clare & Matthew

Love & Kisses

B A Logan

Published 2015. The Reluctant Muslim ISBN 978-1-519-74688-7
Re-published 2017
Printed by YourBooks.co.nz
ISBN: 978-0-473-41813-7 (pbk.)

Project management by Wild Side Design - wildsidedesign.net

Go and catch a falling star,
Get with child a mandrake root,
Tell me where all past years are,
Or who cleft the devil's foot,
Teach me to hear mermaids singing,
Or to keep off envy's stinging,
And find
What wind
Serves to advance an honest mind.

John Donne

Prologue

It was August 1998. The sun sat low in the sky. Ten thousand men, fewer women and still fewer children were gathered on the hot concrete terraces of Ghazi Stadium. For nearly an hour they had been listening to a religious leader preach, and read from the Qur'an over four crackling and dissonant loudspeakers. Hardly listening; they heard without comprehension. The most recent delivery of Taliban justice was being enacted; two men and one woman were to be offered up to the judgement of Allah.

The prisoners were driven across the parched field on the deck of a modern white Toyota pick-up to the southern goalposts: the place of execution. With their hands tied at the elbow, the condemned were compelled to jump awkwardly from the pick-up. Immediately, one of the prisoners was thrust onto the dry dusty earth. Two executioners in white kaftans, without any obvious warning, cut off the prisoner's right hand with one sweeping blow from a scimitar, flashing in the sunlight as it went down. He was a thief. The cries of the hapless creature were annulled forever, on earth and in heaven, by the cry 'Allahu Akbar' from the unhearing crowd.

The second prisoner was made to lie down beside his quietly moaning collaborator. He fared no better. His foot was removed, with more difficulty than his fellow victim's hand, by the bloody, shining and righteous scimitar. The goss in the crowd was that he had been gambling on the outcome of a local football match. He had the temerity to win his bet and the spoilsport loser reported him.

The woman was forced to watch as justice was distributed according to Allah's perfect will. Wearing a light blue burka, her erect and unmoving posture suggested a defiance that had been denied the men.

Stains across the back of the burka could only have been blood from the wounds of a recent whipping. The offending hand and foot were hung on the crossbar of the goal.

The blue cloudless sky and the bright sunlight made it difficult for the twenty-year-old Minnah to comprehend the horror of the scene spilling out on to the sports ground. Having just graduated from university in France, it was as though she had missed out on a decoding process that permitted her to live with understanding on another planet. Bad as it had been, this was not the Kabul she remembered when the Russians had been in control. Justice then was hardly endemic, but neither had injustice been universal.

Now, against her better judgement, she was watching such dreadful pathos with an uncle who had fought for the defeated Northern Alliance. Even though she was a French citizen, Minnah was an unmarried woman and consequently could not have been in the stadium alone. Her brother, Amadullah, was still in Mazar-e-Sharif even though it had fallen to the Taliban weeks before. A fearful surge of anguish gripped her stomach as she thought of what could happen to him.

It was agonising to discover that the women standing in the dusty goal mouth of the sports ground was her old teacher and friend, Afifa. Afifa had continued to teach some girls in her illegal class. She had refused to accept that it was against the will of Allah for girls to be educated. Quite reasonably, in the context of the new religious logic, Afifa was charged with adultery and sentenced to death. The dreadful irony was not lost on Minnah; 'Afifa' meant chaste.

The three accursed creatures were forced to kneel in the penalty area of the football field and bow their heads. Minnah wondered if the symbolism was accidental. It had to be; it was altogether too subtle. Three executioners, each with a ubiquitous ever ready Kalashnikov, stood behind the condemned. Each fired, with what had to be an infernal cacophony, two rounds into the head of each kneeling victim, the woman last. Again, the cry came, 'Allahu Akbar'.

A rush of confused emotions surged through Minnah's body, a swelling black anger rushed to assert its power. Around the ground, compassion dried up as readily as the arid earth drank up the dusty brown blood from the prisoners' wounds. Islam, her Islam, had been turned into a travesty. Indeed, had she not seen the horror spin out before her, Minnah would have declared such an execution in Afghanistan impossible. Where would Afifa find justice now? Surely there must be a higher court somewhere.

Overwhelmed by a debilitating muddle of anger and grief, Minnah filed out of the grounds, tears blurring her vision. She hoped, very soon, she would wake up from a terrible dream. Her university friends, who she had seen only a few days ago, shrivelled from her consciousness like ripening fruit deprived of water. It wouldn't have taken an astute observer to imagine how that day's dark example of justice in Kabul sunshine would shape this young woman's educated and aching heart.

I

"You ever been on time for anything, Roger? You're late again… half an hour. You're lucky I'm patient. I've changed the booking. You've got twenty minutes."

"Sorry Tom, you know how it is. Everything takes longer than it should. Bloody technology. Remember all that buzz about the great technological revolution when we were at school, free time coming out our ears. We weren't taught how to cope with all the leisure in the utopia bound to come. I dreamed of all the booze and sex I'd be getting. I sucked it up. Now we work faster and harder and think we're going slower. I'd say technology was the devil's deception but that would give you an excuse for one of your theological smoke-screens."

"He is, you might recall, the father of lies. Okay I'm placated. I'll turn my mobile off. Will that help?"

"Not much."

It was happening again. Roger nearly always moved from defence to attack so effortlessly it seemed churlish to oppose him. His excuses, Tom was quite sure, were vain explanations muddled by his benign dissembling imagination. But it was small beer. Tom was not offended, and, anyway, half an hour would hardly bring the world to an end.

Tom's faith had the fire of youthful enthusiasm no longer. Nevertheless, he hoped the theology of grace might remain the quiet guardian of his soul. He was sometimes thankful. After all, he came to medicine guided by a conscience informed by the transcendent. Both his parents were doctors. At thirty-nine he treated them with affection, and he certainly loved his sister, Ruth, whom he saw all too seldom.

Roger was a property developer who was making far too much money. Tom wasn't envious, Although, to give Roger credit, he seldom said anything about money. But then fish, comfortably swimming, probably didn't talk much about water. Money, Tom was sure, would only be worthy of conversation to Roger if he lost it.

Squash was the glue of their friendship. They loved playing, twice a week. It was the movement, the dripping salty sweat, the satisfying thwack of the ball on the concrete, and the sheer joy of a winning shot. And then there was the glorious tingling of drying the body with a clean towel after the shower. Good beer always tasted better. Both men liked to believe they were connoisseurs.

They were equally skilful on the squash court. That's what made the contest so much fun. The game and the winning were important. It worked two ways. Each found it satisfying to know when you are playing your hardest, your opponent is forced to do the same. That insight nurtured their friendship, although they seldom saw each other outside the squash court complex. Two or three times a year they would go out for a quiet meal together with their wives. Occasionally they were in each other's house, and then only briefly.

Maybe their bond was rooted in the masculine need for competition, neither really thought it worthwhile to care. But their friendship had an intimacy more intense than either felt inclined to speak about. There was no need. Roger was a sceptic, not a cynic, but he was an agnostic without making an issue of it. He seldom thought about it. Tom thought about it all the time.

"Residual guilt, that's your problem. You're the Protestant version of a lapsed Irish Catholic: still guilty and haunted by the vindictive God who doesn't exist. It's just a story. Life's just a story." Roger had said this more than once. But he was far too successful at making money to think the observation significant. The mind lubricated by money is seldom critical and 'esoterica' religious or academic, so he claimed, got in the way of good decision making.

"Well maybe, but if life is just a story there must be a story teller."

"Perhaps, but my story is going okay."

Roger kept his wife, Brenda, and children happy with lots of goodies. Somewhere in the unexamined tidal shallows of his soul, he might have thought it couldn't possibly last. It wasn't that there was sub-conscious bribery going on. No, it was all very simple. He loved his wife and both his kids so he bought them things. He enjoyed buying them things. The days passed and the money kept coming. No worries.

Tom was more complicated. He wasn't married, not quite. Although if he allowed the theology of his youth to seduce his power to enjoy life, as Roger claimed, he had been married several times. He admitted to serial fornication, but not adultery.

"There's no bloody difference in your world, mate. I went to Sunday school too, you know. One of the last before it became dodgy in the real world. I'm still not seduced by all the post-modern waffle."

Occasionally, Roger's logic worried Tom. He remembered Kaye. He had treated her badly by any standard. Not that she had ever complained. Regret, even a kind of guilt, had been seeping into his psyche over recent weeks without invitation. But then, guilt was like fear; it didn't need an invitation. Maybe Roger had a point. Kaye had loved him and he had taken advantage of her. He hadn't really appreciated her. A young man is reluctant to smother his lust.

They had lived together for three years before she became a well-known newspaper and TV journalist. He wished sometimes that he could see her and say, "Look Kaye, I know we were young and unthinking, but I didn't treat you well. I took you for granted too often. I used you. I'm sorry. I don't want to go into detail, but I'm sure you know what I'm talking about." And maybe he would add, "I heard you've left your husband and that he'd been a bastard."

He anticipated her response with the rising hope of self-indulgence, "Oh, Tom, we all do dumb things when we're young. Yes, I was divorced last year. Perhaps we could catch up. It's been such a long time."

"Right, you up for it then? I'm feeling sharp today. Frustration does that to me." Roger had his squash gear on.

"I'm ready. The waiting has fired me up. You'd better be ready for a hiding."

"Some chance. Not today mate. Best of five?"

"Sure."

It took Roger and Tom exactly three minutes to get on the court for the warm up: some stretching, a bit of feinting and 'good shot' camaraderie. Then time for business.

Roger served. Tom returned with a rather nice drop shot in the right-hand corner. Roger got there but hit it too hard. The bounce was too tempting. Tom dropped the ball beautifully in the left corner: first blood before the sweat.

They had been playing for thirty-five minutes with the score at two games each. Both men were sweating profusely, and making frequent use of their towels with various boosters of necessary invective. They were 'grinning like village idiots', a description from Roger's wife who had recently appeared at a club competition. Both players seemed to think that portrayal a compliment.

"Bugger," grunted Roger as he hit the tin. It was 5-6, he was one point behind. Tom served, but Roger managed an immaculate return. He was in the hunt. The exchange lasted too long for Tom, and Roger drew level. But that was it. The loss stung Tom into action. Before Roger could recover, he was down by two points, and it was all over. It was time for a drink.

"You were bloody lucky, you tin-ass," said Roger in the shower.

"Ah Roger, credit where credit's due."

"No chance. Next time it'll be a real game."

"Can't wait."

"See you at the bar."

"Man, this beer's good," Roger said to nobody. He was still

sweating despite a coldish shower and five minutes sitting at a table in the bar waiting for Tom to finish his excessive cooling down procedures. Roger could never be bothered to take the time to cool down properly, so he continued to sweat while Tom looked refreshed.

"Boy, your face is even redder than usual. You haven't got hypertension, have you? Perhaps you should see your doctor."

"Funny, you know I haven't. Carter's my doctor and he's one of your seedy mates. I bet he tells you all about me. Let's hope I never catch one of those naughty diseases; there's not much chance."

"I hope not. Brenda's too good for you."

"I guess she is. But she has a good life. None of us is checking the bank balance every day. The kids think skiing and sailing holidays are entitlements built into the business of living. New Zealand next winter; Queenstown and Coronet Peak. It's costing me an arm and both legs although I've managed to get cheap flights across the Tasman."

"Enjoy it while you've got it. Life doesn't come with a guarantee."

The cliché wasn't missed, but Roger overlooked it. He knew Tom. There was a Puritan in there not really wanting to come out.

"I've never thought it did. I try not to take things for granted. I suppose I should be thankful, but I've worked bloody hard. Property development isn't the most secure of occupations. I know that. But I'm out of debt now. That's the good news but I'm tempted to take on a new project. Could be a couple of 'mil' in it."

"If I were to dream about money, that's the amount I'd dream about."

"I know. Don't think I didn't pick up your sarcasm, you pious bugger."

For a moment, both men looked directly into each other's eyes. Neither knew what he was looking for.

"Okay, avarice is your sin and hypocrisy is mine. I'll go along with that." Tom grinned, not sure he meant what he said. But it seemed an easy way forward. "Another beer?"

"Why not? This is very good stuff."

"It's new. The manager has a brother who brews it, one of the new boutiques on the market: great after taste, crazy price."

"I bet. It's still good, better even: you paid for it."

"Say, you ever going to get married, Tom?"

"What do you mean? Where did that come from? You've never taken an interest in my love life before."

"I was just thinking. You've got too much nervous energy. You might be easier to beat if you had a few good nights in the pit with a sexy bird."

Tom was not impressed, "On the other hand, I might be better and, anyway, it's none of your business. How do you know?"

"Maybe not. I was just wondering."

"Well keep wondering. I've taken a vow of chastity."

"Of course, you have. You've always had some funny religious ideas. Another beer?"

"No thanks… time for me to go."

"Already?"

"Well yes, I have some case notes to write up before I forget."

"Wednesday then, get ready for a licking."

II

Maybe it was because of Roger's somewhat self-righteous accusation of hypocrisy, but Tom couldn't get Kaye out of his mind. Why on earth was he thinking about her now? He hadn't seen her for almost four years, not since the journalism awards in 2014. Her delicious body had shimmered in the lights that evening as it did now in his mind. She might still be living in that trendy pad of hers, having kicked out that card-board cut-out of a husband. Phone her? Why not? She might have kept the old number.

The phone rang five times. "Hello, this is Kaye. I'm sorry I can't take your call right now. Please leave a message." Tom's tongue refused to move for a moment. It was her voice all right, still traces of that American accent, to the point and polite.

Kaye had arrived in Brisbane with her parents and younger brother Brad at the end of her last year at high school. Her father had been employed as the director of an international company, the name of which Tom couldn't remember. They met in November just after his final exams. Kaye was a new journalist for The Mail, writing a piece on underpaid and overworked medical interns for a French newspaper. It took Tom a while, but he eventually discovered she was a talented linguist, something unusual in Brisbane in the late nineties. Her first four years at high school had been at an elite school in Tehran. Tom thought it was a name something like 'Alborz'. God knows what the school would be like now, maybe no girls at all. But then, Iran was hardly Afghanistan.

If it wasn't love at first sight, it was certainly lust, the more vigorous less responsible half-sister. Tom had been working hard for so long he scarcely remembered what women were like. He was enthralled. The carnal power of Kaye's dark red hair and flawless copper skin only just outshone her obvious intelligence. Within six months they were living together in a one-bedroom flat in Fortitude Valley with no money or air-conditioning, one sheet and no blankets. It didn't matter, it was far too hot for even the sheet most nights. Tom's parents didn't approve of his failure to marry, but they still supplied all their furniture.

"Kaye, it's Tom. It's been too long. How about a drink and a chat sometime? I'm working at the same place in Toowong and I'm still living out at Kenmore, in the bush."

What a dumb thing to do. There was no chance she would ring back. Their last attempt to have a chat had been a dreary fizzer. She didn't even need to lie or think up some lame excuse, just ignore the message. He looked at his mobile to find the time. He had had nothing to eat since lunch time. No wonder he was hungry. It was eight o'clock. No rubbish food this time. It was off to Ho Chi Min's Hideout in St Lucia for the best Vietnamese food in town.

It was the freshness of the limes and the lightness of the food that he enjoyed. His stomach always felt at ease with itself, and his teeth cleaner. And they had a fine range of Sauvignon Blanc and the petite, lovely coffee coloured waitresses smiled with sparkling whiteness. They were such delightfully balanced creatures from another world. There was a bonus waiting. They had a new menu.

It was after eleven when he left to drive home. He was feeling much better. He had shared a bottle of New Zealand Sauvignon with a colleague he suspected might be there. He had turned up his stubby Australian nose at the mention of a Kiwi wine, but by the end of the evening he had changed his mind.

"Never had one before. Didn't know they were so good. If they start making reds as good as this, we're in trouble."

Tom drove home slowly. He turned into his drive to a usual chorus of cane toads, the ugliest creatures God ever made. They were sufficient cause to turn him into a blood-thirsty killer. He parked his car and walked across the lawn to the back door. He managed to whack two toads with a golf club through the fence into the dry creek bed. He kept it in the garage especially for that satisfying target. It was not a good night. The walk across the lawn should have sent at least four toads to toad hell. Dogs went to heaven, maybe, but toads, hardly.

It was a very sticky night, so Tom stripped off and dived into his newly refurbished twenty metre pool. Every house on the street had one of some kind. The salt chlorinator was working perfectly. The contractor had tried to sell him some new magic machine, but Tom was happy with the old technology. Roger would have approved.

It was hot and humid from October to April and swimming was the easiest way to get refreshed. Tom found swimming late at night particularly pleasing. The exercise and the cooling down usually brought sleep quickly. And for Tom, that night, it did. He wondered if he would dream about Kaye.

He didn't, dream about Kaye that is. But he still felt pretty good. Six hours in the surgery, or medical centre as he was now compelled to call it, an hour of squash, an outstanding meal and a swim had to be good. Tom woke up believing things couldn't get better, but they did. The phone rang. It was the landline; hardly anyone ever rang him on that.

"Morning," he had no trouble sounding cheerful.

"Tom, so lovely to hear from you. I'm off to Afghanistan in three days and do you know what? I've been thinking about you a bit. I almost gave you a call. Great minds and all that."

It took a moment but Tom finally managed. "Kaye… Afghanistan, what for?"

"My boss, you know what he's like. Every P. C. reader of the rag thinks he's anti-American. He wants me to find some positive spin on our boys over there. There are still some there you know. I can't guarantee I'll oblige."

"But it's dangerous. You might get killed. You know what happens to western women over there."

"Oh Tom, you really care."

"Okay, that might have sounded a bit wet. But it is a rugged place."

"Yes, but I'll be with our troops all the time, so I'll be fine."

It flashed, just briefly, across Tom's mind how strange their conversation was. They hadn't spoken for nearly five years and it was as though they were still together. An image of their first night together glistened in his mind. They were alone in New Farm Park immediately after a heavy shower of warm rain. Embraced by the soft warm humidity, they walked over a carpet of vivid blue Jacaranda flowers brought down by the rain. Water was still dripping off the trees in the bright sunshine. Kaye was wearing a light red and blue French cotton dress with a low front. Tom couldn't believe his luck.

"Look Tom, why don't we have a meal together before I go? My only free time is tomorrow night. Could you make it?"

"For you and Afghanistan, I'll make a special effort. Don't tell anyone, but I'd love to see you."

"There's a great little Vietnamese restaurant in St Lucia. I can't remember its name. Do you know it?"

"Ho Chi Min's Hideout, I think."

"That's it… eight thirty?"

"I'll be there."

"Can't wait."

Tom put the phone down. A mean-spirited observer might have thought him adolescent. And in a way, he was. His blend of modesty and intelligence with a certain naivety had always make Kaye breathe a little faster. It excited her to play mistress and mother. Tom had no idea of his appeal.

Had he been spiritual in a new age world, he could have been tempted to think the choice of restaurant something to do with Karma or at least a confluence of stars. He wasn't, nevertheless, it was a coincidence he enjoyed.

A wakeup swim was called for. Twenty lengths would be perfect. Of course, by the time he got to about the tenth he lost count. He always did. Not that it mattered. Over twenty or nearly twenty was ideal, just what the doctor ordered. Thank God, the toads were gone, gathered in a hole somewhere maliciously plotting their next assault. The ambitious golf club was still leaning against the pool fence where he had left it the night before.

Tom was early for his first appointment at the centre, although his secretary-nurse, Veronica, was already at her desk. Neither his partner nor his partner's nurse had arrived. Nothing changes. Veronica was always first to open. He'd be in a terrible mess if she ever left. Still blonde but showing signs of grey, she made no attempt to cover up her fifty-three years. She had been a nurse for twenty-two years, but found her present job more agreeable. The hours were better and Tom was an excellent employer. She liked him.

"Good morning, Veronica. Is all well at your place?" Tom's cheerfulness was infectious.

"Yes, it is, thank you. I can see that I don't need to ask you."

"Ah there it is, I'm a man, and so transparent. What simple creatures we are."

"Maybe, anyway, your first patient is Mr. Roberts. I've updated everything on your computer."

"Wonderful, and, as they say, have a good day."

Tom was probably unique in Brisbane. He liked to keep reasonably up-to-date with general medicine, and most days saw a patient who had been the beneficiary of his surgery, sometimes years before. This morning it was William Roberts, seventy-nine and displaying the first symptoms of dementia. Tom had told him what to expect and he had taken it with a kind of resolute composure at first. The last interview had been with him and his wife, Betty. Things had not gone well, tears all round.

Tom's inability to do anything real, except prescribe something in the hope the inevitable be delayed a little, frustrated him. And the number of dementia patients was increasing. Maybe people were living too long.

His own grandfather had gone gaga, but his grandmother had seemed to accept her husband's dotage as normal. He had lived with his grandparents in Ireland for several months when his grandfather's senility was advanced. His grandmother had been remarkable. Even at twelve years old, Tom had been deeply affected by his grandmother's loving care of her husband.

"He's in his dotage, so he is. It's one of the delights of growing old."

There was no question of him going into an institution, even if one had been available. He was grumpy and normally harmless, although sometimes his walking stick would be used to attack an imaginary or, in Tom's case, a real provocateur.

He would go easy on Betty and William this time. It was significant how the memory of his grandparents was influencing his professional decision making. Everything was so sharp in his mind. He imagined his grandmother's life had been shortened by the exhausting kind of attention she gave her husband. She had been a wonderfully tough old girl who could have made a century. Her selflessness, he now understood, was astounding. All very admirable, but was it worth it? That was a question he wouldn't dare raise even with his mother. He dared not explore it himself. It was too foundational, too threatening. He felt ill at ease for allowing it to settle in his mind. Sacrifice, suffering for another, was too big a deal. The doubt seemed to call the existence of goodness into question. He was neither brave nor foolish enough to walk down that shadowy path.

If the day had started raising all kinds of existential questions, it ended with something of a farce. Veronica had a wayward nephew, an eighteen-year-old lad who thought he had caught gonorrhoea. She prevailed upon Tom to help her embarrassed sister. Encouraged by his mates, the boy had visited a prostitute. He had looked up a website and was quite sure he was bearing the justified fruit of his encounter.

"It hurts me when I pee. I think I've got the clap."

Tom's rooms were well set up, so he did a gram test immediately.

There was no sign of the disease. "It's probably a urinary infection," he told his relieved patient. "I'll take a mouth swab just to be sure."

"That's great. I can tell the other blokes it's all kosher. One of them is having his turn tonight."

Tom said nothing to the boy or to Veronica. Perhaps if he was to meet his professional demands, he would have given the apprentice fornicator a lecture on the dangers of visiting prostitutes. But he had neither the commitment nor inclination. It had been a hard day. It was not surprising that desire for a sexual encounter of his own overwhelmed doubtful professional duty.

III

Tom played it safe and arrived at the restaurant early. He wanted to be sure he was waiting when Kaye arrived. If she was still the same girl, she'd be on time. He sat at a table outside, beneath a frangipani tree where he could look down on the car park. It was that time in the evening when the light was subdued, seducing everyone to believe it was making friends with darkness.

Not because he wanted to impress Kaye, so he convinced himself, he ordered a bottle of Pol Roger. Order, was not quite right. The owner was not that well informed on the quality of champagne, Kaye was, so he made sure the restaurant got a bottle in for the evening. With some disquiet, he handed over $120. He smiled to no one in particular, it was a token of reconciliation. He made sure it was in the bucket before Kaye arrived.

Kaye parked her car immediately below him. He stood and waved as she got out of her car. The red hair and the skin on her naked arms and shoulders were smooth and glowing in the warm night air. She saw him and smiled that devastating way he remembered. She stopped, looked at him for a moment and then came quickly up the steps. They embraced, not passionately, but with revealing warmth.

"Tom it's so lovely to see you. It really is. Doesn't the frangipani smell just glorious? I love this time of year. And you... look at you. You haven't changed a bit."

"Kaye, you were a vision coming up those stairs. That dress is delightful."

"Was I? Do you want me to do it again?"

"No, once will do me for a day or two."

"The dress is from a friend in Aix-en-Provence, by the way. She has such exquisite taste."

"Kaye, it's great to see you after all this time."

"Yes, it's been a while."

"Sit down and have a drink. After that running climb, you must need one."

Tom took the bottle from the bucket and poured Kaye's drink.

"Goodness me Tom, you've been lashing out. This was Winston Churchill's favourite. You're not going to propose, are you? You never did, you know. If this is especially for me, thank you." Kaye leaned across the table and kissed Tom on the forehead.

"Well I…"

"Just joking, Tom. Just joking. Now, tell me what have you been up too? I know you're not married. I've had my spies out."

"Mine haven't exactly been hanging about the office either. I heard that your man hadn't turned out as he had so spectacularly promised."

"How right you are. He was a prig and a pig. And that was on a good day. But enough of the pleasantries, I want to know what you're doing now."

"Well the truth is, Kaye, more of the same. Tedious perhaps, but there it is."

"How's the squash? Still at it? Running that loaded developer around the court?"

"Roger? He's fine. Still making pots of cash. I've no idea what his liabilities are though. But you're the one who's off on an adventure. Tell me about it."

"It's all very sudden, but I'm excited. Afghanistan shouldn't be too dangerous for me. I'm going to find the real mood of our troops on the remnants of Operation Slipper. Silly name, must've been chosen by some dull-witted bureaucrat. There's still several service men and a few women there. The word is that they'll all be home soon. I'll try and talk to lads from Brissie first. They might open to someone from their hometown. I'm not entirely sure what the top brass thinks or the kind of freedom I'll have."

"I'm sure it'll be tricky. You could get up the noses of those dull-witted bureaucrats."

"Maybe. I might have to go to the United Arab Emirates yet. That's where the headquarters are. And all in two weeks. The paper knew I had lots of experience with Afghan refugees. Maybe that's why I got the job."

The rest of the evening went too quickly. Tom could hardly remember what had happened, but it had been more enjoyable than he had hoped. Kaye was in scintillating form and it was obvious she enjoyed his company. They had said goodbye in the car park, embracing longer than either had expected. Maybe it was the frangipani. Kaye kissed him briefly on the mouth. Tom resisted the urge in his loins to invite her back to his house in the bush. If he was to ask her he would have to be sure he knew what her response would be. And anyway, they were going to meet again when the Afghanistan adventure was over. He left Kaye, excited about the future.

The drive home was disconcerting. Tom was having one of those periods his mother used to call 'miscellaneous'. As a young teenager, he thought the word described exactly how he felt. So far, he hadn't been able to improve on it. Perhaps it was the sudden unexpected return of Kaye into his life. Somewhere in his sub-conscious, whatever that was, he had hoped for exactly that. It's an odd experience when reality outruns hope. Tom wasn't sure to be thankful or afraid. Maybe because of his childhood, there was something of the cynic prowling about his sub-conscious. He didn't believe the declaration that if the gods wanted to destroy him they would give him what he wanted, but the suspicion hovered about him like a bad smell. It was that feeling of residual guilt that undermined his pleasure. He had forgotten his promise to himself to ask for Kaye's forgiveness. Had he remembered it would have seemed ridiculous, and more important, humiliating.

Tom imagined there was something about Kaye that was new and quite different; a deep seated abstract suggestion of suspicion about men perhaps. As the evening had unravelled she displayed, just so slightly, a kind of cynicism about the world that seemed new. Perhaps it was the fusion of lust with guilt getting in the way and he was misreading things. But there was something he couldn't quite grasp. Despite her declared and obvious friendliness, sometimes during the evening she appeared to be elsewhere.

Tom was so preoccupied when he crossed the lawn to his house he didn't even hear the terrestrial chorus of cane toads. Four dry, leathery lives were saved. They would never know the cause or joy of their salvation.

IV

Two days before Kaye was due home, Tom heard on the news she was missing, probably kidnapped. He was devastated. The intensity of his feelings surprised him, a rare loss of confidence stayed with him all day. Tom, with his tendency to excessive self-analysis, was hardly Australia's latter-day variation on Casanova. He had frequently told himself that self-examination slipped too easily into a kind of indulgence more akin to hedonism than the faith of his youth. Inconstancy, he believed with considerable evidence, plagued the human condition. Recently he had attended a government sponsored course on patient rights where there had been a great deal of waffle about patient self-esteem. It sounded like a hollowed-out version of the old virtue of self-control to him. He had no intention of descending the vainglorious slope of new age narcissism.

His desire to see Kaye remained a sweet and frustrating mystery. He liked that. Really it was all very simple. He wanted to see her and tell how much he missed her. Absurd. In four years, he had seen her once and yet that 'once' was so encompassing. It was a kind of conceit but it pleased him to think his yearning was the stuff of poignant insight. He rang Kaye's parents. Genuinely disappointed when he and Kaye had separated, they were relieved to hear from him.

"We've heard very little," Kaye's father said. "Canberra thinks she might have been kidnapped, but they won't commit. Her newspaper seems to know a damn sight more about her plight. I got the idea that they're expecting a ransom demand. One of the local newspapers in Kabul made a big fuss about her; it's crazy. Kabul has eleven daily newspapers would you believe?"

"How's Kaye's mother? She must be terribly worried."

"Celia's very upset but she wants to talk to you."

"Please, could I?"

"Oh Tom, this is just so awful. We're so pleased that both of you are talking again. Kaye told us. And now this… I'm so worried."

Tom spent nearly twenty minutes talking to Celia and Robert but it was unsettling. They knew so little and had nothing of substance to offer. The war in Afghanistan was something he seldom thought about and he knew little about the Australian troops there. All he could offer were soothing words of concern that lacked real substance, but he meant everything he said. He would do what he could, "We all love Kaye."

And, it would seem, he did. He always had, even during those years of separation. He hadn't admitted it but that's why he had worked so hard. Idle hands and minds get into too much trouble. The squash was therapy, well maybe. He acted as though he was still a teenager at forty. Current academic social analysis suggested he was not alone.

But what to do? That was his problem. He had to do something. Maybe Roger could help. He knew the editor of The Mail. Tom reached for his mobile.

"Roger, it's Tom. You know that mate of yours, you play golf with him I think, the editor of The Mail. What's his name?"

"Bill Williamson. Why?"

"You remember Kaye? She was sent out to Afghanistan a while ago by 'The Mail', and I'm almost certain she's been kidnapped."

"Not good!"

"You could say that. Anyway, I want to talk to Williamson so perhaps you could make sure he takes me seriously."

"I saw the story on the box but I didn't realize that they were actually talking about your Kaye. She had a different surname from what I remembered."

Roger's comment startled Tom. Was she his Kaye?

"Why don't we meet on the golf course, just the three of us? I know you're hopeless, but that won't matter. I always beat Bill anyway. He can have the pleasure of beating you. That'll make him feel good. He always buys the drinks on the nineteenth when he wins something."

"That sounds remarkably sensible. I might be pushing him a bit."

"Sure, push away. He can take it, and, anyway, I'd like to help. Kaye's a great girl. Can't imagine why you broke up with her. She is, as the learned ones say in the trade, a cracker."

"I know."

"What about Saturday morning at six, before it gets too hot and sticky? I've already made a rendezvous with Bill. Not too early for you, is it? I'll tell him I've got a friend coming. He won't mind. We could have a late breakfast at the clubhouse. The food's not bad."

"No, it's not too early. Still St Lucia?"

"Still."

"Right, see you there… and Roger."

"Yes."

"Thanks."

Well, that was something, but what was he going to ask Williamson? What did he know and what would he be prepared to tell and what could be done with the information anyway? Tom's mind was not clear. The last few weeks had been disconcerting, to say the least. Almost five years without Kaye and a kind of peace, and now a few weeks with her back in the frame, and everything was in disarray. He wanted that peace back, but not without Kaye.

V

"There has to be a first for everything, Roger. You can't win all the time."

"I can't believe I played so badly. Even Tom nearly beat me. Now that would've been a disaster."

Bill Williamson was pleased with himself. He had beaten Roger for the first time in nearly a year.

"Thanks for your support, Tom. My game has taken one great leap forward. Not just for me but for golf as well."

"It was 'step' Bill, a 'small step'. Get it right." Williamson's allusion seemed to amuse Roger.

"Was it? Well, it was a leap for me."

"I've no idea how I helped but thanks anyway," said Tom.

"Roger had two opponents to contend with. I managed to just slip past him. He had to concentrate on both. Not a great multi-tasker is Roger."

"What do you mean? I multi-task every day at work. All right, you can redeem yourself. You pay for breakfast. We've just made it on time."

"With pleasure and delight even. I think a bottle of bubbles is called for… if your health permits it Roger. This is one great celebration." Bill winked at Tom, "That'll lessen your pain, Roger."

A waiter, familiar with Roger's extravagant taste, arrived with a bottle of Moet & Chandon Grand Vintage 2009 and poured each player a glass. As one might expect, the late breakfast was a hearty affair. It was an hour from midday and the three men were relaxed. Roger regained something of his composure by thinking about his next game. They sat comfortably in the shade of the veranda gazing out across the course.

"The real thing, Bill, excellent tipple, but don't get carried away. You won't win next time. No bloody chance."

Bill smiled and turned to Tom, "Roger says you're a friend of Kaye Reynolds, our bright and shining star at The Mail."

"Well, yes, I am… for a very long time, in fact."

"I know, you used to live with her. In a moment of weakness and need, I like to think 'need' she told me about you. Don't worry, everything she said made me jealous. I can't bring myself to say she still has the 'hots' for you like some vulgar celebrity. On the other hand, I can't say she doesn't love you either. Her voice used to go oddly soft when she was speaking about you. It was most annoying."

"Really, I'm not sure whether to be embarrassed or pleased."

"Either will do. Or both, they're not mutually exclusive. I've always said I didn't know why you two split." Roger sounded self-righteous, as a consumer of expensive champagne might.

After the second glass, Tom found Bill remarkably easy to talk to. They were all hungry and had ordered variations on the 'big breakfast'. Communication was slowed somewhat. Nevertheless, Tom discovered that Kaye had volunteered to go to Afghanistan and that Bill had been reluctant to send her.

Contrary to what Kaye had told Tom, the assignment was exceedingly dangerous. She knew she would be in constant danger from kidnappers. Tom was baffled. Why had she been so forthcoming the evening of their dinner together and yet mislead him about her reasons for going to Afghanistan?

It might have been that some experience of that tendency to compromise the truth had caused the separation all those years ago, it felt like another life. There had always been something enigmatic about Kaye. He'd forgotten that her emotional ambiguity had been frequently disconcerting. The pleasurable intensity of their reunion had clouded his memory of the past.

"According to the Afghan police, Kaye has been kidnapped." Bill continued. "The ASIS top brass were aware of the possibility. She was on the road from Kabul to Maidan Shahr in the Wardak, only about 35 kilometres away, when she disappeared along with two Afghan soldiers and guide. Although it was common knowledge that rebels were still operating underground in the area Kaye insisted she must go to Maidan Shahr. It is all very worrying. We had heard nothing of Kaye; no ransom demands, nothing."

Williams became almost distraught as he spoke. Although he didn't say so clearly, it was evident he held himself responsible in some way for what had happened to Kaye.

"It's the uncertainty that's the killer," he said.

"It is," echoed Tom. "It makes it very difficult to know what to do."

"Well Tom," said Williams, "I'll do the best I can to help. You can be sure of that. It's all so messy. I'm seldom confident about the Army's ability to tell the truth. I get the impression they know more than they're saying."

"Well the truth is, I felt the same with Kaye. She was a delight but I'm not sure now I was being given the full McCoy."

Three more days went by and still no information about Kaye. Canberra said nothing, and not one of Williams' contacts knew any more. Tom wasn't sure what the catalyst was, but one minute he wasn't thinking it and the next minute he was. He would go to Afghanistan. He couldn't find out anything less than nothing, which was all he knew now. Of course, it was half-witted, but he was a surgeon and could be useful to the locals. There were plenty of other surgeons in Brisbane to pick up the slack. His absence for a month or two wouldn't be an issue. His partner would hold the fort on the medical front; he would have to.

Williams was more than pleased to offer what he did know about the Afghan scene. He told Tom he was crazy but wished him well. He helped with the bookings and arranged a contact on the ground in Afghanistan; an ex-pat editor of one of the local rags.

It was February and likely to be very cold. Most of the rain came in the first four months of the year, so at least he wouldn't be battling the heat and dust as well as bureaucracy and his own ignorance.

Of course, a sensible man would ask himself some sensible questions. Would a mere novice be able to do anything of value in Afghanistan? Received wisdom suggested he'd be more likely to become a liability than a hero. Still he was young... well youngish, and fit and there was certainly a demand for his skills. He would just have to ignore the government travel warning. Kaye certainly had.

Travel in all areas of Afghanistan remains unsafe due to military combat operations, land mines, banditry, armed rivalry between political and tribal groups, and the possibility of insurgent attacks, including attacks using vehicle-borne or other improvised explosive devices (IEDs). The security situation remains volatile and unpredictable throughout the country.

What was going on? A flood of unexpected sentiment overtook him that did nothing to clarify his thinking. He had been so young and idealistic, and Kaye had been the flesh and blood of his lascivious adolescent heat. Possessing its own special elegance, her lithe soft femaleness had given life to the inescapably carnal. It still haunted him. He had to see her. He had to go.

But what if she were dead? That was possible; he refused to contemplate 'likely'. It was impossible to believe she was dead when the sound of her voice and warmth of her body remained so immediate and insistent. That night in the restaurant was so sharp in his mind, it overwhelmed any common sense he might have had.

One last game of squash before he left had sounded like good therapy when Roger suggested it. It would clarify the mind. The heat and scent of burning energy and a cooling sweat always gave him a satisfying view of the world. It was an astonishing thing how sweat and a mobile body made the entire world a more acceptable place. Of course, he knew the biology and chemistry, but he rather enjoyed the mystery of it all. Biology or chemistry in the lab or on paper was one thing but in his own body quite another.

"That was great, Roger. I needed it."

"Well, you're off tomorrow. There won't be much chance of a game in Afghanistan, I imagine."

"I'm not so sure. There's an Afghanistan Squash Federation and there are at least two courts in Kabul. They see sport as a nation builder and the country certainly needs some building. The federation is a couple of years old, I think. Cricket is quite a thing too. They could even have a team at the next World Cup."

"Good, when you get back I won't have to put up with an old, out of form hack. That's a comfort."

"Yes; well, maybe."

"Tell me the truth, Tom. What do you really think about finding Kaye alive? It's been quite a while now and still no word. I know you're a positive guy but…anything could have happened."

"I know it's not your bag and I'm a particular kind of hypocrite, but, dare I say it, I've prayed for Kaye. I want to believe she's alive somewhere. It's impossible for me to think differently. Prayer comes easily when one is up against it."

"I guess. You're a declining religious nutter, well sort of, but nobody could say you're a wimp. I'm afraid I might be if I was in a similar situation."

"Maybe, but it's a funny thing. I think I might have said the same. The truth is, Roger, none of us know how he is going to react in a time of stress or danger. I know that's obvious, but it does seem quite important right now. My desire to go to Afghanistan has caught me by surprise. Self- knowledge, it would seem, is not all that common. It's not original I know, but we're sharp in the self-deception business. Certainty has denied us most of the time."

"You're getting out of my depth Tom. I smell religious chatter. I can do without that and, anyway, it nearly always collapses into gobbledygook."

"Theological chatter perhaps, but that's okay. I won't bore you with the distinction; I'll shut up."

"Good. Too much thinking detracts me from making money

and, who knows, you might get kidnapped and I'll have to pass the hat around."

"Thanks for that cheery note. I had thought of that, it's certainly possible. Getting kidnapped that is, not the hat."

"Naw, I'm sure you'll be fine. But, look, I have this lucky US $100 bill. Take it and tape it into one of your shoes. That's part of the charm. You never know when you might need it. I want it back when you return."

Tom smiled and took the $100. "Silly, but thanks. I'll put it in the shoes I use when I'm working. How does that sound?"

"Excellent. I feel better already."

VI

Kaye was apprehensive when she got off the plane. The leg from Sydney to Dubai on Emirates had been fine, but the stopover was nineteen hours and the paper had bungled the hotel booking. She managed to find a room at an airport hotel for $US390 out of her own pocket. That frustrated her and made her crotchety as well as tired. The trip on FliDubai to Kabul didn't help either. It was very bumpy and the meal wasn't served.

Kaye had done her homework. She had had two passport photographs ready for her foreigner registration card. She was ready when her Australian passport was examined in a tacky little office behind a soiled and barely readable notice, 'Duty-free'. She had fully expected to have to pay a bribe but since the introduction of the US into the country, bribery was less common.

Most people when they arrive at an airport would have no idea of its history, but Kaye was not most people. The old one had been built by the Soviets in the 1960s. They had controlled it until 1989 when the Taliban eventually took it over until it was bombed by the US after September 11, 2001. The new grey stone building, hardly beautiful and with its name in English, had been opened in 2009. A new second runway had just been started with Japanese money.

Kaye felt pleased with herself despite tiredness. Her knowledge of the culture and familiarity with the prevailing language encouraged her to feel safe. And she needed as much comfort and safety as she could get. If only her editor and the people back home knew what she was up to they would be appalled. They simply wouldn't understand, couldn't understand. The assignment for the paper had been a godsend. It meant she could leave Australia without anyone's suspicions being raised. She was confident she could get a good story back to the paper and then get on with the real work.

Amadullah's text told her where they would meet the next day. She walked quickly out into the reception area where Williams' representative was waiting.

"Robert Jones; it's Kaye, I assume."

The deeply lined face was cheerful. Jones reminded Kaye of W. H. Auden, the poet she was particularly fond of and whose deeply lined face had always fascinated her.

"Good to see you in Afghanistan. Australian women are thin on the ground here and attractive journos non-existent. Pleased to see that boss of yours had the sense to send someone at last who fulfils both criterion. I've been at him for long enough. Your profile will be a big help back home. The ordinary Aussie really doesn't have a clue what's going on over here."

"I guess not. I hope I can help."

"That's the idea. Anyway, let's get you to your hotel."

It was very cold outside, with fresh thick snow covering everything. Attempts had been made to clear the streets of the most recent fall. Kaye's taxi drove along fitfully through a mix of winter clad pedestrians and unruly traffic. As she got out with Robert's help, three women, in full light blue burkas, floated out of the hotel. Against the snow, they created a surreal image. Kaye found it difficult to believe that there were bodies of breathing women inside the flowing dream.

The Serena was better than expected. The garden view room turned out to be spacious and clean, and the woman at reception spoke excellent English. Her orange headscarf could have been a concession to a hijab or a suggestion of rebellion. When Kaye responded in Pashto she was the receptionist's friend forever. The full red lips and white, even teeth were dazzling. Kaye thought rebellion more likely than concession. Perhaps the blurb was right. The hotel was 'an oasis of serenity'.

As soon as Kaye entered her room tiredness overwhelmed her. Although there was only a six-hour difference between Kabul and Brisbane, all the travel through Dubai was catching up. The evening meal with Jones in the Silk Road restaurant was not until 20:00 hours. That gave her a full eight hours. Kaye helped herself to the water from the fridge and was asleep immediately.

A loud knocking on her door at about 19:00 hours wrenched Kaye out of deep sleep. She felt terrible, hot and sticky. The air conditioner was manual and it had been running warm all night. A large white envelope shot across the floor from under the door. She stared at it in an uncomprehending way. Just for a moment, she had forgotten where she was.

Slowly she reached down and picked the letter up, holding it loosely on one corner turning it over several times. Her imagination was running ahead. Kaye thought of plastic explosives but the envelope was so thin it seemed empty. Silly. She opened it. A hand-written note on a small piece of paper was from Amadullah, giving a time and place for their meeting.

For a moment, she was shocked. They were to meet in the hotel lounge at 9:00 hours the following day. But then, why not? Amadullah must know what he was doing. She'd make a point of talking to guests and staff, after all that's what journos did. She had no option but to wait.

Kaye's lingering shower was her first detour into the sensual for some time. She washed her hair and shaved her legs. It was satisfying. Afghan women probably didn't shave their legs but then who would know what went on in that very private female Muslim world? They allegedly bought sexy lingerie, and, who knows, a little vanity under the covers could lead to all kinds of hidden passion. And anyway, this might be her last chance to indulge herself for months. Just for a moment she was afraid, but very quickly dismissed fear as unproductive.

She was here to do a job that would have seemed exciting to any Australian. She was confident. Fluency in the local main language and her years of experience with the refugees had to be a plus.

Jones had already ordered wine when Kaye arrived.

"Kaye, how lovely to see you again. I've taken the liberty to order the wine. I hope you don't mind."

"Certainly not, Robert, but I did think that booze was forbidden in Afghanistan."

"Yes, it is, but the law is applied unevenly. You will discover very soon that everything is uneven in Afghanistan. In theory, it's possible for this hotel to be raided by the National Police, but unlikely I think."

"I'm pleased to hear it. It's very nice; goodness me, Cotes du Rhône even here?"

"Yes, the French are nothing if not entrepreneurial. They have had a successful trade going on here in Afghanistan for some years."

"I think I'd heard."

"In all sorts of things. There are rumours that Marseille is used by Taliban gun-runners."

"Really?"

"Okay, let's order and get down to business. I don't want to rush things but I'm away all day tomorrow. I was hoping we could start things when I get back. The remaining Australians are in Tarin Cot in the Uruzgan province. As I guess you know, they're part of the Provincial Reconstruction Team. It's too dangerous to go by road so we'll have to fly first thing the day after tomorrow."

"That's fine by me. I need to get the feel of the place anyway."

"Be careful tomorrow. It will be cold but don't wander too far from your hotel. You'll be safe enough but a woman alone is not a frequent event here. You could be harassed in quite an unpalatable way."

"I'll cope."

The meal was unexpectedly agreeable and the wine excellent. Perhaps Kaye's perceptions were the consequence of an ignorance she had kept to herself. Robert was a convivial and informative host.

First up, she was to meet the commanding officer which 'would be no problem'. He had done all the spadework.

The last three or four days had been something of a haze that had protected Kaye from the reality of what she was doing. She remained excited and afraid. Sure, she had government support, but she would also be guilty of deceiving her employer and Robert as he made plans for something she knew would not happen. Quite simply, tomorrow she would disappear and throw the newspaper into confusion. Her parents would be worried too. But she had thought about it for months and, anyway, there was no going back now. Everything had been set up.

"Robert, I think I understand the process. It's not very complicated really. I just get permission to talk to a selected group of soldiers and then write up my articles for consumption back home. I could be finished in a week."

"I guess you could. But take it easy tomorrow and, as I've said, this is Kabul and women do go out alone but very rarely. Remember where you are. Take it easy tomorrow, swim and relax. This hotel has one of the only heated pools in Afghanistan. With the snow outside it's rather lovely. I'll be here the day after tomorrow at 8:00 hours."

The meal ended with something of an anti-climax. Kaye was tired and Robert gave the impression he had done his duty. They shook hands and in less than half an hour Kaye was in bed.

VII

The following morning, just before 0:900 hours, Amadullah sent another message to Kaye's room, delivered by a child. He was in the lounge waiting to see her at her convenience. 'At her convenience', how graciously old fashioned. She was impressed and went out to see him immediately.

"Ah Miss Reynolds, you are very prompt. Thank you very much." Amadullah bowed as Kaye approached. Sharia marriage was still the social foundation of Islam and the pre-feminism honorific was not news to her. It was clear that Amadullah thought it important to be aware of her marital status.

"Not at all, Amadullah. I'm excited and I want to get on with things. This is a big deal for me."

"It's a very 'big deal' for the women of Afghanistan," responded Amadullah, picking up the idiom. "It could be the saving of our country. I pray to Allah daily that it will be so."

"If I was a believer, I suspect I would pray too."

Amadullah said nothing but he did seem to look at Kaye with something like pity in his eyes. Her reflexive agnosticism had been a mistake.

"You will work mainly with two women. One is my sister, the other a very good friend and relative. Both are fluent in English and, of course, Pashto. I've arranged for all of us to meet about forty kilometres from here. They haven't met you publicly because it would be too dangerous. The base will be in my village and, as you know, for most of the time you will dress like an Afghan woman. We have no desire to disguise who you are but just to make it more acceptable to the ordinary women you should dress as they are."

"Of course, that's easy to understand. I didn't expect anything else. But I would like to have the opportunity to buy some local clothing myself; perhaps this afternoon."

"I anticipated that you would, so I've organised a visit to two different shops. As you can imagine, we don't want to advertise your presence. There are many people who will be hostile to what you're doing."

"I know and, I must say, I'm beginning to be scared with the enormity and sheer bravado of the project. I'm worried about my parents especially. They'll be very concerned. It's all very messy, I'm reluctant to admit it, but I will be deceiving them."

"Well, Miss Reynolds, we have thought of that too."

"Amadullah, please call me Kaye. Miss Reynolds sounds so strange. Do you mind?"

"Certainly not, Kaye, if that is what you want."

"Well, I would feel more comfortable if we were a little less formal."

Amadullah smiled and, without thinking, Kaye embraced him. He stiffened and Kaye knew she had made another mistake.

"Oh, I'm sorry, Amadullah. I've embarrassed you. I just want to show how much I appreciated you."

Amadullah relaxed, "I understand. I was educated in France so I'm familiar with Western customs." He nearly said decadent customs, but thought better of it. "From now on we have a job to do, you are my Afghan sister."

"Great, that makes you my brother." Kaye felt rather silly stating the obvious, but it seemed to please Amadullah.

"Tomorrow you will go missing along with me and a couple of friendly Afghan soldiers. That will be the official release. Robert Jones will receive a note saying so. After twenty days, your parents will be told confidentially that you're safe. That's the best we can do I'm afraid and anyway you will need considerable time to get things going."

"I understand, but I suspect my parents will not be convinced. Still they won't be left without hope. That's something, but I still can't help feeling anxious and just a little guilty."

"Well, Kaye," said Amadullah with noticeable sympathy, "you knew what you were getting yourself into. It's dangerous and there's a price we all must pay. Later it might be possible to contact them so they can hear your voice. That should be a help."

"I know there's a price. I'm not complaining, just thinking aloud. It's a little dilemma I have. This, what can I call it, adventure? It all seemed so rational and exciting in Brisbane."

The trip to Amadullah's village proved cold and uncomfortable. He talked very little. The Toyota Hilux had lost its suspension on the bumpy roads. Kaye felt conspicuous in her new clothes; three quarters of an hour had not given her much time to choose. A modest black hijab was a default purchase. She recalled reading what Allah had said somewhere in the Qur'an. Remembering and following the essentials wasn't going to be easy. She unfolded a paper to read for the last time. She tried to imagine the passion of Islam had seeped into her bones.

The believing woman, Kaye read, *should lower her gaze and guard her modesty that she should not display her beauty and ornaments except what (must ordinarily) appear thereof; that she should draw her veil over her breasts and not display their beauty except to her husband, her father, her husband's father, their sons, her husband's sons, her brothers or her brothers' sons, or her sisters' sons, or their women, or the slaves whom their right hands possess, or male servants free of physical needs, or small children who have no sense of the shame of sex; and that they should not strike their feet in order to draw attention to their hidden ornaments. And O ye Believers! Turn ye all together towards Allah, that ye may attain Bliss.*

How had she managed to talk herself into all of this? A compelling mixture of anger and compassion would drive her to fame or death. Was that a cliché? If it was, it didn't help; she was still afraid. But here she was with eyes wide open as her father might have said. Altruism of some kind had swamped her fear.

From the beginning, the entire project had been outrageous but so appealing. Surrounded by war, she was going to be involved in making peace. For several years now, the CIA and the ASIS had been working secretly together on the entire concept. The idea was to appeal directly to women in Afghanistan. They had been operating covertly for months with the Revolutionary Association of Afghanistan Women (RAAW). It was not encouraging, as Kaye discovered that its last two leaders had been assassinated.

The whole idea was simple but fraught. It was slow progress but more women, defying opposition, were becoming educated and increasingly dissatisfied with their lot. Even under the American supported regime, women were still being punished for attempting to escape domestic abuse. Amadullah had told her getting to talk to the women was the problem. Too often they had to rely on the local translator who was frequently a man related to the women they wanted to talk to. It was obvious the women were not always forthcoming, and the translator was frequently not accurate in his translations.

Despite the violence against them, the women remained ambivalent. Initially Kaye was surprised, but it didn't take long for her to understand. Why should the women want the freedom that characterized the West when they thought it decadent and tainted by sexual excess? This was going to be a long-term and difficult assignment. So much seemed to depend on the persuasive power of a few hundred educated Afghan women. It was more fantasy than real politics.

The project was daring and fool-hardy. By speaking directly with educated women, they could be encouraged to influence other women and consequently their husbands. If Kaye had been able to use 'liberal' in the classical sense, the educated Afghan women were the most liberal of Muslims. They wanted peace more than anything else, especially when the American and Allied forces left. And, while it was never said, everyone knew that if things deteriorated, the West would have an effective body of sympathetic women as a soft fifth column unlikely to be influenced by extremist propaganda. Kaye was fluent in Pashto and that was why she had been asked to help. Speaking to the women in their own language was a big plus.

"Minnah and Rokhshana are going to meet us when we arrive," said Amadullah, breaking into her musing. "They both speak excellent English, and Minnah is a French trained doctor. We are very proud of her. Pashto and English-speaking female doctors are rare in Afghanistan. My sister and you will be the only fluent English speakers in the area."

"I can't wait to meet them. I'm sure we'll do great things together."

At last, Amadullah pulled up outside a soiled creamy coloured house with a curved roof. It was larger and in better condition than most of the other mud houses Kaye had seen. It was surrounded by a stone wall about shoulder height. Amadullah had hardly turned off the engine before Minnah and Rokhshana rushed out to meet them. Minnah embraced her brother with such instinctive affection that Kaye felt the awkwardness of an intruder.

She needn't have worried, because both women embraced her warmly too. Immaculate in their Punjabis and trousers and taller than Kaye, they would have turned more than one or two heads in Brisbane or Sydney. Minnah's prevailing colour was blue while Rokhshana favoured some tan Punjabi and cream trousers. Both women wore elegant shoes and long colourful scarves, hardly Kaye's somewhat limited image of Islam.

Minnah was the first to speak, awkwardly perhaps, "We're overjoyed that you have come to help us. It's quite wonderful to have someone from your country prepared to take the risk you are taking. Afghanistan is a suffering nation." Tears moistened her cheeks. Kaye knew, at that moment, she was doing the right thing. The seriousness of her new life burst in upon her. Quite unable to hold her own tears back, she embraced both women. Later she would remember the tears in a turmoil of grief and loss that experience was yet to teach her. She was to discover that the tears they shared had their source in a grief relieved only by the anticipation of success. The tears were

innocent, like those of a child. There was something quite lovely, otherworldly in their embrace.

The next twenty-four hours went by all too quickly. Kaye discovered that there were several hundred women fighting for their rights
in Afghanistan. All of them were in constant danger. Some were supported by husbands and family, but just as many were not. Her role
became clearer. Women could talk to her in their language without
the presence of a man. They could speak the truth and not have
the embarrassment of a male translator censor what they wanted to
say. It came to Kaye afresh, she could supply the kind of intelligence
not available any other way. She could not resist a wry smile. It was
woman to woman power, but Western feminists had no idea of the
kind of family dynamic that confirmed their solidarity. As the women
shared their desires, Kaye's confidence soared.

It was daunting and obvious, trite perhaps. She would be a bridge
between the women she spoke to and the world outside. The women
were strong, but they needed encouragement and the world needed
to know the truth about what was really going on in the intimacy
of Afghan family life. Men who were suspicious of Western notions
of sex equality were still looking over their shoulders. Amadullah,
it would seem, was a rare Afghan. He too had received his university education in France on money their father had earned fighting
for the Russians, but her parents had been murdered by the Taliban
two weeks after Minnah's graduation. Both Amadullah and Minnah
hated the Taliban and their mindless self-righteous holy ignorance.
Irony was endemic in Afghanistan. The whole country seemed to be
embedded in the ambiguity of religious dogma and complex family
loyalty. That complexity was one constant that Kaye, perhaps too
hopefully, thought she could grasp.

Minnah had married Maurice Muetton, an engineer from France.
He had been captured by her modest beauty and subtle mind. It
hadn't been hard for her to convince him that their future together
had to be in Afghanistan. They were proving a formidable team. The

murder of Minnah's parents had been a potent catalyst to action for her friends and relatives as well.

"They work together like hip and thigh," Rokhshana told Kaye. "Maurice understands Afghanistan more than any foreigner I've ever met. He's a believer, I can accept so easily why Minnah loves him. I don't know what she would do without him."

The first working meeting Kaye had was in a village somewhere in the Wardak Province, southwest of Kabul. Several women and one man were gathered in a house pock-marked by bullets. Apparently, the man was their 'protector', but he was keen to leave the women to talk about 'women's things' and chat to Amadullah.

Without warning, Kaye felt something that would have been called a panic attack back home. But this was Afghanistan, and panic attacks were a luxury reserved for the effete in the West. There was no panic attack, but she was out of her depth. She didn't share Tom's prodigal faith and she struggled to understand Islam. Religion confused her, so she undervalued it. She was a modern secularist with no coherent means or desire to criticize her own perspective. When Minnah asked her one evening, very seriously, why Jesus taught believers to love their enemies, she was lost. She had never thought about it and was only vaguely aware of the command. Its uniqueness to a Muslim mind had passed her by. She was unable to understand why it seemed so important to Minnah or why she would be familiar with, or even interested in Christian scripture. She could, however, just about understand, now that she had been made aware, why the command to love your enemies, could fascinate an educated Muslim woman like Minnah.

It came to Kaye that perhaps she was in Afghanistan with little more than a sentimental altruism to sustain her. She had never really examined her motivation closely before. Like so many of her contemporaries, she had presumed a generalized ethic of tolerance and doing good to be self-evident. Western democracy and a liberal mind were the way to salvation and peace. It was common sense.

Reasonableness and the liberal mind were synonymous. Submission to Allah, or Jesus for that matter, had never occurred to her as possible or even desirable. Maybe that's why Tom had annoyed her. His languid faith, which kept waking at the most awkward of moments, seemed little more than superstition or even hypocrisy.

As the days went by, Minnah and Rokhshana were a growing revelation. Educated at universities in the west, they remained boldly Afghan. Both were familiar with firearms and physically competent in a way Kaye had not experienced. Necessity had made them strong. But they were still women; creatures who nurtured and wanted to survive. Both were married with loving husbands and Rokhshana had three children under six. Minnah was still trying. Indeed, her childlessness was her greatest anxiety. Maurice saw his wife's childless pain and grieved with her. It was that strength in grief that caused Kaye to sense a spiritual strength in Minnah that fascinated her.

VIII

Tom had no idea that Kaye's plans were well advanced when he arrived in Afghanistan. Her fear was being dissolved by the gutsy power of the Afghan women. Possessing few resources and with virtually no freedom, they carried themselves with a dignity quite beyond Kaye's experience. For reasons that contradicted all her liberal reasonableness, they made her proud to be a woman. She dared not yield to such false doctrine, but to the Afghan woman, sacrifice and womanliness were inseparable.

Bill Williamson had been keen to assist in planning that Tom be met by Robert Jones, the colleague who had met Kaye. Williamson knew that Tom didn't have Kaye's inside knowledge and any help would be appreciated. But, it still took Tom two hours to clear the bureaucracy of the airport and pay for $160 for a visa he thought he already had. When he finally did meet a patient Robert Jones, he was tired and decidedly grumpy.

"Ah Tom, I'm Robert Jones. You're easy to recognize; Bill's description was spot on."

"What a relief to see a friendly face. I can't say I've enjoyed my first two hours in Afghanistan."

"Yes, the arrival business can be tedious. Australians and American's are still an easy target. You probably gave somebody a month's salary. Anyway, let's get you to your hotel where you can freshen-up."

"That'd be great. The second half of the trip was exhausting, so a few hours' sleep will be more than welcome."

"I see you're booked in at the same hotel as Kaye. Bill put you on to it?"

"Yes, he did. I have to say, he's been very helpful."

It took thirty-five minutes from arriving at the hotel to the deep sleep of exhaustion. Tom didn't care where he was, all he wanted was sleep. He saw very little and was only marginally aware of the cold. For eight hours, he enjoyed a dreamless sleep. He had no idea, but news travels fast in Afghanistan. Half way through those eight hours Kaye learned that he had arrived in Kabul. For a brief time, she wondered what she should do, but the answer became obvious: nothing. Her swirling murky Rubicon had been crossed before, that lovely meal with Tom and when she had been tempted to tell him everything. The past and Tom's gentleness had come back to her. He had been her first 'real' lover. That was impossible to forget and, anyway, she didn't want to. She would ask Amadullah to keep an eye on him.

She felt responsible even though there was no chance that he would ever find her. It would be just too easy for him to come to harm as he blundered about the countryside in his search for her. Any information he received would be unreliable. He was a foreigner and would be treated as somebody not to be trusted. It was almost inevitable that he would annoy someone enough to be disposed of.

The power of her position was stimulating. The man she once loved, and probably still did if she knew her own mind, was putting himself in danger for her. It was all very amateurish, but rather romantic. But then the Romantic has always been an amateur. Whatever the truth of the situation might be, Tom's appearance in Afghanistan made her feel an even more significant player. Kaye had a job to do but at the same time she had become Tom's secret protector.

Nevertheless, there was no place for a double mindedness that would lead to danger and failure. She had been through everything repeatedly in her mind. The obvious imposed itself; Afghanistan was not Australia. That she would be a different woman in Afghanistan was something she had only hazily anticipated. Her identity, she had assumed, was in the freedom of her mind, or at least freedom as she understood it. But now she was responding to those around her in a way she couldn't have foreseen. Identity was not something one lived out alone like a latter-day narcissist. Freedom for the Afghan women was earned and lived in community. Kaye's dependency on those close to her was changing the way she saw herself in the world. Freedom and dependency, she was learning, were not mutually exclusive.

Kaye had never seen herself as a group member. She was not a joiner. Indeed, she hated clubs and voluntary groups because, she thought, they diminished her. Now the close friendship of the women around her was having the opposite impact. Leaving them, not being with them, diminished her. Without them she was lonely.

It was difficult to find satisfying explanations for the change. For days, she ran them over in her mind. The women were together in a task that made friendship necessary. In Afghanistan, one could never work alone. What had once seemed critical wasn't critical at all. For a self-contained, modern Australian woman that was more than a little disconcerting. She was not her own person at all.

It was about how the women loved one another. The irony was breath-taking, or was it simply absurd? Their religion isolated them from any man who was not in the immediate family. It was as though their ordinary human decency transcended the demands of their religion. Their affection and concern for each other overpowered any dogma. Yet, their affection for each other was given opportunity by their religion. That was expressed in what Kaye was forced to identify as the affection of humility, there was no other way to understand the elusive irony. The deprivation and isolation of the women from men had become their strength. She respected and loved them despite their foreignness. In an abstracted way, she was nearly guilty of veneration. They might be second class citizens but they had a dignity that rose above it. And yet, in the face of every older woman a certain sadness was impossible to ignore. It increased as they submitted to the toughness of their lives. What might once have been relieved by poignancy could so easily became tragic. Kaye grieved without the relief of spiritual insight or religious understanding. Maybe reality demands that tears don't always need to be understood.

IX

Tom woke early for his first full day in Afghanistan. Before leaving Australia, he had arranged to meet the head surgeon at the Kabul Emergency War Centre. There was no doubt his skills would be useful.

He telephoned the centre and asked to be put through to Michael O'Reilly. It was no surprise when a Dublin accent responded, "This is O'Reilly." When they met, a mere thirty minutes after the call, O'Reilly completed Tom's benign stereotype of the Irish. Michael was talkative, amusing, and he had red hair.

"Quite a CV. I've done my homework. Sure, you're just the answer to a maiden's prayer. I hope you know what you're in for. The only fellow we had with your experience was sent back to France last week." O'Reilly was sure that Tom was set to start work immediately.

"Look," said Tom, "I need to come clean, I think."

"Come clean? Now, that's something I haven't heard in a little while."

"Silly phrase, but I am not here because I'm imbued by humanitarian spirit. I'm here to find a woman from Australia who has been missing for weeks."

"Is that a fact now? So, you'll be coming in and out then."

"If that's all right."

"Sure 'tis, Tom, once you have been here a while you'll understand the tyranny of necessity. It drives everything, it does."

"I'm sure I don't really understand, but I do know that this isn't Australia."

"It's the smell of an oily rag stuff here. You'll be understanding that soon enough. Not a sniff of patient rights here or how to complain. When you don't have much, a little is a lot."

"Yes, I daresay." Michael was not saying anything Tom didn't know, but when his anxieties were reinforced by somebody who knew what he was talking about, the possibilities of the next few weeks became more daunting.

"The woman you're talking about wouldn't be that Australian journalist woman now, would it? It's been in all the papers here because she was working for the Australian Army. It's a thin air job as far as I know. But then they all are. Kidnappings are common. It's only when somebody with profile disappears that it makes the papers."

"Kaye Reynolds?"

"That's the name, right enough."

"I'm talking to a few people tomorrow, but if you ever hear anything I'll be very grateful."

"I certainly will and the best of luck to you. I'm sure you've thought about it. You can't be stupid. Be careful who you talk to and how you ask your questions. There's a kind of law here, but it doesn't say much about protecting the weak, the infirm, or foreigners. Strange really, because the ordinary Afghans are kind and hospitable; necessity and survival I guess."

"Thank you. I'll try to take your advice."

"You can start as soon as you like. But just remember, if you start something you'll probably have to finish it. There's no experienced backup here unless you count me."

"I understand."

"I hope so. Try not to get your two jobs mixed up. Make sure you let me know if things get overheated. That's important for both of us."

If the hard nose of Afghan realism was thrusting itself defiantly into Kaye's ideal world, it was starkly imposing itself in Tom's imagination.

"It's in shambles out there. You can't trust the police. Something like ninety per cent of heroin consumed in Europe comes from

Afghan opium. There were fifty-eight reported murders last year and at least twelve kidnappings. They're the ones we know about."

"I'll keep my head down."

X

Tom had been in Afghanistan one month when Kaye learned that he had taken a bullet from the side of an important tribal leader sympathetic to the Taliban. She knew very little about the man and Tom would have known even less. She wasn't sure whether she should be pleased or anxious. On the surface, such an act should offer Tom some security, but one could never be sure. Everything she knew, including the information about Tom and the action around him, had come from the women in her group. It wasn't that she doubted them; it was just that so many of their other stories were grotesque and unbelievable. She hated it. Lack of reliable knowledge was bringing back those first sensations of vulnerability. It didn't help that Tom's position would be a lot more precarious than her own. He couldn't speak the language and he knew a lot less than she did about the country. Ignorance would be his greatest danger.

Even now, although the Taliban had limited power, they were still quite capable of murder and extreme cruelty should anyone who looked like an enemy fall into their hands. They no longer had the opportunity or power to dismember those who broke the law at halftime in the sports ground during a football match. But she was fearful, nevertheless. Tribal leaders, like the one Tom had operated on, might not have been Taliban but they were usually sympathetic to many of their aims. Everyone was anticipating the departure of the Americans, so preparation for the future was an exercise in self-preservation for most Afghans.

Comfort of a kind came from the women she was learning to love. Strong stuff maybe, but then everything was strong stuff in her new world. Kaye remained baffled by the paradox that engulfed her. Hospitality, cruelty, loyalty, genuine familial affection and downright grotesque violence struggled for supremacy. Everything was so raw, crying out for healing, but too sensitive to touch.

It wasn't possible to contact Tom no matter how much she might have wanted to. The message of her safety had reached her parents, and she was quite sure Tom would be talking to them soon enough. At the very least, he would know she wasn't dead. It came slowly but she was feeling increasingly ill at ease. The deceit, so much part of her everyday existence, was gnawing at her confidence. The rewarding confidence she had expected was becoming progressively illusive. It could become a problem but she didn't have immediate time to consider moral subtleties. Too much introspection would make her a risk to herself and others. And things, so far, were going well. Tom, with a little unobservable help from her friends, would just have to look after himself.

Kaye had her own work. She had already spoken with women from five separate cells of ten. Each woman was in contact with other cells as well and each could pass on information and listen to the women in those other cells. Although Kaye had spoken with only fifty women, at least five hundred had heard what she had to say. Many of the cells had been operating for several years but it was only recently they were becoming politically informed. Those years worked in their favour because they were still seen by their men as mere women concerned with the virtues of family life. That was true. It would have been unthinkable to suspect them of anything political at all. That was not what Muslim women did.

XI

Kaye was to learn how quickly unexpected events could change life in Afghanistan. Four weeks after Tom's arrival he was kidnapped and Maurice, Minnah's husband, was murdered. The suddenness of the events intensified her vulnerability, her limitations were displayed with brutal clarity. A dreadful incident she remembered from her childhood made her more sensitive. A friend, only three months older, had drowned in her parents' pool after being told not to swim without supervision. Kaye imagined, perhaps with some self-gratifying melodrama, she was as helpless as that disobedient little girl drowning alone. She dreaded speaking with Minnah. What could she draw on to offer comfort?

A distressed Amadullah had brought both appalling revelations at the same time. For a second time, she embraced him but this time there was no embarrassed stiffening of his body. He melted into her arms and wept; Afghan honour was swamped by grief. The embrace might have lasted ten seconds, but the impact would reverberate for days. Amadullah disengaged and stood straight, attempting to gain his composure.

"Sorry," he couldn't use Kaye's name, "I won't do it again."

"Amadullah, you're my brother, remember?"

"Ah yes, how could I forget? In Afghanistan, one doesn't often make such a friendship with a foreigner as I did with Maurice. Neither does a man weep like a woman."

"If it helps, I've forgotten your tears already, but what happened?

Is there a connection between Maurice's murder and Tom's kidnapping?"

"I'm almost certain. Do you remember that Tom operated on Ahmed Bakir? Well, we know he's a Taliban sympathizer. It's likely he'd been planning Maurice's murder for a long time. Bakir hated Maurice. He might have known about Minnah and what she's doing. I don't think he has a clear idea, but it was enough for him to think she is, and even more so her husband, an insult to his own vision of Islam. Maurice was failing to keep his wife under control, and that is an unforgivable sin. I'll find out… be sure of that." Amadullah's authoritative presence had returned.

"Where is Minnah now?"

"At home with Rokhshana and several of the other women. I don't dare go to see her yet. At times like these we men like to keep our distance."

"But Amadullah, Minnah will need you."

"Soon, soon I'll go."

"Well, I must go now. Will you take me?"

"Of course."

It took twenty-five minutes in Amadullah's old truck to get to Minnah. Kaye was not prepared for what she saw. The women were 'lamenting' like a chorus in an ancient Greek play. Awkwardly aware of her inadequate emotional and religious vocabulary, Kaye couldn't think of another word to describe the scene. 'Lamenting' sounded archaic and yet the scene was just that. The wailing and weeping was loud and frightening. Such cultural and familial intimacy was beyond her capacity to absorb, the wailing more than she could endure. The entire scene was so… well, alien, threatening even. Kaye was ashamed of her own limited emotional range and inadequate vocabulary of grief. She wanted to get back into the truck with Amadullah and drive off. But Minnah saw her friend and rushed to embrace her. Kaye was transfixed by her red and swollen eyes.

"I'm so sorry to hear about Tom. It's so unfair. He came to help and now he's in real danger."

Had Kaye been asked, she would have had no coherent explanation, not to weep was impossible. Minnah's husband had just been murdered and yet her first words to a foreign woman expressed concern for a foreign man. What was it that shaped this woman's heart?

'Dear God, I have a lot to learn,' Kaye said to herself. 'I've no idea what I'm doing here.'

"Kaye, I'm so pleased you could come."

"I'm so sorry, Minnah. I don't know what to say... dear Maurice."

"There's nothing to say. We can pray to Allah for mercy and that he chooses not to increase our burden."

"Of course, Minnah, I'm sure we can." Kaye had not prayed since she was eleven. She had asked God to spare her very lovely sick grandmother who, she pointed out to the Lord, was only sixty-three. Kaye's grandmother was a believer who knew men were sinners and that they needed to be saved. Over the years, she had given Kaye several Bible verses to learn by heart. The critical one at the time was about man's allotted span being three score and ten.

But either God had not read Ecclesiastes or he had forgotten. Kaye's grandmother died and the last thing the eleven years old Kaye had said to God was that she hated him. Now that childish hatred was reinforced by adult anger. She was no longer a child but the swelling powerlessness of her anger was just as ineffective as her childish hatred. She was without inspiration of any kind in a country overflowing with a religion and customs so alien they were terrifying. And yet here was a woman who loved her. Minnah was a rebuke, as far as Kaye could fathom, to the macho religion that engulfed her. But that was the point. Of course, it was. That was why she was in Afghanistan: to support the women who were the heart of their nation and acutely tired of violence. Children disfigured and killed, husbands and brothers blasted by landmines were wearing them down and sapping the will to live. The women were tired of suffering.

Because Kaye could not bear the intensity of the suffering, she sought protection in a restraining intellectual abstraction, an abstraction, deliberate and necessary. It was a limited kind of relief. Those fellows in the sixties might have been right after all, Pinter, Stoppard and the rest, and Becket of course. Life was like waiting for somebody in your pyjamas, or whatever, who was never going to turn up. But we keep bloody waiting.

Kate, like her educated contemporaries, had absorbed her morality in the abstract. It was easy. One could be moral without having to be personally disciplined or sacrificial. The moral woman was green, believed in climate change and equality. She loved whales and believed in gender theory. It hadn't occurred to Kaye to think that there could be a difference between a sentimental morality emotionally aroused, and one with a foundation that demanded personal restraint and discipline. It was coming to her slowly. Liberal piety might be psychologically satisfying in the lecture theatre or chattering around the dinner table, but it wasn't much use in Afghanistan. Pain, anguish and death were terrifyingly intimate. Paradox was real. Flesh and blood was warm, terrifying, cruel and loving. She could never be sure what kind of flesh and blood she was likely to encounter. Her own warm blood could cease to flow and her flesh could grow cold. In Australia, she had imagined living forever. In Afghanistan, each day alive was a kind of victory that demanded thankfulness.

Thankfulness, what a strange thing for a grieving heart. Who would she thank? Her mother, her father, Tom perhaps, the God who wasn't there? But neither was anyone else. There was no one, and yet she felt the need to be grateful. She embraced Minnah and wept with her. For the first time in her life she was enfolding a bereaved woman in her arms. It came to her... this was the tightest she had ever held on to compassion. It was so real. Kaye was alone in a hostile country surrounded by death and suffering and guileless humanity of comforting another. She hadn't anticipated how deeply it would confuse her. How could she?

XII

The day before Kaye learned Tom had been kidnapped, he had a visitor at the hospital late in the evening. Ahmed Bakir had returned to thank him for saving his life. Something of an overdramatization, but Tom accepted the gratitude. But from that point on everything went crazy. Bakir asked Tom if he would go to France for a week or two, 'to do some important lifesaving medical work.' Payment would be very generous indeed. He suggested twenty thousand euros. The proposition seemed absurd.

"Surely there are thousands of excellent surgeons in France."

"Ah yes, but I need someone I can trust." Bakir was not convincing. It was hardly surprising that Tom suspected something shady.

"No, I'm afraid I can't help. Too much to do here," Tom's refusal was too emphatic.

"Well my friend, I don't have time to waste."

Two large men appeared from nowhere and bundled Tom along the deserted corridor to a waiting van. It took place so quickly, Tom had difficulty believing it was happening. It wasn't quite a dream but it couldn't possibly be real. But it was. He struggled as a dusty fabric was forced into his mouth and handcuffs on to his wrists. Ahmed Bakir moved into the front seat beside the driver. No attempt had been made to blindfold Tom.

"I'm sorry my friend but we need your skills immediately. In a little over eleven hours you will be in Marseille. You are flying out of Afghanistan as an undesirable alien on a special flight. There will be no use appealing for help on the plane because no one will believe you and few will understand English. If you determine to be uncooperative then we will not hesitate to silence you with the necessary drugs. I'm sure we won't need to."

It would have pleased Tom to think he was being brave, but he was dealing with a powerful man. He tried to convince himself otherwise, but he was scared. Some of the ground staff and maybe even the aircrew could have been bribed. If there was a consolation in any of the absurdity, it seemed he was more valuable alive than dead. But what a mess. He had come to Afghanistan to find Kaye, who was either dead or kidnapped, and now he was abducted and being taken out of the country. It sounded like something out of a teenager's thriller. Bakir was a tribal leader of some kind. He knew that but nothing else.

It was early morning when the plane touched down at Marignane, after a two hour stop in Istanbul where Tom was forced to remain on the plane. He had been to Marseille once on a university rugby tour, so his memories were pleasant if a little foggy. He knew where La Notre Dame de la Garde was and maybe the hotel where he stayed. That was about it. A bus had taken the team to the grounds where they played. He had managed to get lost every time he went out. And now here he was, with a couple of heavies on either side. They had his passport but as they approached the non-EU queue one heavy slipped it into his hand.

This was his chance. For a brief period, as his passport was checked, he would be a metre away from both heavies. But he hadn't counted on the infrequent offhand style of French passport control. He was through before he had worked out what to say. His only chance was to run for it. But that impulse was immediately quashed. Bakir had moved in right behind him with what felt like a very hard object in his back.

"Now, my friend, we need you, but not absolutely."

The implication was clear. Tom decided to conform for the present. It was a mystery to him how Bakir had managed to get a firearm into France and apparently carry one on the plane. Maybe he had a contact in French customs to supply him with one. Maybe it was all bluff but Tom was not yet ready to risk anything in such an unfamiliar environment.

A car was waiting outside: a large black Citroën with darkened windows. He was placed between the two, now familiar, heavies in the back seat, going to some shabby hideaway, no doubt. One of his heavy-duty friends said something to the driver, probably in Pashto. Tom had learned to recognize the language's rhythm and intonation. The driver thought it very funny, whatever it was, and laughed far too loudly to soften Tom's discomfort. He thought it vulgar.

Tom was contemplating the nature of the civilized mind when a somewhat dusty cotton bag was forced over his head.

"Waste of time, mate, I'd never remember the way there or back." Still, the bag was a good sign. If they were taking the bother to conceal the way to wherever they were going, it was unlikely they intended disposing of him. That was a kind of comfort. There was another laugh, a little less intimidating than the other. Perhaps the brightest spot so far was that he could still breathe comfortably. No one spoke for what must have been about half an hour. Tom tried to count the minutes but got confused and gave up. The car stopped.

Someone said in English, "Okay, this is as far as we go."

With not too much force, Tom was taken from the car and led for about thirty metres until he was inside a building. When his hood was removed, he was confronted by a smiling Ahmed Bakir.

"I hope you haven't been too uncomfortable Tom." Bakir's use of Tom's first name annoyed him. "But it's your own fault. You could have agreed and we would all still love one another." Bakir sniggered at his little joke. That annoyed Tom even more, but he remained silent.

"Come, you have a job to do."

Tom was lead down a dull, dusty corridor to a set of double doors. He noted that they were considerably superior to the rest of the building he had seen so far. Looking very pleased with himself,

Bakir led Tom through both sets of doors to display an operating theatre that would have been credible in any medium sized hospital in Queensland.

Inside there were two men all scrubbed up and looking tired. Tom assumed that one of them was the anaesthetist and the other perhaps a surgeon. Both were young, no more than thirty.

"Hassid and Muhammad will inform you better than I could what you must do. They will be guided by your superior skill and experience. I will leave you in their care."

The man lying on the table looked about thirty-five. Tom wondered if he was Bakir's brother, the resemblance was so close. But why here? Why did Bakir not want to use a French hospital or surgeon?

And even more confusing, he was to discover, the patient was already attended to. The young medicos had done everything necessary. Apart from making the obvious noises of approval his task was complete. Bakir had other plans unless he had merely underestimated the skill of the two young men. Anyway, Tom was exhausted. He had no idea who had been stitched up. Whoever he was, he had been a mess. Caught in an explosion, he would have been dead if he had not been attended to immediately by Hassid and Muhammad. They had done all they could. But Tom remained perplexed. Why had Bakir needed him? Certainly, he was experienced and good at his job. Perhaps Bakir's experience with Tom caused him to believe Tom was more skilful than he was. But again, why get him when there were so many surgeons in France so much more experienced? That question irritated him.

After his remarkable non-appearance in theatre, Tom woke suffering from what must have been jetlag. It was either that or he had passed through a window on the horizon to a new kind of fantasy. A fantasy unhappily concluded by a very large man with a luxuriant beard who brought Tom's breakfast: fresh fruit, cereal, milk, yoghurt, two croissants, orange juice and coffee. A mouth must have been somewhere inside the beard, but it chose not to reveal itself by sight or sound.

Tom ate nearly everything. The coffee was unexpectedly good. It was then, the beard having left, that his immediate situation imposed itself. He was in a plain but comfortable room about six metres by five metres. There was one door and two windows both with bars on the outside, normal in France. The walls were matte white with several photographs pinned to one wall. The fierce bearded and mouth-less one stared out from one picture; Tom was quite sure his eyes followed him about the room. 'All very odd,' mused Tom. Muslims, he understood, wrongly perhaps, had profound religious objections to the camera.

He closed his eyes and attempted to assess his predicament. 'Assess' was wishful thinking. He had no reference points. Another photograph claimed his attention. It was Bakir with his arm around another man. Tom was sure it was the wounded patient he had attended to and he did look like Bakir. Both men carried rifles. Tom knew they were Kalashnikovs. The Australian army, as far as he knew, still had F88s. They were the only rifles he could recognize with confidence. Maybe, for some perverse reason, the pictures were there for his benefit. The door opened again and Ahmed Bakir entered. He smiled.

"Ah Tom, I see you're awake. I hope the breakfast was to your liking."

"Yes, it was," said Tom, awkwardly submissive.

"I believe I owe you an explanation. You might be tempted to think so, but you're not in the hands of lunatics."

"That's a comfort," Tom's voice sounded almost normal. It had lost the annoying obsequious tone.

"Good, I see you have recovered somewhat. We are going to see much of each other over the next few weeks, so it's important that we are able to cooperate with honour."

"Honour? I'm hardly here out of the goodness of my heart."

The last two lines of a poem he had learned at high school, somewhat irrationally, flooded into his mind. The poet, he was almost certain, was female: 'I could not love thee dear, so much/ Loved I not honour more.'

Tom was quite sure the poet's honour was not Bakir's. Honour demanded truth and love. The indoctrination of his childhood, if indeed it was indoctrination, was giving him confidence. There was something deeply encouraging about a childhood conviction realistic enough to sustain the man.

"Indeed, but you were offered an opportunity to come with dignity. Nevertheless, I do regret the necessity of our actions because I believe you are a good man. Let me show my respect for you by telling the truth. This little institution is very important to us. We are in Marseille because this is where I attended university and I know the city. Oh yes, I'm not an uneducated primitive as you might find it comfortable to believe. I simply want to see Afghanistan free from foreign soldiers, be they Russian, British or American. We cannot risk French surgeons working here. They are too familiar with the environment and would very clearly be missed by their colleagues. It would be far too messy to employ them, and we would always have to cover our backs."

"I see. I'm useful but disposable."

"If you insist. That is the necessary truth. However, you will be well paid. Every week 4000 euros will go into an account not in your name but entrusted to you. I'll give you all the particulars in due course. As long as you remain accommodating all will be well."

Accommodating? What a bland word for the circumstances.

"And eventually I'm free?"

"I hope that's the case."

"I see. The alternative is obvious."

"Tom, let's not think of that. I'm in your debt, consequently I want to treat you with justice. I understand how you must feel. I too have been a prisoner but in less congenial surroundings, believe me."

Tom nearly said something he knew he would regret. He was going to point out that Bakir's notion of justice was somewhat skewed, but he thought better of it. He was in one world and Bakir in another. 'East is east and west is west', and all that. Bakir's East would consume his West. The debate would have been delicious in more agreeable circumstances.

Tom, of course, had no idea of the man who held him prisoner. Had he known more, he would not have been seduced by Bakir's apparent bonhomie. Born in Algeria, Bakir had been abandoned by his father before his tenth birthday and brought up entirely by his mother. He loved her and hated his father. It was that deep hatred that informed his need to see himself as a victim. Power was his god. Both men despised weakness. It was hardly surprising that Muhammad was his model warrior.

Drugs and arms had made Bakir rich, very rich. An enemy might have said ideology was giving him his energy and a greed massaged by religious dogma was giving him his motivation. The enemy might have been right. Whatever the case, Bakir had an excellent memory and he was, indeed, a master of duplicity. Like his fraudulent mentor who chose to rule on earth rather than serve in heaven, Bakir chose to reign in Afghanistan rather than serve in the world as he pretended to do. In Afghanistan, he had gained the confidence of some senior officers in the US army. The Americans were concerned that their final departure from the country be orderly and not smell of defeat. They needed reliable friends they could leave behind. As well as that, transporting heavy weapons out of the country was expensive. If some could be left in the hands of friends, all the better. Bakir was that friend.

The Americans were not complete strangers to duplicity. They could be, like everyone else, competent liars. But unlike Bakir, lying was not built into their philosophy. That was their weakness and Bakir's strength. If he required it, he could lie with Allah's approval. There was no need to be compromised by guilt. The American's were not in the same class. They might not have been God's army but they retained a residual, if irrational belief in the virtue of truth even when they lied. And, what was of even greater importance to Bakir, they believed others were the same. Bakir, they had concluded, was trustworthy.

XIII

It was the day after Maurice's burial when Minnah told Kaye who had killed him.

"We're certain that it was the same man who abducted Tom, Ahmed Bakir. He's taken Tom to France. Amadullah found out, he has ears and eyes everywhere."

"France, why?"

"The only reason that makes sense is that Bakir needs Tom's skills in France. Amadullah thinks that Tom's surgery on Bakir was a mixed blessing. The successful surgery just gave Bakir a good reason to get on with things."

"But why France?"

"Not sure, except Bakir has friends in Marseille. In the old days, he ran his drug distribution from there. Amadullah is quite sure he is planning something that must involve Tom."

"What about Maurice? Oh Minnah, this is dreadful. Who is this guy?"

"He's a tribal leader with ancestors in Afghanistan, although he was born in Algeria. He fronts as a devout Muslim but he's only interested in money and power. He has hated Maurice for years because Maurice had support from some moderates who want reform. The opportunity came to get rid of a thorn in his flesh and he took it. I'm sure Tom's little trip to France and Maurice's 'execution' are not directly related except they happened on the same day."

Minnah's composure was remarkable; the mild sarcasm was unexpected. It seemed so out of character. But then, of course, she was an educated woman on a mission. Her husband's death would make her more single-minded. Kaye had never found a woman she admired so much. She couldn't help herself. She embraced Minnah with a deep sense of pathos, but not without a slight discomforting ache. Afghanistan was not her only unfamiliar country. Kaye was the first to speak.

"So, what do we do now?"

"We go to France, that's what," Minnah was emphatic. "Amadullah is obsessed. Revenge and honour are all he can think about. I don't dare let him go alone. He'll take the most extraordinary of foolish risks. With me he'll always think twice; that's the kind of man he is, a real one."

"But what about your work here? You'll be missed."

"Yes, but this is the heart of things. I won't be in France forever. I'll be back. Evil has to be destroyed in France as well as here."

"Has it? Is such a thing possible?" Kaye had no idea. Her question was genuine enough; she had no hidden agenda. Any concept she might have had of evil was still vague, coloured by years of abstraction. She had no capacity to accept that evil might have a powerful and personal existence.

"It has to be. Evil must be defeated, otherwise we're all lost. All religions are not equal."

"Aren't they? I think the consensus back home is that they might be in the end."

"That's because they don't live in the naked brutality of a country like Afghanistan. They take refuge in theory and conjecture. They live on the surface, money is their anaesthetic. I wonder if they'll ever wake up to discover they've lost the plot. It's the great Western disease. They've forgotten the old story of sin's power, so they have no touchstone anymore. If evil does impose its presence on them, they think it's just over here and not a threat to their own hearts. They're such hypocrites. They preach freedom for all but insist on legislating their own bankrupt ideology of democracy on the rest of us."

Kaye was astonished. She was a little girl being lectured by her mother. She neither understood nor liked what she thought she was hearing. Wasn't Minnah wanting to work with the West? What did she really want?'

"You say you'll go to France. Does that include me?"

"Of course, Tom is the man you love, is he not?"

Minnah was irritating; her certainties were breath-taking but Kaye didn't dare question her. She had grown up in a world where all personal problems and questions of guilt were deemed psychological, for Minnah all personal problems were moral. Sin and guilt were real and deep, not always evident on the surface.

Kaye was subdued, "Of course I'm coming. I've no idea what I'll do, but then I came to Afghanistan in the same condition. Why change a good thing?"

Minnah smiled. "Indeed, why change? Your minders will be concerned, but you'll still be working with us so they won't stop you. Anyway, Amadullah will keep them sweet for a while at least."

"I'm out of my depth Minnah. You're going to France to 'execute' Bakir. Have I got that right?"

"I certainly hope so, Kaye."

"Just like that?"

"Just like that!"

Kaye's re-education continued. How on earth could she handle this? How did she get here?

"Kaye, please understand. We don't expect you to be an intimate part of our little mission, but we will need you to draw out Bakir."

"Really, how?"

"Bakir must be using Tom for his surgical skills. Don't be fooled. He will have known about you in Afghanistan, but I suspect only about your official business as a newspaper reporter and perhaps your association with us or with Tom. As soon as he knows you're in Marseille, and he eventually will, he will seek you out. His vanity will insist that he does. It gives him another card to play in the game he's playing with Tom. Believe me I've known this man a very long time."

"Minnah, you're using me, and do you know? I don't care. All my life, until I came to Afghanistan, I had no idea how exciting it could be to live life on the edge. My life had no edges; it was all centre… me. It was so bloody boring and the irony was I didn't know I was bored. Can you believe it? Now I'm really going into the unknown. It's exciting. Am I mad? Don't answer that!"

"I won't, but in the next few days you'll have to learn how to use a handgun. Are you up for that? It was on the agenda anyway."

"Why not? Absolutely. I spent two weeks before I came to Afghanistan being put through the paces by SERE, you know, survival, evasion, resistance and escape. I'm not a novice."

"Good girl."

Kaye, yielding to instinct, enjoyed 'good girl'. She was a little girl being praised by her teacher. Ignoring any possible accusation of sentimentality, she found the hint of tears heartening. She had never considered her present life possible. She was being offered insights that lay outside all previous experience. That essential grieving that nearly always accompanied any entry to the sublime had eluded her. Perhaps now a glimpse was being offered. For the first time in her life she was experiencing a sense of wonder about the nature of the world or something like that. It was less painful to keep any revealing insights vague; it was easier that way.

It was one week and three days later when Kaye, Minnah and Amadullah landed at Nice Côte d'Azur Airport after a short flight from Rome. Amadullah didn't want to land in Marseille because, he claimed, Bakir had too many friends at the airport.

"There's one little flaw here," said Kaye as they walked towards border control. "I'm a tourist on an Australian passport. I'll be so easy to identify. You just walk into the country. Bakir will find me before I'm ready."

"Don't worry. I know Bakir's methods," said Amadullah. "He won't treat you like Tom, although I suspect Tom's safe enough. As soon as he knows you're here, and I'll make sure he does, he'll try to chat you up to find out what you know. Believe me, he can be very charming: sweetness and light."

As it happened Kaye's Australian passport was given less attention than she expected. Italy was an EU country and once in the EU, Kaye was to find out, few border control officers were interested. As soon as they were in the TGV to Marseille from Nice and everyone was feeling relaxed, Minnah looked directly at Kaye from the seat opposite. She placed her hand lightly on Kaye's knee and said, "Kaye, I'm sure you understand. We need to contact Bakir because we must know where Tom is and what Bakir is up to."

"I guess so, it's just that I'm not up with the play like you guys. All this cloak and dagger stuff is new territory for me."

"I know. Just remember why you're here." Minnah kissed Kaye on the cheek. "You're going to stay at a middle of the road hotel, Mama Shelter. Like the name? Amadullah and I will be staying less than a hundred metres away. And, if you don't mind, please wear this."

"What is it? It looks like a watch."

"It is, but it's also a simple tracking device so we always know where you are."

"I see." Kaye's fear was swamped by the realization she was important to the entire mission, a pivot even. Well perhaps that was an exaggeration, one of the pivots. It was an appealing metaphor. But what was she? It wasn't too long ago that she thought she was in control and quite able to shape her own life. She was neither. She was a woman pulsating with life in a way she had not thought possible. Forces were at work, sure they were, and they were pointing her in the way she wanted to go. It was liberating.

XIV

Tom's first week at the 'clinic' was uneventful and, when he thought about it, tedious. There were nearly fifty DVDs in the room, left behind by others perhaps. But there is a limit to how many old films one can watch in a day. He had never liked 'Lawrence of Arabia' but some of the old westerns were fun. 'High Noon' was even better than he remembered, and 'The Magnificent Seven' somehow, he had missed. The Marx Brothers were a surprise. Groucho restored his faith in human nature. He wondered if Muhammad had a moustache. When did beards become obligatory for Muslims?

The films had to be old. Modern movies would be too salacious for the pious mind of the good Muslim. Maybe the odd Terminator movie would have passed muster. Two movies, however, proved thought provoking. One was from the early 1950s with James Mason, "One Way Street". The morality implicit in the film was remarkable. On the surface, it seemed to be about reaping what you sow but, really, it was about the acceptance of one's wrongdoing with a kind of gracious resignation. Another, "Istanbul" with Errol Flynn, of all people, had a similar theme. Personal responsibility seemed to be important, even to the villain. Tom suspected they would have been sentimental and implausible to Roger.

Perhaps he should be more appreciative; the food was still good and he had his own bathroom, which was kept clean by a woman he heard but never saw. Tom thought it was a woman. The adjoining door was always locked as she worked. He had listened once and imagined he had heard a female voice complement the noise of running water and scrubbing.

Week two was to be much more exciting. He had two broken limbs and a suspected concussion to attend. The highlight was a visit from Bakir, apparently to see if Tom was happy enough. Bakir decided he was. Well into the exchange of pleasantries Bakir asked, almost as an aside, "Tom, do you know a journalist from your home town, Kaye Reynolds?"

Tom was baffled. The question came from nowhere. Wisdom suggested he proceed with a precise but limited truth.

"Yes, I do. She's very well-known back home." Tom congratulated himself; he nearly slipped into the past tense.

"Do you know her?"

"Not as well as I would like. She's a very attractive woman."

"You know she was in Afghanistan when you were there. Did you ever see her?"

"No, I didn't, but it would've been impossible not to hear about her. Her kidnapping was big news in Australia. I didn't see her but I would've been very happy to have done so."

Bakir looked intently at Tom with an expression more quizzical than hostile.

"I could have been convinced that the appearance of both of you in Afghanistan was a coincidence. I'm certain you had no contact with her there, but now we have a small problem, Tom. Miss Reynolds is in Marseille. What can you say about that?"

"Not a lot. I have no idea why she's here. And as you've just said I had no contact in Afghanistan and certainly none since I've been here. If surprise is the issue, then I'm as surprised as you seem to be."

"Yes, I'm inclined to believe you. There are other reasons that could have brought her here."

"Why not ask her? She is a journalist after all. If she's been in Afghanistan, she might know who you are and want an interview."

"Perhaps, we shall see."

When Bakir left, Tom's mind was raging. Kaye was alive but she was up to something. The whole kidnapping thing was subterfuge. What on earth was the woman up to? He was angry or relieved, maybe both, he couldn't be sure. Obviously Bakir knew more than he had revealed. That was certain. But what did he know? Did it matter? Kaye had gone to Afghanistan to do a job for a newspaper. That would hardly have been threatening, so why should Bakir be concerned? What was Kaye up to and why the phony kidnapping? Thank God, she was alive. What was going on?

No matter which way he looked at it, Kaye had deceived him. That was upsetting. After that night in the restaurant he had thought a new start had been possible and he was sure Kaye was thinking the same. He was disappointed. Now he just wanted to see her and hear an explanation.

He had to get out, but with no money and no credit cards it would be difficult to get away quickly even if he did make it out of 'prison'. He still had the tourist's impression of Marseille. It was a lawless place with cut-throats on every corner. Desperation could easily take control of his mind. He had no idea where he was, and in the middle of the night in Marseille anything could happen. Careful... then he remembered. He still had his work shoes and Roger's money with Benjamin Franklin's face was taped inside the left one. It was enough for a taxi, providing he could find one. The US dollar might still have some clout in France. Dear Roger, he could have had no idea how his odd gesture could be a possible life saver. Perhaps he had!

The window in the shower was the only window that had no bars either inside or outside, but it was high up and small. There was just a chance he might be able to squeeze through. But how to get to it? That was the problem. First up in the morning, before the cleaner came, he would test things out.

Tom was wide awake at first light. He took the only chair he had into the shower and attempted to reach the window. He could just reach, but he still had to pull his whole body up and through the narrow opening and even then, it was doubtful if the window was large enough to allow his shoulders through. He needed more height, but how? He took the chair back to its position in the room and flopped down on the bed knocking his head on the edge of the wobbly bedhead. It was just leaning against the wall, unattached to the bed. Tom put the chair back in the shower and balanced the lower edge of the bedhead on the seat of the chair. By standing precariously on the upper edge of the bedhead, he could reach the window comfortably. His shoulders just might fit through.

Emboldened, Tom practiced the manoeuvre several times before placing the chair and the bedhead back where they belonged. He would attempt his escape as soon as it got dark. Every night he had been left to his own devices; there was no reason to suppose that was going to change.

Of course, Tom couldn't know that while he was contemplating his escape Bakir contacted Kaye. He had sent a hand-written message to her hotel suggesting they meet at a place she chose. Although expecting, and even hoping for such a message Kaye remained anxious. Minnah's encouragement strengthened her.

"Look Kaye, it's very unlikely Bakir knows of your contact with us. He'll be sounding you out, probably about Tom. I'm sure that he's not suspicious; he has no reason unless he knows why you were really in Afghanistan. And even if he did, it's unlikely that would put him off. This is our chance to find out where he is and maybe something of what he is planning in Marseille."

"I'm trying to keep calm, but I don't find it easy. I would like to think I was one of James Bond's girls, one who survives at least."

"Look, Amadullah has been talking to an old friend in the Police Nationale. They trust him and they know Bakir is here, although they are no wiser than we are as to why."

"I'll go but you fellows keep a close eye on me."

"Of course, we've already thought about that. So, meet him at your hotel for breakfast. Just sit in that outside area. Use the second table from the left. We can have a listening device installed."

"You are organized."

"Yes. We'll hear everything that's said. It's too dangerous to place a listening device on you. The tracer watch is enough if you happen to go on an unexpected trip."

"I suppose I should be pleased about that. Do the police know what we're up to, by the way?'"

"No, not yet, although I'm not entirely sure what they might have gained from Amadullah by osmosis, body language being what it is. By the way, Bakir will be watching yours, and I'm not talking about your cleavage, although I guess he'll be watching that too. He's a randy hypocrite with a great deal of charm."

"Of course, he is. The extremists are always the best cheats."

"Your prejudices have some use after all, Kaye."

"Yes… well, I guess. It's a mystery how you're so civilized and he's such an apparent low-life. It's hard to believe you're both Muslims."

"Perhaps; every faith has its hypocrites. Christianity has had more than its share. They started with Judas, remember? I doubt myself frequently. I suspect Ahmed seldom does. But then some doubt is not all that bad. Thomas made it okay, if you remember."

"Minnah, your Biblical knowledge surprises me. Why are you so interested?"

"Ah, one has to know what the opposition is up to. By the way, something I'm sure you don't know, the Qur'an mentions Jesus more often than Muhammad."

"Really? So, Christianity's not the opposition then."

"Ah, you speak like one who hopes the world can be made better if we were all just that little bit more tolerant. Yes, I'm afraid, my very dear friend, it is the opposition. Two absolutes can't share the same world, nor enemies the same bed. But don't worry, I wouldn't expect you to have thought about that. That's a problem we share. Western liberals are seldom either/or people when it comes to religion."

"It's all very polarising, a 'no go area' among my friends as I remember. They're light-years away now. Afghanistan has filtered them out, if you know what I mean."

"Only too well I'm afraid, Kaye. I expect the filter's clogged, if I can steal your image. Afghanistan bewilders Westerners. Americans make heavy weather of it all. The Muslim brand of religious faithfulness is beyond their notion of good order. Thou shalt be democratic, is the first commandment. They're not good at having their backs to the wall. And anyway, they've spent the last few decades consigning religion to the political compost bin. They don't remember what compost is supposed to do."

"I don't understand."

"Well, they know so little about Islam. Few in the US hierarchy understand the ambiguity of the Muslim mind. It just seems so irrational to them. They can't grasp the consequences of the obvious; religion is married to politics in Islam."

"Is it? For the moderates like you and Amadullah too?"

"Yes, Westerners, certainly the French, have faith in the supremacy of the rational, but rationality alone will not discover God, or lose him for that matter. One believes that He is. Jews, Christians and Muslims agree on that at least. The hard question is the next one. Who is he? The Christians have a head start; God became the man Jesus."

"That's my problem."

"What do you mean Kaye?"

"Well, a Muslim attracted by Jesus? Isn't that a bit odd?"

"Oh. It has become the love story for me."

"Really! I'm not sure I understand."

XV

Tom waited until he was sure he wouldn't be disturbed, and arranged his escape mechanism silently. He balanced delicately on the edge of the headboard and tried to get his shoulders out through the gap, too tight. He stepped down, took off his shirt and covered the upper part of his body with soap, kindly supplied by Allah. He climbed up again and poked his head and arms out through the window. There was a fall of nearly two metres onto the road. Slowly the soap worked its slippery purpose and he was out as far as his waist. He would have to land on his hands and hope he didn't break a wrist. He placed his hands against the wall and reduced his fall to less than a metre.

Tom's hands slid down the wall as slowly and as far as he was able. By keeping his legs apart in the opening, he could use them to delay the drop. And then he fell. For a moment he lay still, expecting loud shouting and rough hands… nothing. His legs were bleeding from scraping along the window frame and he had cut his left forearm on a sharp stone in the wall. Picking himself up in a response that more closely resembled Pavlov's dogs than the intelligent action of an escaping man, he was to comment later, he ran as fast and as far as he could.

It was early morning and Tom was exhausted, bloody, soapy and shirtless. He had no idea where he was or what to do. He walked for at least an hour with a mind passing between wild anger and subdued relief. He was angry at Kaye's deceit and the sheer waste of emotional and physical energy she had demanded in some oblique way he couldn't quite explain. Her career had always come first. That annoyed him. Maybe that was the nature of journalism at the top. Its demands were irregular and tyrannical, and time was always going to be absorbed in unexpected ways.

Eventually some kind of normality had to return. Tom examined street names. They meant nothing. Rue Berthelot and rue Pasteur sounded familiar, but every village, town and city in France had a rue Pasteur. And then a major road: Chemin du Moulin du Diable. Devil's mill, appropriate perhaps but hardly helpful.

It was nearly daylight before Tom found a taxi willing to pick him up.

"Le Gendarmerie, si'l vous plait. Vite!" shouted Tom, flashing the lucky 100-dollar bill and using nearly all the French he knew. He had no idea of the difference between the police and the gendarmerie, if indeed there was a difference. The driver was, Tom discovered, from Algeria and a sympathetic man. He assumed Tom was a tourist who had been mugged. It didn't take long before the driver pulled up outside the Police Nationale on Boulevard Mireille Lauze. He helped a very tired and bewildered Tom out of the car and up the steps.

Eventually, after much explanation to a haze of faces, the fog lifted. He found himself in a shower with an unremarkable white robe given to him by a pretty and kindly policewoman who introduced him to a certain Commissaire Fabien Bartholdi. After the shower, his injured leg and arm were neatly bandaged. The $100 with Benjamin Franklin's face had been more than helpful.

Bartholdi was about fifty, his remaining grey wavy tresses well-groomed. Marginally under six feet, in the old measurements which Tom still used, his presence in the room was imposing. He looked more authoritative and stronger than he might have if Tom had seen him in a more routine situation. Uniforms have that effect, Tom thought. His English came with an easy confidence.

"Well, Mr. Grace, you've been having quite a time. We're aware of Monsieur Bakir, so your story interests me. You must be exhausted.

I'm going to have you taken to a hotel for the rest of today and to-night. You are an important man and in need of some good French hospitality. Tomorrow you and I will have a long chat. For your safety and peace of mind, I will have your room guarded by two of my men."

Tom could think of nothing significant to say. "Thank you. I am tired," was all he could manage.

"I would like you to stay in your room for the next day or so. Ar-rangements will be made to bring you food when you request it. I want you fresh tomorrow; we have much to discuss."

Tom's hotel room on the sixth floor was large with a view of the harbour and across to the Notre Dame de la Garde, a building he could remember from his rugby touring days. But he was too tired to reminisce. He was in bed sound asleep within fifteen minutes. The col-our of the walls and the bed clothes faded to a muddled forgetfulness.

Tom slept for almost ten hours, the first time since he was a teen-ager. Maybe it was the security of the hotel room and the guards outside after being a prisoner for over a week. His bed back in those teenage times had often seemed like a cocoon. Leaving it had always been difficult.

But leave it he did for a very enjoyable breakfast. His guards sat at a table nearby, but they spoke only occasionally to him. Both were in their late thirties or early forties and talked quietly to each other. Tom tried not to look too much in their direction, although he had no idea why. He wasn't afraid, just out of his comfort zone. And that, for Tom, was to be a continuing experience.

Tom mused that Providence seemed to have a sense of fitting the scene rather neatly together without informing the actors. 'Provi-dence' was a rather poor attempt to avoid the 'G' word. His spiritual vacillation didn't encourage the sensation of a protector overseeing his life. His mother would not have been at a loss to describe his state of mind.

Just as Tom was reflecting about Commissaire Bartholdi and the virtue of various appellations for God, Kaye was nervously waiting to meet Ahmed Bakir. She was not prepared for what she saw. From any perspective Bakir was impressive. He was immaculate in a dark blue, pinstripe single-breasted linen suit with deep splits in the back of the jacket. A silver blue striped tie sat immaculately against his white linen shirt. As he approached Kaye at the table, he walked with a naturalness that made her feel at ease until she saw, up close, the deepest blue eyes she had ever seen. They were disorientating, alarmingly hypnotic. She was bewildered. Algerians don't have blue eyes. Kaye had no way of knowing that Bakir's eye colour probably came from his ancestors, the Shawia in Eastern Algeria.

Whatever the case, Bakir knew his eyes had the power to fascinate. He greeted Kaye with a warmth that if it wasn't genuine it was so seductively contrived it was impossible to discern any duplicity. He was so unexpectedly non-threatening Kaye wondered if she should tell him that everything he said to her would be recorded for training purposes. His presence was so benign she felt like confiding in him. Now, she understood how Eve would have felt on that fateful day.

Neither did Kaye expect Bakir to be accompanied by another woman. She was older than Kaye and immaculate.

"Kaye, I would like you to meet my very good friend Maeva Hassan. Maeva, this is the charming Australian, Kaye Reynolds, we have heard so much about."

"Enchanté Kaye. You live up to Ahmed's description."

"Really," Kaye responded, wondering just what that description might be.

"Maeva has a business not too far away, so I took the chance for her to meet you, Miss Reynolds. I hope you don't mind."

"No, of course not. It's a pleasure."

As it happened, Maeva only stayed a few minutes, business called. She left hoping to meet Kaye again.

"It's very kind of you to meet me. What a delightful hotel; the staff are so young and energetic. Pity it's tucked away, it's so hard to find." Kaye watched, intrigued, as the apparent Muslim terrorist helped himself to bacon, eggs, saucisson, and tomatoes. When in Rome perhaps, well Marseille anyway. Ahmed made two cups of coffee on the espresso machine and gave one to Kaye.

"Now Kaye, may I call you Kaye?"

"Of course."

"Please call me Ahmed."

"Thank you."

"Now let me tell you why I wanted to meet you. I am going to be honest with you. You are an intelligent and competent woman and I'm not going to waste your time."

Kaye noticed in Ahmed's favour that he didn't add 'and I don't expect you to waste mine.' Altogether too smooth an operator.

"You're an important journalist and I seldom get the chance to speak to journalists on neutral ground, certainly not good ones. I hope you understand."

"Yes, I think so... I hope so."

"Good. Some of us from Afghanistan get a very bad press. Few Western writers understand Islam. I suspect you're better informed than most. Yes, and before you ask, I have been doing my own checking up on you. I'm encouraged."

"Really, you're very kind."

"Not at all. The truth is, I'd like you to write an article about us in Afghanistan and give the story a human face. It would have an influential audience in Australia, the US, and maybe Europe. I should say too that I know you are fluent in my own language. I admire you for that."

"To do credit to such a story I would have to return to Afghanistan. I'm not sure..."

"I'd be more than happy to cover all costs."

"That's very generous. I'll have to think about it. I'm not sure I want to go back." The conversation was not going in the direction Kaye had expected. Bakir was moving too fast.

"This is an important work for me. Perhaps we can meet again very soon to discuss your decision?"

"Yes, thank you. That would be helpful."

Bakir had captivated Kaye. Again, he was not what she had expected. His eyes were all wrong and he just so... nice. Silly word, but in this case, it seemed to fit. Seldom had a suit of any colour draped itself so fittingly over such a lean and muscular body. Bakir was just the right age to be interesting to a woman like Kaye. Genes, sunshine, and exercise gave his clear skin that elasticity and shading she wanted to touch.

"Now tell me, Kaye, a little about yourself. You are, if I may say so, a fascinating woman."

Bakir sounded so sincere and interested in her that Kaye couldn't resist offering an obsequious smile. She wanted to believe what he said. He was just so outrageously handsome and smooth it was difficult not to yield to his charm. It irritated her that she was so receptive to that charm even when common sense might have suggested caution. It embarrassed her to enjoy telling Bakir so much about herself. But tell him she did, he was such an attentive listener. She told him about her education in Iran, and how she became fluent in Pashto. She nearly told him about Tom but checked herself. She talked about her parents and her work as a journalist. She couldn't believe that this was the man that Minnah wanted to kill.

"Now maybe a little about yourself, Ahmed."

"Next time, after you have thought about my offer."

"Ah no," Kate was feeling brave. "You will have to do better. I can only work for someone I know."

For some reason Bakir found that remarkably funny and laughed too loud and long for Kaye to retain her ease.

"All right, I'll be ready next time we meet. I have another meeting, so I hope you don't think me rude. It's been a pleasure. Until next time; Au revoir, enjoy Marseille."

Bakir kissed Kaye's hand and was gone, leaving her, if not dumbfounded, then certainly bewildered. She stumbled into the lift and swayed back to her room where Minnah and Amadullah had been listening.

"A sly dog, Kaye," said Minnah. "Is he not? You told him everything and he told you nothing."

"Not quite."

"Anyway, it was all good. He wants to trust you. His vanity was flattered by your attention. I'm sure he expects a good story after all that."

"But why the woman friend, and all that patter about me?"

"There's something you need to know, Kaye," intruded Amadullah. "Bakir is playing two different games with the same players. Here in France he heads a cell of young fanatics prepared to do anything he tells them. I'm confident that my intelligence is reliable. The French suspect him, but they have no evidence of any cell. There is even talk that he has powerful protectors in Paris. He distances himself from everything."

"But he seems so nice."

"Well, just yesterday a lone suicide bomber blew up five people waiting at a bus shelter in Lyon. My information is that he was one of Bakir's young fanatics."

"But why? What can he hope to gain from that?"

"Well, he keeps the French police on their toes and it breeds fear. That's the idea. Breed fear and destabilize. The lone bomber is a ploy to have the French think it's a one off. It encourages the press to think fanatic rather than jihad."

"Why don't the French just kick him out?"

"Yes, they could, quite easily. Normally someone like Bakir wouldn't last long here. The French don't have legal inhibitions like those that surrounded the Abu Qatada case in England. No, they're after the whole deal this time. That's what Bartholdi says. He'll strike when he's ready. It would be amusing if it wasn't so strategic. In Afghanistan, Bakir feigns the American sycophant. The Americans think they're using him to do what they want. The reverse is closer to the truth. The Americans still think everyone will eventually want to play the game like them. They would deny that, I'm sure, but it's true nevertheless. They might be enlightened latter-day liberals in their heads, but they are still boy scouts in their hearts. They think the democratic spirit, rather than deceit, is lodged in the human heart. They don't understand the subtleties of Islam."

"I'm not sure I do," said Minnah very softly. "Anyway, what are you thinking about the story Kaye?"

"I'm not sure, I need time to reflect."

For a moment Amadullah looked puzzled by Minnah's doubt. "The detail is still sketchy. There was an explosion outside the Supreme Court complex in Kabul last night. At least twenty people were killed, including six children. Some forty have been injured and three buses were destroyed. It was another suicide bomb attack."

"Was Bakir involved? Writing this story could be dangerous."

"Can't be sure, but he could have been. Whatever the case, he will lament the cruelty of the calamitous event and promise to give the Americans all the help he can. He wants to be in a strong position when those remaining finally leave."

"How does he manage it?"

"He plays to win because he is convinced he can."

"Ah," said Minnah, "Defeat is impossible for Bakir. He laughs at the Americans and their infatuation with the separation of church and state as revealed truth. It makes him confident that they can't win. He's sure that democracy is the weakest kind of government."

XVI

A car called for Tom at nine thirty. By nine fifty-five he was in Bartholdi's office wearing the fashionable clothes left in his room. He was certainly getting the treatment.

"Good morning, Tom. A good rest, I hope; and a fine breakfast? Here, sit down and relax."

"Thank you. Yes, to both questions." Tom took Bartholdi's advice and sat down on the black, comfortable leather chair.

"Excellent."

"I'm curious, why you're looking after me so well?"

"Well, let me start at the beginning. You've had a difficult time, so let me give you some good news. You're a windfall, I hope you don't mind being called that, you've given me something solid to hold against Ahmed Bakir. And, as you're a reluctant visitor to our country, it's the least we can do. I'm assuming you will be happy to give evidence should the need arise."

"Certainly, although I'm somewhat ambivalent. I have a grudging regard for the man. That must sound a bit crazy to you."

"Well, let me say, as time goes on you'll find out what he's really like. You're an educated man and your ambivalence, I hope, will dissolve quickly."

Fabien Bartholdi had spent several hours finding out as much as he could about Tom, and he liked what he'd heard. He'd been in touch with the Australian Police, his special connection in the CIA, and the British. He knew more about Tom than Tom knew about himself. For an hour or two he had entertained the rather absurd idea that he could have been a Bakir plant. He was sure now that was not the case.

"The problem is, Tom, Bakir's elusive. Although he was born in Algeria, his parents are French citizens. His mother is still alive. The entire scene around him is a political nightmare. He's able to get in and out of Europe with ease. He can fly in a private plane to Italy or Spain, to Greece maybe, and just drive into France. It's very difficult to keep him under surveillance. Influential French and American friends make him particularly slippery."

"But can't you get the Italians to grab him? They won't want him either."

"I'm afraid corruption at some smaller airports is not unknown. He has far too much money to throw around. And, anyway I'm not quite ready to show my hand."

"How can I help?" Tom knew his limitations. "There's no way I can understand the political complexities around Bakir. I can only guess the problems you have to deal with."

"Well, for a start, I'm hoping you might be able to recall some of your nocturnal ramblings before you were picked up by your cooperative taxi driver. By the way he left you some change, thirty euros. You overpaid him."

"Ah, an honest taxi driver. I liked him. Perhaps we'll meet again. Your hope, I'm afraid, might be in vain. I didn't even think to look at street names until I was well away from my 'detention centre'; I'm not sure what to call it."

The Commissaire shut his eyes, leaned back on his leather chair, and scratched his brow. "I'm not interested in arresting Bakir just yet, but I would like to know what he's up to with his 'detention centre.' Private hospital would better fit the description you gave us yesterday."

"There's no doubt the place is being used to patch up friends of Bakir who run into trouble. How does he keep all that away from the press?"

"So far, that has been Bakir's ace. He flies well under the radar. Wealth can certainly give you a high profile, but in Bakir's case he uses it to keep his dark side well hidden."

"Perhaps if I could get back to where I was picked up I might remember something and be able to find the place. Believe me, I want to help."

Bartholdi was warming to the straightforward Australian. He was tempted to trust Tom more that his professional reserve would normally allow. Bartholdi was something of a loner in his department, largely because he knew more about Islam than any of his colleagues, and he despised the prevailing climate of appeasement. He was even beginning to have some sympathy for *Le Front Nationale,* God forgive him.

Before Marseille he had worked in Carcassonne, and there he had become mixed up in a bureaucratic shamble over escaped Muslim terrorists. Political ideology and official prevarication had been a frustrating problem. He had learned the hard way to reject the official claim that Islam was essentially a religion of peace. He made it his task to learn the religion's history and he was familiar with the Qur'an. Of course, there were millions of Muslims who wanted peace and to go about their daily life like everyone else. But these people, he believed, were better than the demands of their religion. Few would have read the Qur'an. And then there were some like his good friend Amadullah, who seemed to have accepted an idealized Islam. It was all very complicated.

Tom found himself enjoying the interview. Bartholdi confirmed that Kaye was in Marseille with Amadullah and Minnah, and that Bakir despised both. It was likely that Minnah's husband had been murdered by Bakir or, more likely, by one of his puppets.

"French law gives me considerable discretion, Tom. In this situation, I'm going to stretch it more than I ever have. I am going to meet with you, Kaye, and her two colleagues, Minnah Muetton and her brother Amadullah. I have known Amadullah for a long time. I wonder if we can be something of a team. I know I'm taking a risk but, I'm going to confide in you. I'm worried about worms in my own woodwork. I'm not sure who I can trust. We live, as they say, in perilous times."

"I understand, and I'm flattered. My decision to go to Afghanistan in search of Kaye is having a remarkable fallout."

"It's an uncertain business these days, being alive."

The Commissaire was buoyant. Evidence had been building slowly for months. And now, if only they could find the 'hospital', he was quite sure they would find much more than an operating theatre. Almost certainly it would be a storage place for smuggled weapons. Bartholdi was positive that Bakir was dealing in arms in a big way, but so far, he had no hard evidence. Sure, he had enough to put him away for a while, but he wanted to suffocate Bakir's entire organization. He wanted to stand over its rotting corpse.

XVII

Ahmed Bakir's sexually nourished bonhomie drained from him on his return to his lock up theatre. Tom's escape had just been discovered by one of the guards. Any memory of Kaye's skills or body was shredded into a convenient recycle bin his mind had for such contingencies. The bed end and chair were still in place and the window open.

"Who would have thought that such an inoffensive Kafir would be so enterprising? How, in the name of Allah blessed be his name, did he get out that window? It's so small."

Ahmed examined the opening and allowed himself a smile that might have been sardonic. Traces of soap were still evident on the windowsill and frame. Tom's unexpected and creative escape prompted admiration. Bakir admired enterprise. He had no compelling reason, yet, to suppose so, but he wondered if he had judged Kaye Reynolds as accurately as he should have. Was it just coincidence that both these instalments in his life were forced on him in such a way on the same day? Allah was speaking to him, teaching him to be patient.

They were two of a kind. How could he have thought otherwise? Both were in Marseille and both in Afghanistan at the same time. They came from the same city in Australia.

"Something is going on, my dear Miss Reynolds. What are you up to?"

The breakfast he had just had wasn't really his initiative at all. The Reynolds women had been far too easy to find, too available. But why? Was it simply that she wanted a story? Bakir suspected she knew more about the good doctor than he had thought. It wasn't a surprise.

"We shall see, Miss Reynolds," he mumbled to himself with rising anticipation and some irritation. Frustration was not permissible in his business; it undermined efficiency. The Australian journalist was not important enough to worry about but it was likely that, *'le docteur'* would contact her. Or more likely, she would contact him. The police would have found him by now. Careful, irritation could easily slip into anger. There was too much at stake to stop now. There was no real danger. Tom Grace would have no idea where he had been. Once through that window he would have run mindlessly through the labyrinth that makes up that part of Marseille. But, just in case, he would go to Cassis and leave only the theatre operating. It would be unfortunate if it was discovered, but not the end of the affair by any means. He would make sure all the important merchandise was removed to the cellars in Brignoles. In the meantime, he had a flight to catch to Doha.

XVIII

Surprises were coming too rapidly for Kaye. Bartholdi had told Amadullah that Tom was in Marseille and, as they suspected, Bakir had abducted him, but somehow, he had managed to escape.

"I hadn't thought Tom to be the escaping type," Kaye said to Minnah, and then felt immediately embarrassed she had underestimated him. "He hasn't been hurt. That's a relief."

"Could change the dynamic between you and Bakir though."

"Bakir," said Amadullah, "is going to be annoyed. He'll still want to go ahead with his little propaganda exercise though, more than ever. The dragon's tail has been trodden on, but he will puff out more than a squeak."

"He'll be on guard now and maybe more dangerous," said Minnah. "You're not obliged to meet him again, you know, Kaye."

"Yes, but this makes me keener than ever, and I have to see Tom."

"We need to talk to Bartholdi. There's no doubt he'll listen to what we have to say." Amadullah was showing renewed enthusiasm. "Timing in our business, it's nine tenths of the contest."

"Kaye, you're the one to contact Bartholdi," said Minnah. "Your friendship with Tom is an obvious place to start, and he'll be interested to discover how you know about Tom's escape. It might be that Amadullah lets out a few trade secrets, but that's a small price to pay. He and Bartholdi are not unknown to each other."

"Phone Bartholdi, mention Tom and you'll get straight through," said Amadullah. "I can give you his direct line."

Kaye looked mischievously at both her colleagues. "What a weird trinity we are." Amadullah's eyebrows might have risen, and Minnah's eyes created a suggestion of a smile. Religious sensitivities were always close to the surface for Amadullah. "Okay, I'll telephone this fellow who seems so important."

"Try this number; here, use my phone," said Amadullah, enjoying his inside knowledge.

Kaye spoke to a certain Capitaine Grimaud, Bartholdi's right-hand man according to Amadullah, who declared he didn't like 'le Capitaine tordu'. The Commissaire would welcome a visit as early as the next morning. Grimaud said nothing to Kaye of Bartholdi's intention to speak with them. But he did say they had already spoken with Tom Grace.

Bartholdi had chosen a pleasing room for the 'chat': completely white, with black carpet, and three inoffensive modern paintings thoughtfully placed. The southeast wall was nearly all windows looking out on to the water and the newly scrubbed buildings that had adorned the European Cultural City for the previous year. La Musée des Civilisations de l'Europe et de la Méditerranée stood bold and black against the purple sea and the bleached rock of the Château d'If in the distance.

The Commissaire's desk and chairs were French oak. A green and orange couch was a contrast to the black and white. Introductions were unexpectedly informal. Capitaine Grimaud introduced himself and then the Commissaire. He was younger than Fabien Bartholdi and not appealing to Kaye at all. There was something devious about his eyes. On the other hand, the Commissaire was thoroughly charming.

"This meeting, as I'm sure you must know, is unusual. But we are in an odd situation." Bartholdi continued, "This week, representatives of the Taliban are meeting with a high-powered US military delegation in Doha. Absurd, one would have thought, but according to officials it's a milestone. Washington has even dropped the demand that the Taliban renounce its relationship with al-Qaeda. Maybe the Americans believe al-Qaeda are yesterday's men. They might be right. Iran is a new centre of power. Although the threat of ISIS has diminished it still seems to be everywhere. Believe me, the Arab Spring was over-rated. Anyway, Afghan peace negotiators will also be in Doha speaking for the Afghan president who has had authority for all his national forces on the ground."

"It won't be easy for him. Just a few days ago, a suicide bomber blew up three buses and killed about twenty people. Many more were injured, including children. We are almost certain that our 'friend' Ahmed Bakir was involved. We know he's left for Doha."

"I don't want to tell you your business, Commissaire, but why not arrest Bakir? You must have plenty of evidence."

"Bakir is important, Minnah, but I want to get the whole outfit. I want to tear their hearts out. I'm a patient man and, in this case, I'm sure it will pay off. Unfortunately, I'm not my own master. I have Paris to appease."

"Well, Monsieur Bartholdi, when it comes to Ahmed Bakir, I'm not a patient woman," Minnah was emphatic. "How can we help? I can't think of anything better than for that terrible man to get what he justly deserves."

Bartholdi had found three fellow travellers who wouldn't care about his bureaucratic restrictions. For five years he had been trying to come to grips with Bakir's 'jihad', if that was the right word. The bureaucrats around him displayed all the frustrating ignorance of political obfuscation. He had had the feeling for a long time. He was in a game where the rules kept changing and the conflicting ideologies swirling around in Paris were undermining his resolve.

Amadullah had already proven useful in helping him understand the complexities of Islam. Now Minnah, with her cross-cultural knowledge, could be a godsend. Informed subtlety was what he wanted. Tom was simply caught up in the drama. But he was intelligent and likable. Anyway, he couldn't be let loose yet. And Kaye?

He wasn't sure. But the big plus in all of this was that he had useful people outside the system. For some time, he had suspected there was an informer in the Paris office, or maybe even Marseille. By feeding selected information that only he had access to would make it easier to trace the mole. He was playing a rather dangerous game, some would have said foolish, but he wanted an untainted arm he knew he could control. These three foreigners had a common interest and he liked them. They trusted Amadullah as much as he did. Tom and Kaye might be new, but they were worth the risk.

"For the next few weeks I'm going to insist, I'm afraid, that you, Tom, Kaye and Minnah go into one of our 'safe houses'. Amadullah is big enough to look after himself and he will be working directly with me anyway. I need his expertise. He has been helpful in the past. Capitaine Grimaud will settle you in."

Settling in proved to be trickier than anyone imagined. The house was, in the idiom of real estate jargon, comfortably modern. They had a bedroom and a bathroom each, but a developing awkwardness between Tom and Kaye was becoming obvious to Minnah. Both were less than frank with each other. That was a pity and something of an enigma, because their friendship must have had deep roots. Kaye had never been completely convincing in Afghanistan that she had really left Tom behind. Was Kaye was running away from him? She did seem to be running away from something. Or was it towards; redemption in Afghanistan?

"I'm sorry, Tom," said Minnah on the evening of the third day of mute awkwardness between Tom and Kaye. "I should mind my own business, but there's an unease between you and Kaye that makes me uncomfortable. Watching muddled passion isn't easy, if indeed, that is what I'm watching."

Tom knew that something had been lost, but coming to terms with the night in the St Lucia restaurant wasn't easy. He had pursued Kaye halfway around the world because of it, and now the closeness of the safe house mocked his pursuit. He imagined Kaye was instinctively self-centred. That might have been the easiest way to explain things, but it was hardly satisfying.

"I'm sorry you're not comfortable, but I'm not sure what to say."

"I had my laptop stolen a few weeks before we left Kabul," said Minnah. "It upset me more than I might have expected. I kept thinking it would turn up. It sounds silly, I know, but life without it didn't seem quite the same. I'd been attempting a diary. You know, writing little insights about my world. What I had written became more meaningful to me after I had lost it."

"I'm not sure I follow; laptop?"

"Well, we think we have an ordered life and then something, even a little thing, seems to change everything. That's what I'm saying, Tom. Time goes by, and what was once so meaningful becomes less so. One cannot backup one's life like a laptop."

"No, I guess not, but change is inevitable. Is that what you're saying? I'm sorry, but I'm still at a bit of a loss."

"We don't control our own lives; that's what I'm trying to say. We react to events. Stuff happens and we react. It's how we respond and how we understand that response. We are shaped as we learn to cope with suffering."

"I'm sure, but I've heard all that before. It's a truism from my childhood."

"Well, yes, it is, but like many other truisms, it's frequently ignored."

Minnah was not happy with her conversation with Tom. She must have sounded banal. It annoyed her that she couldn't say what she wanted to say. Tom could have no idea of what it was like in the real Afghanistan, no idea of real privation and suffering. Had she described what she was feeling, it would have sounded too much like an accusation.

Tom wasn't quite the uninformed Australian that Minnah suspected. He knew she had experienced more suffering than he could even imagine, she was not like any other woman he had ever known. Sure, he had a theoretical insight into what kind of woman Minnah might be, but that was all. He sensed a compassion, wisdom perhaps, in her that had to be the consequence of suffering. Tom's admiration for her awakened an irrational need to protect her, in spite of her being, almost certainly, more psychologically and spiritually robust than he had ever been. Now that was a serious discomfort. A game of squash would have been welcome. The taste of sweat on his lips and the sting in his eyes was good, honest masculine stuff.

"Minnah, I remember watching my father saying goodbye to my grandmother when he was leaving Ireland to come back to Australia. We'd had a long holiday in the village where he was born. I didn't know at the time, but he'd gone with my mother to Ireland to see her before she died. Perhaps he wanted my sister, Ruth, and me to learn something."

"I'm sure you did."

"Yes, well… Sarah, that was my grandmother's name, was ninety-two years old and weeping; I was eleven. Even then I was disturbed by the tears of someone so old. I remember her saying to my father, 'I'll never see you again William.' In my own childish way, I sensed the bleakness of her deep sadness. It was the first time I knew there was such a thing in the world. I grasped then, even though I was a child still, that losing someone you loved was the greatest sorrow. Maybe that's why I have sympathy with your 'lust' for revenge, even if I believe it will end in tears."

And Minnah certainly did have a lust for revenge. Killing Bakir would be her lust's most gratifying consummation. Simple lust, she believed, was such a compelling sin: enjoyable in anticipation and fulfilment. Lust for revenge was more complicated, but it was certainly as pleasurable to anticipate the climax. It gave her a kind of energy that frightened her in those better moments. If passion was a defect in her educated armour, she was not inclined to repair it.

"You know, death and sex baffle the West. You're so odd." Minnah was on a roll. "You're obsessed with one and hide from the other. The irony is explicit. You talk about sex of every kind until ennui overcomes you, but you can't confront the most inevitable event in life. You have so many books on sex and its performance but hardly any about how to die with dignity, or do I mean resignation? All those attempts the Dutch and the Belgians mumble about to make assisted suicide dignified are laughable."

"I'm not sure about that, but isn't that where the irony lies? You know, suicide bombers and Islam, I mean."

"Irony, indeed, we can't escape it. Europe spread the story of Jesus the Redeemer and his victory over Death itself. Now it's the Europeans who try to euthanise death. You said that the greatest suffering is to be permanently separated from those you love. Doesn't Christ promise to unite believers with those they've loved? Apostasy is so dreadfully confusing. Tell me, Tom, do you believe that scandalous claim that Jesus is the Saviour of the world?"

"If push came to shove, that's what my parents taught me. It's something that I find astounding, but I still believe it. Christians are the only people left in Australia who can be mocked with immunity. I suspect it might be safer to declare you're a child abuser among some of my academic friends than to admit being a Christian. Child abusers can be counselled and presumably cured. Christians are irrational bigots, especially if they suggest there's truth in the power of sin to seduce."

"You know, Tom," responded Minnah, "I've been watching the unravelling of Europe from the side-lines; if you will allow me such an image. Europe, and maybe the entire West, has lost its guts. It has turned the good political idea of equality into an absurd moral imperative. That's why Bakir thinks he'll win. The West will just submit, roll over and put its pallid, diverse face to the wall. He's not alone in that assessment. Nearly every terrorist thinks the same."

"I should be concerned somewhere in my psyche, but I'm tempted to wonder if it really matters."

"Tom, you've been seduced by the utopian platitudes of the puritanical liberal levellers. Please don't prove my point."

"Perhaps, but it's a convenient way out."

"That's the problem,' sighed Minnah. "Apathy surrenders the high ground to the self-absorbed fanatic. What would Kaye say about all this? I wonder what she learned in Afghanistan."

"Not much, I suspect. She must be hiding away in her room still. I'll have a look."

"Good idea."

Tom climbed the stairs and knocked on Kaye's door. Silence. He knocked again, still no response. He opened the door a little and called out. It took a moment before Tom knew that Kaye was not in her room.

He called out down the stairs, "Kaye's not here."

"She must be."

"No, she's gone."

It took a moment for the seriousness of Kaye's disappearance to set in. She had sneaked off, contrary to all warnings. Minnah and Tom were angry.

"I'm not surprised, Tom. Kaye has been bored with both of us over the last few days. You must have noticed."

Tom hadn't. He had assumed that Kaye's offhand manner was the consequence of frustration at being confined to the apartment. He wasn't entirely wrong, but the intensity of Kay's boredom had escaped him. That did little to placate his anger. Kaye's thoughtlessness was putting everyone in danger.

XIX

The longer Kaye was in the apartment with Tom and Minnah, the more she had wanted to get out. Here she was, trapped, in France's oldest city, a European cultural centre. There were museums, galleries and shops everywhere and all that enthralling graffiti disorder of sun and seediness. They were all out there. Tom was slipping into somebody too ordinary and the lovely Minnah was so disciplined. She had been in Marseille over two weeks, having seen almost nothing of the city. That was more than any sane red-blooded woman could bear.

The issue was how to get past their minder. He nearly always had a revitalizing snooze after lunch, but the code to get out still eluded her. She had watched as closely as she dared, but so far had managed to discover only three digits of the four-digit code. It wasn't a simple process of just inserting the first three numbers and then trying out the range from zero to nine. After three failures, an alarm would go off; an embarrassment she wanted to avoid.

However, the fear of embarrassment proved weaker than the desire to get out. Why not start at zero and work her way through two numbers at every opportunity she could get? That way she would avoid the buzzer. The first attempt was a failure. The second, although more exciting, was an unsuccessful follow-on. By the third attempt, on the following day, Kaye was aroused by the game. Expecting another failure, her index finger pressed 6; the door clicked and opened as though by magic.

She was outside on the street immediately, exhilarated and only slightly aware of her disloyalty. The door clicked behind her. She would face a telling off. Minnah would be the worst, and Tom just might find the courage to look at her in that new disappointed and annoying way of his.

The street was narrow and dusty, not at all what she had imagined in the heat of her domestic rebellion against the boring and ordinary. Cars drove one way slowly or tooted as a van stopped to let down or take on a package or two. There was a lot of chatter, but no one seemed hostile. It was such a relief to be outside, boredom was forgotten.

Kaye threaded her way through the cars and vans to Tapis Vert; the street sign at the end of her street informed her. It was exciting even though the buildings still looked tatty and grimy. Many of them, in places she thought inaccessible, were defaced by graffiti. Parked dusty cars lined both sides of the narrow street leaving little space for delivery vans moving through them. There was more honking of horns and swearing, not always in French. Vitality and decay struggled for ascendancy, Kaye mused with some pleasure at the accessible image.

Tapis Vert, Kaye was to discover, was the heart of the Marseille wholesale rag trade. Shops lined both sides of the street and spilled over into several of the side alleys. It was invigorating and a long way from the miserly choices she had had in Kabul. What a difference! It was another world. Afghanistan was a lifetime away. What on earth had she been thinking about? Not a great deal, it would seem. Life was here. Not that there was no life in Afghanistan, but it was life of a different kind. The street was alive with expectation and possibility. Bunyan might have been forced to imagine the grimy bling of 'vanity fair' but Kaye was not embarrassed by the revitalised lust of her flesh.

Although the street was dusty and occasionally stained by dried patches of human urine in the doorways and other carelessness, Kaye was excited. There was something in the air: an enticing sleaziness

that evoked forbidden pleasures. Kaye had always found the suggestion of vice poignantly attractive. For some reason, seamy cabaret
music flowed through her mind. It was that amoral union of sleaze
and youthful vigour that had fascinated her. The advertiser's apt but
annoying phrase, 'shabby chic', sort of made sense. Whatever it was,
the French did sleaze with flair. Then, an intrusion:

"Kaye, Kaye Reynolds, I believe."

It took Kaye a moment and then, "Oh, hello, this is a surprise. It's
Maeva isn't it?"

"Well done to remember my name. What are you doing here? You
going into business selling French fashion garments in Australia?"

"I wish. It might be less stressful than journalism."

"Perhaps, but not so exciting, I think."

Kaye was tense. She had been on the street a mere ten minutes
and had already met a friend of Bakir. The coincidence was disorientating. Minnah and Tom will have live ammunition to shoot at
her now, providing she told them. She comforted herself with the
thought that telling them wasn't necessary.

"Have you seen much of the old city?"

"Not much, I hope to though."

"Here, let me show you our shop. You're right outside it."

Like so many business premises in France, the outside gave no indication of what was inside. Only six or seven metres wide, it was easy
to miss. Both women stepped inside a brightly lit sales area. Maeva
showed Kaye through three floors of rooms all painted a matte off
white with lightly stained floors. The mesh steel stairs were painted
a shiny black. Rack after rack of brightly coloured woman's clothing
contrasted perfectly with the walls. Two or three assistants were taking items off the racks and packing them quickly and efficiently into
cartons. From time to time, Maeva took a sample from one of the
racks and said, "What do you think of this?" Kaye had no need to
pretend. The garments were lovely.

"Nothing for Australia yet, maybe you could be our first client there."

"I don't think I would have the expertise to sell these, although they do look lovely."

"Actually, you've been overtaken. A woman from New Zealand bought eight hundred items just yesterday. An Aussie beaten by a Kiwi; not good, I think.'

"You're well informed about my part of the world."

"I've spent time in both countries. Indeed, we very nearly settled in Sydney."

"Really?"

"Here, look, this is an Italian label. They sell themselves; forty euros here, two hundred in the shops. What's that in Australian dollars, nearly three hundred I believe? There's a special discount at the end of the season. Just when the summer is starting in Australia. Look, choose one. It's a present."

Maeva, Kaye observed, was either generous by nature or trying very hard to be friendly.

"That's very generous. I'm tempted to accept."

"Tempted?" Maeva laughed. "Try one on."

Kaye did. She chose an abstract floral, somewhat flamboyant layered dress with sleeves that flared from the elbow. Shorter than she would normally wear, it was orange and green with a suggestion of blue. It hung softly on her hips and seemed to flatter her tummy to a very gentle curve. She felt positively Provençale.

"Beautiful, you look magnificent. I should be paying you to wear it. It does something for your eyes. You have excellent skin."

"Brilliant," she said as she looked in the mirror. "I feel twenty. I'll wear it back... around the city." Kaye almost said back to the apartment around the corner. Maeva gave no indication that she noticed anything.

"Excellent. I'll put your old dress in a bag. Look, how about a drink? There are a couple of little bars just at the end of Tapis Vert on Le Place des Capucines. 'Layabout Place', some call it. I have breakfast there most days. We could sit in the shade and chat, provided you don't want to use a toilet; they're terrible."

"Sounds like fun, why not?"

La Place des Capucines was bathed in dusty sunlight which was just as well; it needed it. While not threatening, it was hardly inviting. More delivery vans and cars fought for the road and parking space.

"The Marseillais are a motley lot," said Maeva.

Kaye watched. People mixed without touching. A pale red-headed woman, closer to sadness than wasted, was slumped over a table right beside a brasserie doorway. It wasn't clear whether she was begging or offering the use of her body, such as it once might have been. Maeva ordered two coffees and looked directly into Kaye's eyes in the way an old friend might have.

"It's a big village, really, Marseille I mean, and France's biggest port. All the Corsicans, Moroccans, and Algerians become Marseillais in a very short time. Sure, we have our problems with crime, but the city can be very friendly. Watch your handbag."

"I will."

"So, when will we see you again? I'm positive Ahmed would love to see you. He talks about you enough. I'm not embarrassing you, am I?"

"No, not at all. I've had no invitation."

"Perhaps I should encourage him."

"No please, that would embarrass me."

"Don't worry, I won't say anything. Does he have your mobile number?"

"I believe so."

"Maybe the best thing would be for you to phone me when you are able. I would love to show you around Marseille."

The conversation continued. Maeva was friendly and flattering. Kaye would have been suspicious had she been more astute, but she had neither reason nor desire to be either. Maybe it was just the change of company, or discovering that Ahmed had found her interesting. She was a little excited. Whatever else Bakir might be, he was certainly colourful.

It was a good half hour into the conversation before Kaye recalled where she was and what she was doing. She tried to avoid the silent accusation that she was compromising anyone's safety. The chance of meeting Maeva must have been thousands to one. How was she to know that Maeva's shop was just around the corner? Anyway, no harm had been done. She waited for an appropriate moment and said goodbye as cheerfully as she could and went, as they say, to face the music.

And it was a cacophony. Tom and Minnah were angry.

"I just went to buy a dress. Look, I've got it on. I was very low, remember? Not much chance in Afghanistan."

The bold adolescent foolishness of Kaye's excuse was so absurd they were silent. Tom was so overcome by Kaye's thoughtless idiocy he burst out laughing. Minnah acquiesced. The minder watched, bemused.

"You weren't followed?"

"No, Minnah. I'm sure I wasn't."

"Well, that's a relief," said Tom.

"It is a lovely dress Kaye, I'm jealous."

That was that. For the rest of the day, no one spoke much to Kaye. Tom and Minnah chatted quietly and their minder continued to read his book explaining why the euro would not collapse and the European Union endure, Brexit or no Brexit.

Kaye, unfortunately, had been followed. Maeva had phoned one of Bakir's colleagues who managed her second shop. He was sitting at a table fewer than twenty metres behind Kaye when she left Maeva. It was just too easy. He was one hundred metres behind when Kaye was admitted to a building on Rue de la Providence through an unkempt door. She had no idea she was being watched. Despite her training and time in Afghanistan, she just wasn't thinking.

By the time she was back inside, Bakir knew where she was. He had recovered from his mixed success in Doha and was attending to the most important task he had had for a long time: getting the most substantial shipment of arms he had ever managed to his brothers in

Afghanistan. Kaye was a pleasing diversion and a potential threat. The situation had not changed. He should keep an eye on her.

Bakir thought he had the ability to examine and admire his actions from another's perspective. He saw himself as the wealthy arms dealer allowing his life to be complicated by a beautiful woman. But, always, he was in control. Although he would never say so, even to himself, he was the principle actor, producer, and director of his own award-winning documentary.

It was impossible to phone Kaye in the apartment, so why not ask Maeva to invite her to the villa in Cassis? He could meet her there on friendly territory, and there would be no need to feel uncomfortable. If he was to convince Kaye that he was a friend, it was important that she felt at ease.

Maeva was a step ahead. She told Bakir that she expected a call from Kaye within the next week. She knew what kind of woman they were dealing with. It was likely that she was in the 'safe house' with our doctor friend and maybe Meutton's wife. The whole deal was beginning to look a trifle incestuous, Maeva mused.

Maeva, as it developed, had assessed Kaye accurately. It took her four days before boredom overcame her again. She rang Maeva and the rendezvous was set: a look around Marseille and then dinner at Maeva's villa in Cassis. It would be a big day, so Kaye, if she wished, could stay the night. Perhaps this time it was fortunate, but Kaye's judgment failed her again. All her phone calls, like everyone else's in the apartment, were recorded for Bartholdi. It was not surprising that he turned up for a chat the next morning to discuss the phone call.

"It wasn't the wisest of phone calls, Kaye, but we can make it work to our advantage and we can even attend to your boredom. Don't think you're the only person ever to behave as you have."

"Thank you. That makes me feel a lot better."

"Good, go ahead with the day out and stay the night if you want to. I think Maeva and her friends just want to keep you close, assess your position and find out who your friends are."

"You really think Kaye won't be in danger, Commissaire?" Tom was concerned.

"Yes, in fact, I think we can now allow you and Minnah considerably more freedom. You can come and go as you please providing I know where you are. It's important now that you look relaxed."

"And I can see Amadullah? I miss my brother."

"I can't see why not, but not here; at his hotel."

"Well, this is certainly a move forward," declared Tom. "It's such a relief not to be tied down, after nearly a month."

"There is something you should know, Kaye. Maeva and her husband are very wealthy. Just recently they bought a villa in Cassis at a knock down price. Originally, it had been sold to one of the nouveau riche Russians who still haunt the Cote d'Azur, Vasily Ryolovlov. He paid two million deposit but, rumour has it, he couldn't get the remaining five million fast enough. He lost the villa and his deposit, although he was apparently rescued by Bakir."

"Wow, is there that much money in the rag trade?"

"No, there isn't. We're not entirely sure where their money comes from. Bakir will be there in the background. Compared with prices in, say, Villefranche or Cannes, Cassis is small beer, as the English might say. There's a lot of talk about Mafia money but it's not easy to circumvent the French money laundering laws."

"I don't want to tell you what you already know, Commissaire," said Minnah, "but Bakir is a big player in the manipulation of Islam in France. Qatar is the latest player in the funding of mosques. I suspect he's involved in a devious scheme."

"He is. With the weakening of the influence of Algeria and probably Morocco, Bakir has been forced to look for new funders."

"That's a worry, because Algeria and Morocco were moderate even into the nineties," Minnah asserted.

"There's been a shift in the power structures within Islam and in France. For years, Islam has been manipulated by a range of different players. That had its own benefits. It kept extremists under control.

That, unfortunately is becoming less true."

"I hate it, but extremism is more prevalent in every Muslim nation these days. The crazy surge of fundamentalism muddies the water everywhere. Islam must go back to its roots; that's the new maxim."

"Tell me, Minnah," asked Tom, entering the conversation. "Does that make sense? If Islam were to go back to its roots, wouldn't that make it even more aggressive?"

"Ah Tom, such a provocative question. Be careful where you ask it."

"Well, I was just thinking. Christian reform did involve going back to the New Testament; I imagine it still does. That's what gives the faith its vitality. I think Christian reform had the opposite effect that any real reform of Islam would have. It was born out of violence. The pivotal issue in Christian reform, if I remember my history, was the issue of authority: the priesthood or Scripture. What's the pivotal issue for Islam?"

"It has to be… Mohammed is God's last prophet," Minnah was thinking out loud and not responding to Tom's question. "Submission is the issue."

"I suspected as much. That's what modern Islamists are doing?"

"Yes, and that's the problem," said Bartholdi. The increasing militancy can be defended from the Qur'an. The young pious bomber can find a defence for his actions easily. Self-righteousness encourages neither good exegesis nor self-examination."

"Now, that really is the problem." Minnah's eyes, Tom observed, were glowing. He was not embarrassed; neither did he have any desire to stop looking at her. "Muslims don't need to be redeemed. All they must do is obey the Prophet's law. They have no need for a foundational theology of forgiveness. Jesus and Mohammed are opposites."

They? What was Minnah saying?

"Are they really?" Kaye thought she should say something just to prove that she wasn't out of her depth. She had failed to notice the significance of Tom's silent question.

"It was Jesus's command," said Minnah, "'to love your enemies' that really upset me when I first compared it with Islam. It was impossible, if not downright silly; a warrant guaranteeing self-destruction… and yet."

"What would Amadullah think about all this?" Tom was worried that Minnah would say something she might regret.

"I'm sure Amadullah doesn't think about it at all. I love my brother, but I fear we are beginning to travel along different roads. What really overwhelmed me, when I first read it, was the story of the three women: Mary of Magdala, Joanna, and Mary, the mother of James. They were the first witnesses to the resurrection, even before Peter or John. You need to be a Muslim woman to understand just how liberating that is. Women are second rate citizens. In court, a woman's testimony was worth half that of a man's. In Islam, it still is.

"But here, three ordinary women are the first to see their risen Lord. Do you understand how the emotional and spiritual power unite here to excite a woman? That would have been impossible in Islam. That story is liberating to an educated Muslim woman. Right at the beginning, the dignity of women is declared. No wonder early Christianity attracted so many Roman women."

"You know, I've not thought of that," Kaye's interest was aroused. "What happened? We've been fighting for equality ever since."

"Ah Kaye, you confuse equality with dignity. They're close but not the same."

"What do you mean?"

"I'm much more concerned with my dignity than my equality. It is God who gives me my dignity, while the state or Islam declares my equality or lack of it. Equality is the consequence of dignity, it is not the other way around. I don't think you have to be a Jew or Christian to understand that."

If Kaye understood or disagreed, she offered no clue. But Tom was beginning to believe there was something otherworldly, prophetic, about Minnah; she astounded him. Her insight and spiritual vision were remarkable. Kaye, in her Western confidence, was like a little girl beside her.

"A woman can retain dignity surrounded by inequality. I saw it all the time in Afghanistan. I think you did too."

"I did, I must admit."

Kaye met Maeva, in her dark blue Bentley Continental, outside Mama Shelter. Although it was the first time she'd driven in such an expensive car, she played it cool. It was a mystery how such a big vehicle managed to manoeuvre around many of the narrow Marseille streets. Parking it would have been a nightmare. It must have limited use. Still, she felt agreeably urbane sitting beside Maeva and gazing out from her air-conditioned comfort. Kaye had always suspected there had always been something of the snob in her psyche. Its residence was becoming increasingly comfortable.

"Today, Kaye," declared Maeva with plain good cheer, "you're the tourist and I'm the guide with one difference; the guide pays for everything."

"That's too generous."

"I insist. It'll be fun. I don't get the chance to do this kind of thing enough." Maeva meant what she said. She was generous by nature and she was enjoying herself. Her wealth gave her natural generosity a satisfying practical reality. Quite apart from all the business with Ahmed, she liked Kaye and she wanted to be liked. Kaye was not a follower of the Prophet, blessed be his Name, but she could be. At the very least she could be an extremely helpful go-between.

If Allah was watching, it is difficult to know if he smiled at the irony or whether he was outraged at Maeva's first visit for the day, Notre Dame de la Garde. Because of its Byzantine style, Maeva was less offended by it than its namesake 'museum' in Paris and, anyway, it was important that she be the moderate she claimed to be and, if the truth was ever to be known, she probably was. If she was going to win Kaye's confidence, overt propaganda wouldn't help. Nothing was ever said but she knew the suspicions Kaye might have. It would be rather odd for a guide not to show off one of the city's most spectacular sights.

Kaye was enthralled. She had never seen anything like it. Her experience of old church architecture had been the darkness of the Gothic and Baroque, and it helped that the church was in such good condition. The colour and the light inspired her romantic notion of the spiritual. A rare sense of awe melted something within her. She was uncertain whether to be pleased or sceptical. Usually old churches were just museums, but this time the museum was alive. To her liberal pseudo-protestant mind, a charge she admitted to, Catholicism had always been a superstitious fusion of pagan myth with the sublime.

The rest of the day was a whirl of galleries and museums. The vin rosé laden two-hour lunch was delightful, but a mistake. Kaye wanted to sleep, but was kept awake by a furious shopping splurge along *La Rue de la Republique.* The need for money reminded her that pay from the newspaper had ceased going into her account. They probably thought she was dead. She wondered what she would get if she ever got back to Brisbane.

Whatever the case, lack of money made shopping a lot less amusing, and keeping up in the heat became a chore. Her host's generosity only served to sharpen her self-pity. After shoes, jeans, and perfume it was getting embarrassing. It was a relief when Maeva said they were heading off to Cassis and that it would be an hour's drive. She told Kaye to have a snooze in the comfortable, deeply reclining leather seat.

Kaye woke just as they were turning up a curving white stone drive to what looked like a very expensive modern pink villa built to look as old as possible. All the large white framed windows had shutters.

Some were open. Had it been in Australia the villa would have been pretentious and bad taste, but it worked magnificently in France. Most of the south wall was covered by a creeper Kaye didn't recognize.

"Here we are. I see the welcome party's out for you." Maeva's husband was smiling benignly in the large double doorway.

"*Bonsoir*, Kaye. Maeva phoned and said you were coming."

"*Bonsoir, Monsieur* Hassad."

"Omar, please. This is a pleasure. Here, let me take your bag. I'll show you to your room while Maeva puts her car away. You can freshen up after such a warm day wandering the streets. I know what Maeva is like."

The bedroom was large, white and airy; furnished in harmony with the rest of the house, 1920s' style. The cupboards and bed were Art Deco, Kaye observed. The adjoining bathroom was perfect in black and white tiles. The bath and shower were huge. Kaye didn't wait. She flung her clothes on the bed and stood in the warm foaming water for ten luxurious minutes. She watched herself in the large mirror with that kind of vanity that in Minnah might have awakened something akin to guilt. Hand in hand, the shower glass and the substance of any guilt misted over. She had lost weight since leaving Australia.

Kaye stepped from the shower and wrapped herself in a massive, soft white bath towel. She walked to an open window and looked out across the lawn to the largest private pool she had ever seen. The still blue water seemed to flow over its far side down into the even bluer Mediterranean. Cars on the waterfront road moved with a silent smoothness. It was all very agreeable.

The gentle knock at her door did nothing to intrude on her pleasure. "Kaye, it's Maeva. There's an aperitif waiting when you're ready, don't hurry. We're in the reception room to the left of the main stairs."

Kaye hadn't thought about it in Afghanistan much, but just then it became embarrassingly evident. She loved luxury. She revelled in it. Afghanistan, her bland apartment in Brisbane and the 'safe house' were impoverished and unworthy. She would hide it from herself no longer, Afghanistan had been a nightmare. Not for the first time in her life, Kaye experienced the intense nurturing frustration of avarice. It hadn't quite surfaced, but she was discovering, somewhere in her spirit, that ideology is no defence against unfulfilled desire.

The reception room was just the right size to be inviting. Maeva was there with two men, her husband Omar and Ahmed Bakir. As she entered Bakir, turned to her and smiled. Dear God, he was handsome. Maeva's husband held out his hand to Kaye. "You remember Ahmed, of course?"

"Yes, I do." Instinctively, she offered him both her cheeks as he took her hand. A wave of musk pleased her. Something about her friendship with Tom unsettled her.

"I'm delighted to meet you again, Kaye. What a fortunate meeting you had with Maeva. I'm sure it was God's will."

"Yes, I'm sure," responded Kaye without thinking or believing. "It's lovely to see you again, Ahmed."

"I hope there will be many more, Kaye."

"Kaye, what would you like to drink?" Maeva was smiling with warmth that was genuine.

"A Martini, please."

"White?"

"Thank you. Tell me, you all speak such excellent English; I can't help wondering why. I hope I'm not being impudent."

"Certainly not," said Ahmed. "None of us is French in the absolute sense. I was born in Algeria and I do have a French passport. I went to Afghanistan with my parents when I was only two years old, but we returned to Algeria, where my parents lived for a very long time, my mother is still there. Quite simply, English was essential. Maeva and Omar are from Egypt."

"I spoke English as a child," said Maeva. "I was sent to school in England, and I met Omar at university. Perhaps I should whisper it, but I feel more English than Egyptian."

"England and France have treated us well," said Omar. "Our

business ventures have been very successful; with help from friends like Ahmed, I must say."

And so, the evening went, affability all round. Kaye was stimulated by the easiness of Ahmed's company. Self-control, had it even managed an entrance, would have been an unattractive option. She had never met a man who oozed such enticing sexual authority. That she was attracted to a man who Bartholdi had declared a womaniser was irrelevant. Fear and fascination, as they often do, conspired to make the sinister appealing. Now that was the kind of challenge worth facing.

Bakir left a little after midnight, insisting that he and Kaye meet again. Kaye excused herself politely from Maeva and Omar and went to her room. What a delicious evening, Kaye mused, as she slid between the sheets of her large bed in her large room with large windows. She was agreeably aware of her firm shapeliness and the way Bakir had looked at her. The satin sheets were cool and smooth on her skin. Surely Ahmed wasn't the man that Minnah and Bartholdi described. It was impossible to believe that he could have murdered Minnah's husband and abducted Tom. There must be more to both stories. There had to be more. Perhaps that was something she could find out getting to know Ahmed. This spying business had potential to be lots of fun.

The morning started late. Breakfast was slow after a late morning swim, so it was almost mid-day when Maeva and Kaye drove out through the gate and headed towards Marseille. This time in a much smaller car: a Porsche of some kind.

"I prefer to drive this car. It's so much easier to get around."

"I must say, Maeva, I could live in this part of the world and not miss Australia one little bit. Everything seems so soft around the edges, if that makes sense."

"Yes, it does. Australia promises a lot but somewhat hard and sharp, a little too brash, if I may be permitted that little criticism. Think about living here, it's not impossible. I know Ahmed is impressed by you. Believe me, he is influential in France, and elsewhere for that matter. He is, if you pardon the cliché, a mover and shaker."

"Employment would be a problem for me, I think. I need to earn a living."

"Of course, you do. I understand you know little about the fashion business in France, but you would soon pick it up. My company needs a woman like you."

"Really, that sounds like a fantasy to me. What would I do?"

"Well, you speak English and French and, goodness me, Ahmed tells me you are fluent in Pashto as well. That combination is very marketable, believe me. In a beautiful European woman, it's almost unknown. You could start with a *Carte de Sejour* and then citizenship, eventually. I think that's how it works."

Kaye's stomach gave a nervous heave. A new world was there to be grasped. It was astounding. She had no idea how to respond, although a pink and white villa on the *Cote d'Azur* was a concentrated stimulant. She was here to learn. Afghanistan had reinforced the belief that the world of extravagant wealth was a vain and foreign country. But now Afghanistan was distant. It was almost as if she had never been there. It was unsettling. She wanted what Maeva had. And, what was more exciting, it was beginning to seem possible.

"You know, Maeva, the idea of staying in France really appeals to me. I'm not sure that after my paper finds out about my performance in Afghanistan the editor will be happy." Kaye said nothing about the pretended kidnapping. "I suspect you know I was supposed to write up a story on the Australian troops there."

"Yes, I believe Ahmed did mention such a thing. He was hoping you might write something for him."

"He did suggest that, and he was very generous."

"Well, Kaye, you've got some thinking ahead."

For the rest of the day that was all Kaye did. She wandered around Marseille in a daze. She spent little money and reported back to the others well into the evening. She imagined herself a double agent in a spy novel. Perhaps that's how it happened. The grass on the other side really was greener. But what could she tell the others? Nothing had happened. She didn't need to mention Bakir. There was nothing ominous in an offer of employment. She was making use of her talents, that's all.

"Well, it was all very interesting, but I don't think I learned anything," Kay said to Minnah as they had their first coffee together.

"Nothing about Bakir?" asked Tom.

"Nothing," lied Kaye, not expecting the wave of discomfort.

"That's a pity. I was hoping we would have something useful for Bartholdi," said Minnah. "He really wants to know what Bakir is up to."

"I might meet him soon. Maeva said something about a party at her villa."

XXI

A mere six days passed for Kaye and 'partner' to get an invitation to Maeva's party.

"Partner?"

"Why not?" Minnah came to the rescue. "Bakir is waiting in the wings. He loves doing what people least expect. Intrigue appeals to his sense of control. It's likely that he wasn't too upset about Tom's escape and would enjoy renewed contact. He expected Tom to be Kaye's partner and Maeva is a willing collaborator."

"As Bakir's victims go, Tom, you were treated well. Maeva might have sent the invitation, but Bakir will be at the party. It is all part of a show of strength and a challenge to Kaye."

"Man, he's a bold bastard, isn't he?" Tom was astonished. "I must say though, I must go, if only to show Bakir I'm not intimidated."

"Exactly, Bakir knows his players." Minnah was smiling. "It won't be dangerous. He knows you would fancy playing James Bond's understudy. Let's get Bartholdi's take on it when he calls."

"Yeah, that's sensible I guess."

It was almost mid-day when the Commissaire arrived. Like Minnah, he was not surprised by the invitation.

"The whole thing", he claimed, "is more amusing than sinister and it has the potential to be useful. There's no convincing reason why either of you should reject the invitation. I know where you are and my men will keep an eye on you. There's no real danger. Indeed, the friendlier Kaye is with Maeva and Bakir the better. We must build up as much information on Bakir and his friends as possible. The net, when we finally do spread it, must be without a way of escape."

"I've no idea what I'm doing," said Tom after reading Maeva's response. "The situation is getting crazier by the minute. I'm going to meet someone who has threatened to kill me."

"Tom, I know how Bakir thinks," said Minnah. "Your escape might have annoyed him, but he gets over minor irritations quickly."

"Minor?"

"For Bakir, I mean. Sorry, Tom, none of us saw your abduction as minor... anyway you know that. It's different for Bakir. He's cool in the old-fashioned sense meaning of the word, and likes to think he is in the modern sense as well."

"Is he?" Tom was not expecting an answer.

"I wish I could go with you and Kaye."

"Minnah, that's not such a bad idea," said Bartholdi. "I'll have men situated at as many vantage points as possible. I want to photograph everyone going to that party. You will probably know some of them. Amadullah will be with us but, as you say, two heads are better than one."

"Now, that does sound like fun. You know, of course, that Bakir will expect you to be watching him."

"Yes, he will and he'll be trying furiously to confuse us. Maeva will have invited a wide cross section of the coast's 'Who's Who'. Bakir will send cars to pick up people who have flown in and he'll make sure strangers meet on the way to the villa. A kind of necessary affability and guarded aspiration will fill the backseats of his cars. Some will be his cronies, others will have had very little to do with him. We take pictures as they arrive, but we have little idea who his real associates are. It's frustrating and time consuming and leads to a lot of dead ends. It's one of Bakir's little jokes."

"Ah, I could be of use in identifying the, well, hard core."

"That's what I want. I expect much of you and Amadullah."

"Thank you, as an uninvited guest of the French taxpayer, I feel useful already."

Maeva's handwritten response to Kaye's acceptance was enthusiastic. It was completed by simple directions to the villa 'in the unlikely case she and her partner got lost'.

The days leading up to the party passed without incident. Bartholdi organized a car for Kaye: a white Renault Megane hatchback, the best the long-suffering French taxpayer would permit. But even that surprised Tom. His Australian free enterprise spirit would never come to terms with his distrust of French socialism.

The Commissaire knew he couldn't let his 'collaborators' get bored. Tom was given a subscription to a gym and lessons on how to use a handgun. Minnah's needs were slightly different. Bartholdi knew she was at home with firearms. He also knew, from Amadullah, she carried a Ruger SR9. She liked it, he had said, because it was modern, light and slim as well as being accurate. Bartholdi had no intention of taking it off her, indeed he arranged for her to obtain a French license.

Anything would have been exciting for Tom. Leaving the tedium of his confinement was such a relief he was prepared for anything. He was missing squash so a chance to use the gym was a huge relief. The handgun training was welcome and, even better, he was a fast learner. Cane toads came to mind. Perhaps he could hit them into the air with his golf club and shoot them before they hit the ground. The fantasy was most satisfying.

By the third week of training Tom had lost his reservations about meeting Bakir and, what's more, he was 2 kilos lighter and fitter. The handgun training had given him a different kind of confidence; a new kind of power. He was sane enough to realize such confidence might be misplaced but he enjoyed it nevertheless. The standard police issue SP2022 suited him. It sat rather nicely in his hand. It charmed Tom that he had access to a handgun with *Propriete de l'Etat* printed clearly on the barrel. He had not experienced it before, but holding a handgun and shooting at a target excited him. The developing intrigue of meeting Bakir was alluring. The Commissaire was certainly unorthodox and influential. Tom couldn't help reflecting, yet again, on the astonishing nature of his present situation. His decision to go to Afghanistan had proved life changing. Here he was, in Marseille, enjoying himself with the intensity of his student days with the same kind of energizing anxiety he recalled from imminent exams.

The company of two beautiful women was more than agreeable, even if he didn't understand either. Their sexual attractiveness gave his adventure a piquancy he rather enjoyed. Tom had always found the lithe female form more exciting than was probably good for him. It remained a mystery why certain shapes could suggest so much pleasure. Someone had told him once there were no straight lines in nature; he could believe it.

And he was beginning to like Amadullah. He was a man of his word and he carried himself in such a dignified way. Tom had never presumed to understand Islam, but Amadullah had to be Islam at its best although he displayed none of the religious curiosity of his sister.

It was clear to Tom why Amadullah despised Bakir. Not only had he killed Minnah's husband, he was an ugly stain on the character of Islam; he was a talented and handsome opportunist. He was an Islamic Pharisee addicted to power. His cardinal religious ethic was control and he was lucky; events had been kind to him. The growing Islamist revival gave him a context to manipulate and to find his place in the world. He could pull the strings and not be seen on the stage.

Everyone waited for the evening of the party to arrive. Tom was at ease. He understood Bakir's need to display his wealth and assume the mantle of productive citizen. Hubris was not always ugly, at least on the surface. Sometimes others would benefit from the largess that hubris might appear to give to others. Pride wanted to be loved but her lover's adoration was always unrequited. It was reassuring for Minnah to remember that it came before a fall.

XXII

Tom's vanity was not wounded by the role of pawn on Bakir's skewed chessboard. He was happy to be a minor player in a new game. Maybe it was that uncommon humility that made him so engaging. Tom, if it was possible for one man to be the opposite of another, was Bakir's counterpart. That, Minnah mused, was the most delicious of insights. She had neither intention nor inclination to attempt an explanation.

Bartholdi knew that Bakir used lavish parties to impress the rich and famous. They became unwitting weapons in his extensive charm offensive because they created a responsiveness among those he wanted to manipulate. Revelry was his first instrument of seduction; nothing new there, Tom might have mused. That felicitous union of bonhomie and the venal hearts of his acquaintances tended to bring the outcomes Bakir wanted. It allowed him to remain in control as he spoke softly to his quarry, shrunken by avarice and swollen by expensive booze. Bakir knew the extravagant display of wealth created a drama that undermined a friend's judgement and an enemy's defences. He was urbanely courteous and he knew human folly and enough French history not to go beyond the bounds of good taste.

Kaye, on the other hand, would have been angry had she believed she was a minor player in Bakir's game. There was no way she would be a pawn in anyone's game.

Bakir smiled benignly at the outward signs of Kaye's conceit. He flattered and he lied so well he convinced himself that he was creating a permanent and compliant friend. Like any practicing tyrant, the irony of his own vanity was lost to him.

When not distracted by the compelling range of varying passions, Bakir would recall that checkmate was the climax of his game; it was not just a playful little war game with the odd captured knight or bishop. Only the queen would satisfy him before the end of the game. He played his game not with the precision of a competent chess player, rather more like a cat with a mouse. Rules were made to be manoeuvred.

Kaye and Tom drove in Bartholdi's Megane to Cassis. They were nervous, unsure what to expect of either Bakir or, of each other. Satisfying chatter was not immediately forthcoming. When partners imagine they have fallen out of love, a wearisome static fills the air to scramble the conversation. It was as though each had learned to speak a foreign language the other couldn't understand. But the alien tongues did nothing to diminish their desire.

Nervousness and rising uncertainty do little to sharpen the mind, and Kaye had no desire to be reflective. One would have thought, that a woman as attractive and sophisticated as she, would have had more self-knowledge; apparently not. Kaye's world of fresh possibilities was just too enticing to be diverted by either knowledge or doubt. The sensual static bent any light that might have entered her mind.

"Ah, Kaye, lovely to see you again, and your friend." Maeva was radiant and, as usual, perfectly groomed. Tom was consumed, just for a moment, by her wealthy elegance. Was she ever anything else but immaculate? Although well off by Brisbane standards, he, like Kaye, had never been in such opulent surroundings. It was another world, even for a Brisbane surgeon. The men were relaxed and stylish, tanned and fit. He couldn't see a fat woman anywhere or one admitting to over the age of fifty. Was this just a to-do for the beautiful people? Of course, it was. This was the Bakir's own special slice of the *Cote d'Azur*, not Surfer's Paradise.

"My friend, another Australian, I'm afraid... Tom Grace. Tom, this is Maeva. I've told Tom about you already, Maeva."

"*Enchanté*, Tom. Australian, how lovely. You're among friends here."

"I'm pleased to hear it. Delighted to meet you at last, after hearing so much about you from Kaye." Tom could hardly believe what he was saying. Kaye had hardly mentioned Maeva. Need he be so facile? There must be something in the air; a Provençal variation of nitrous oxide in the air conditioning?

"Let me introduce you to the Carters. They live here in Cassis but come from Scotland." Maeva guided them towards a couple, taking a drink from one of the waiters on the way.

"Stella, Robert, meet Kaye and Tom from Australia."

Stella and Robert were from Edinburgh. Robert had been a land developer in Spain before the great collapse.

"Yes, we got out just in time. Could've lost everything. It's the luck of the draw I guess," declared Robert, exposing his penetrating grasp of economics and the market all at once. Tom disliked his glib analysis. This guy's not in Roger's class he mused. But he didn't muse for long. The prospect of boredom was banished by the shock they expected.

"Kaye and Tom, how pleased I am to see both of you, and together too."

Bakir was smiling broadly and holding out his hand. Tom was so astounded that he shook the Afghan's hand like a half anaesthetised patient. He watched helplessly as Kaye was greeted with an enthusiastic kiss on both cheeks.

"Tom, I want to apologise. I regret that our last meeting was not as I would have liked. Necessity sometimes makes a man act against his best instincts. Please don't think too ill of me. I have been worried about you for some time." Bakir drew Tom aside from the others.

"Here, I have a little something for you." Discreetly, Bakir handed him a thick plain envelope.

"I... what is it?"

"Just something I would like you to have a look at. Not now, later, when you get home. It is a peace offering of sorts."

"I'm not sure," Tom wanted to be indignant and angry. Bakir had abducted him and here he was smiling that smile with the programmed confidence of extraordinary wealth. The grasp of Mammon was already at work, even on Tom.

"Look, Tom, circumstances threw us together in a way that started badly. I want to show you I'm genuinely sorry. I could state the obvious and say that Afghanistan is not France."

"But you did mess me up somewhat." Tom was starting to feel braver. "I'm not sure..."

"And Tom, I must say I did admire your creative escape, even if unnecessary."

Bakir's continued smile and conversation was so charming that Tom was in danger of being completely disarmed. Residual anger dissolved. His determination to hold onto it weakened. He loathed his own fleeting moral precision. He wanted to tell Bakir that his actions were deplorable and that he was a bully and a hypocrite. He wanted the others to see he could stand up to the bully and expose the hypocrite. But he didn't. He was not encouraged.

"You and Kaye enjoy yourself, that's what this evening's for. Meet new friends. You never know what might happen. Treat this house as your own home. That's what Maeva would like."

And, with that, Bakir was off to enlighten the lives of others. Kaye returned, but probably not to enlighten him.

"You know, Kaye, I would have denied it before, but being in the presence of absurd wealth does have its own kind of impact. It could make one willingly obsequious."

"But not you Tom, not you."

"I'm not sure. I hope not, but the temptation's there. Lust is not just about sex."

"Oh Tom, you're mumbling the obvious. Now, that's just plain silly at your age."

"Maybe. It's one thing to resist temptation in theory, quite another in practice."

"What do you mean?"

"It's easy not to be a thief when there's nothing to steal."

"Does that mean we're all thieves at heart?"

"I think it might."

"Tom, you're starting to sound boring."

It wasn't sour grapes. Tom convinced himself that he didn't envy Bakir's wealth or his good looks and charm. Lucifer, after all, was the angel of light. Evil always begins its seduction by looking plausible. It wasn't the abduction; it was something about Bakir. Tom remembered a movie from his early adolescence, a Hollywood version of Bizet's Carmen. The bullfighter had become a boxer and Carmen was a beautiful black woman. She had enthralled Tom, but her murder devastated him so much he had to leave the cinema. The innocence of a thirteen-year-old was not prepared either to confront the consummation of evil. It had frightened him. The child came back and, just for a moment, Bakir frightened Tom.

Everyone at the party was friendly enough, and some seemed to take a genuine interest in him. One Russian, Vasily Ryolovlov, was most curious about Australia; a great place to invest money he understood. Seized by some inexplicable fit of magnanimity, Tom gave him Roger's contact numbers. He was never sure why. What would he say when Roger asked him?

'Well, you're the only person I knew with millions of dollars in his pocket,' would have to do.

Whatever Roger might think should they ever meet, the Russian was thankful and insisted Tom take his mobile number. That had to be a positive of some kind, although he couldn't imagine a time when he might want to use it.

After the initial misgivings Tom warmed to the lush surroundings. The bottomless champagne glass made its contribution. He had never tasted such a wide range of tasty food. Neither had he ever seen so many beautiful women under one roof, or an entire collection of roofs for that matter. The warm evening encouraged the exposure of tanned clear skin and so many of the women were easy to talk to. That was a surprise. Tom hadn't quite grasped that a single Australian surgeon had exotic appeal in France. He had always imagined beautiful and extravagantly expensive women would be intimidating. They would have had 'hands off' tattooed, tastefully of course, on each firm breast. Maybe they assumed he was one of the favoured rich, one of their kind.

It was to Tom's credit that, although it might have been difficult for an acquaintance to accept, he was not conscious of his athletic good looks and easy manner. Female vanity intrigued him, but male vanity appalled him. He believed it was more deeply rooted in a dark narcissism that needed to control everything in its shadow. Bakir, Tom was quite sure, would prove to be an excellent example. Either out of wisdom or cowardice he kept it to himself, but he thought female vanity rather amusing and not entirely unattractive. It was an appeal to be loved or at least noticed. Male vanity, he was quite sure, was ugly and frequently violent.

It was mid-evening when Kaye deliberately lost contact with Tom. She was having, she said to Maeva, 'tremendous fun'. Bakir introduced her to a fascinating tall blonde Russian, Anna Tolstoy, who claimed to be a great-great grandchild of the famous man. Kaye tried to do the sums but gave up. It was then she knew she'd had too much to drink. She was a bit of a failure at arithmetic as well as a spy but it didn't matter as she had no intention of passing on information to Bartholdi anyway. Tom could do what he liked.

"Kaye, I'm sure you appreciate good art." It was Maeva. "I've been collecting for years now. Would you like to see some rather special pictures in my little gallery upstairs?"

"Love to."

Maeva led Kaye to the third floor and unlocked an inconspicuous door slightly to the left of the stairs.

"I like to keep quiet about this room. I sometimes sell paintings, the less the opposition knows the better."

"I'm very flattered that you're showing me."

"Ah Kaye, I trust you. I know what kind of a woman you are. You're an intelligent idealist."

"Am I?" asked Kaye, feeling flattered as Maeva smiled.

The carefully lit room, slightly cooler than the rest of the house, was not large. Kaye counted twenty paintings on three pale green walls.

"This is my favourite."

Kaye saw a dark long-haired woman looking straight at her, her right hand resting lightly on her cheek. A blue dress with a yellow halter top, revealing strong shoulders, flowed over her body.

"Matisse, isn't it magnificent?"

"It's lovely."

"You know there's a rumour out there that this particular painting has been burnt, the same as with this one."

Maeva turned around and crossed the floor to another painting almost opposite.

"This Lucian Freud is a close second."

The painting was a portrait of a rather masculine looking woman with her eyes closed. Kaye didn't like it, but she was captivated by the pain the face seemed to hide. The woman looked so sad, she thought.

"Really, are both paintings supposed to have been burned?"

"That's the gossip in the art world."

"Why don't you put them right?"

"Ah, Kaye that's a long story."

"I see," but, of course, she didn't.

"Kaye, I have something to attend to downstairs. I hope you don't mind but I'll leave you for a few moments. Just enjoy yourself while I'm gone."

Kaye sat down in one of the black leather couches and looked at the favourite painting closer. She was feeling a little tipsy so it wasn't easy to focus. Maeva had been away fewer than five minutes when the door opened. It wasn't Maeva returning; it was Ahmed Bakir.

"Kaye, Maeva said you were here. I hope I'm not intruding."

"No, no, of course not," Kaye hardly recognized her own voice.

"You're very fortunate. Maeva shows few people this room. What have you done to encourage such trust?"

"I'm not sure, but I must say Maeva has been very kind and helpful."

"It's certainly a pleasure to see you again. You're more ravishing every time."

"I'm not sure what to make of that, Ahmed. I could continue the cliché and say, 'I bet that's what you say to all your women'."

"Kaye, believe me, I know a lot of women but I'm never tempted to be extravagant with my language; with my champagne, perhaps."

Bakir moved beside her as she continued to look at the painting of the woman with closed eyes. He was so close she could feel the heat emanating from his body.

"I don't like this very much," Bakir volunteered.

"It upsets me," responded Kaye. "Sexual ambiguity has never appealed."

"You're all woman. That's why."

At any other time, Kaye would have been on guard and recognized Bakir's seductive style as sophisticated sleaze. 'All woman' appealed. Ahmed was more handsome than ever. Any machinery she might have had to discern between charm and seduction was not well oiled.

"Really?"

"Here, let me show you something. It's my rather philistine answer to Maeva's paintings."

It was beginning to occur to Kaye, too slowly for her own well-being, that she was being subjected to a barrage of pick-up lines. But she didn't care. Everyone was wanting to show her something.

"Sure, can't wait."

Bakir looked directly at her and smiled.

"Excellent. Come with me."

Bakir took Kaye's left arm and lead her downstairs out onto a small terrace on the west side of the villa. He gave her a pair of binoculars.

"Look down there, out beyond the harbour wall. You will see a yacht moored about two hundred metres from the beach. It's too big to bring into the moorings of the inner harbour. I call it 'The Shark'. I bought it only last week, beautiful. Would you be my first guest?"

Things were getting serious. Kaye's suspicions, dulled by champagne, were not aroused.

"Sounds like fun."

"Be out in front in twenty minutes and I'll have a car take you down, it's a short drive. A boat will take you out to the Shark. I'll follow after I finish a little business here."

Kaye returned downstairs, not sure what was going on. She could see neither Maeva nor her husband. Standing at the foot of the stairs, the hallway was hazy. Each person was real enough, flesh and blood, but each person fused into a noisy smog. Kaye might have said she was disorientated; in fact, she was drunk. For some reason, it had to be perverse, she remembered an image of a severed wasp head sucking juice from an over ripe pear. She had no idea what it could possibly mean. It meant nothing. It made no sense. She wasn't sure what to make of Bakir's invitation. Why couldn't he take her? Was he just making a point or was he simply used to having somebody do his menial tasks?

"Where have you been? I wondered if Bakir had abducted you just to keep his hand in." It was Tom.

"No chance. He's going to show me his new yacht though."

"Be careful. You haven't had too much to drink, have you? You look a bit... well... out there."

"I'm perfectly fine. I've never been on anything like Ahmed's yacht. It'll be exciting. I hope you have the car keys. You might need them. Don't worry about me. Ahmed will get me home if necessary. I know him."

"Ahmed?"

Kaye left Tom to himself again. It was becoming a habit. Had Kaye been sober she would have been closer to a state of shock. She couldn't believe what she had just said to Tom. 'I know him.' She had no idea.

XXIII

"Hello, I'm Patricia. Welcome aboard. I look after the guests on the yacht. You're the first, so a special welcome to you."

Kaye was welcomed at the wharf by a tanned twenty something blonde nymphette. 'Dear God,' she thought, 'Does Bakir go for this sort of thing?' Just for a moment she hesitated to step on board.

"Monsieur Bakir told me I'm his first guest."

"Step down and I'll take you out."

Kaye stepped down into the little Shark. Patricia fired the motor and the pup, if that's what you called little sharks, seemed to fly across the surface of the water. It was only a matter of seconds before they reached the sleek grey mother.

"Welcome aboard. Let me show you around. Monsieur Bakir will be here presently."

Kaye stepped on to a wooden lattice platform at the stern. She was incredulous. She was not prepared for such luxury on a boat. There were three or maybe four decks; she couldn't quite work them out. Every room was so light and airy and agreeably curved with superb woodwork. The main bedroom with subdued lighting, she supposed it the main bedroom, was huge with two large paintings and a modern stained-glass window. It would be spectacular in daylight. The walls of the adjacent bathroom were covered with pale yellow tiles. Provocatively, the wall between the bedroom and bathroom was lightly frosted glass. Kaye wondered if it had blinds. The stateroom, a new descriptor for Kaye, was the most spectacular room Kaye had ever seen on land or at sea. The pool was half as big as Tom's in Brisbane. The gymnasium seemed remarkably excessive. What do these guys do on their boats all day? She had a vision of the poverty in Afghanistan recalling that Ahmed was an Afghan by adoption. The incongruity of his wealth was astonishing. Kaye imagined there was virtue in observing the contrast. She possessed that remarkable skill of being able to enjoy wealth and disparage it at the same time.

"Ah Kaye, I hope Patricia has made you welcome." Bakir, as he had promised, appeared in a white bathrobe, almost exactly thirty minutes after speaking with her on land. Kaye had no idea how he managed to get to the Shark.

"Ahmed, yes, very welcome. To tell the truth; the yacht astounds me. It's so beautiful. It's a long way from the plastic fantastics of my youth in Australia. The workmanship is breath-taking. It even looks like a shark, so threatening, grey and sleek."

"*Merci*, Patricia. I'll take over from here. *Bonne nuit.*"

"*Bonne nuit, Monsieur.* I'll sleep on board tonight. Bernard and Anton are on board as well. But I think you know that."

"I do, thank you. Excellent."

Bakir turned to Kaye. "I hope you enjoyed Patricia's introduction. She knows more about the yacht than I do, having worked for the previous owner."

"She seemed very competent." Kaye's first impressions had changed.

"Oh, she is. Everyone one on board is an expert in some way or another. I'm very careful about who I employ."

"I'm sure you are."

"Now, we must have a drink to mark your visit. Patricia has opened a bottle in the master's cabin, I believe."

"Tell me, Ahmed, how did you get here? I heard no other boat."

"I swam Kaye, hence the bathrobe. I have made a little pact with myself. I'm going to swim to and from the boat as often as possible and create the fastest time. Perhaps you would like to compete sometime. Just for fun, I thought I would run a little competition for my guests. Do you think that's a good idea?"

Kaye was feeling brave. "And what happens if I beat you?"

"We will have to see. I'm sure I could find a very worthwhile reward."

Kaye had that glass of champagne with Ahmed (Or was it more?) in the master's cabin, with the glass bathroom. Bakir smiled at Kaye satisfied she could be one of his most satisfying seductions. Of course, he didn't admit to himself or to anyone else that he was in the business of satisfying his sexual appetite when he felt so inclined. But with or without insight he knew that this time it wasn't going to be simple. Kaye was an exciting woman and he certainly wanted her in his bed. Anticipating entrance to the body of a Western woman fluent in Pashto was exhilarating. She was already on his side and, if not yet, she soon would be.

"It's been a big day for me, Kaye. What about joining me in the pool? There will be something that fits you in that locker."

"I'll look."

"Please do. I'll see you out there."

Kaye found an elegant, white one-piece costume. It was neatly modest, but on her body promised more. It didn't slip her notice that it might just have been waiting, chosen for her. Whatever the case, it made her look the woman she wanted to be. The mirror confirmed it. Tom admired her back in those New Farm days and Ahmed would approve, she was quite sure. He was already in the pool when she arrived and dived gently alongside him. The water, colder than she expected, forced her to gasp involuntarily. As she slid past him, Ahmed caught her and very gently kissed her briefly on the mouth. She had no desire to resist. Neither spoke. They swam alongside each other for several minutes without a word, even when their eyes met. It was, as her Irish uncle might have said, 'a brave soft night'.

"I'm going to have a shower, Kaye," said Bakir very quietly. "There's a shower adjacent to mine. Press the blue button on the left of the door and the blinds will close."

Kaye gave Ahmed some time before she followed him out of the pool. Just fitfully, she wondered if she could trust an inordinately rich, wine consuming Muslim. Self-centred hypocrisy came to mind but she had no intention of dwelling on the intuition. She went to the shower on the port side of the bedroom, pressed the blue button and climbed out of her wet costume. The warm water came quickly with gentle soothing pressure. That and the alcohol in her blood made her as relaxed as she had been for a long time. As she rinsed off her body, shampoo her hands explored a body that she recognised as still desirable. She stepped out of the shower and slowly dried herself. It was then that the blinds started to rise, slowly at first and then much faster. She looked out through the lightly frosted glass. She could just make out Bakir lying on the bed.

Kaye made no attempt to cover herself with the very large towel in her hand. She calmly finished drying her body before covering herself with delicious smelling moisturizer. She walked out of the bathroom, nipples noticeably firm, across the bedroom floor and into Bakir's bed.

"It was a risk," said Bakir, "but I knew you were a woman who appreciated enterprise."

XXIV

Tom drove home alone, angry and disappointed. He tried to convince himself he had no good reason for either. Kaye, after all, was just doing her job: finding out as much as she could about the Arab. He parked the car in the hotel garage and went to his room and slowly into bed. Sleep did not come quickly. The party might have been fun for Kaye and revealing to Bartholdi, but for Tom it was frustrating and unsettling. He felt like an appendage to all the action; not something he was used to. Minnah and Amadullah were waiting when Tom came down for breakfast.

"We saw Kaye going off to get aboard Bakir's grandiose status symbol," Minnah sounded just a little miffed. "I hope she knows what she's doing, Tom."

"I doubt it."

"Anyway, Fabien is pleased with himself," said Amadullah. "He knows a little more about Bakir and his colleagues in the arms trade. Any gun runner worth anything on the coast was at his party. I've known who he works with for months, but now Fabien is on the same page. I'm almost certain Bakir's getting a shipment of the latest stuff off to Afghanistan via Pakistan very soon. The problem is, the police don't know where the arms are stored or how they leave the country. The illegal arms trade is worth billions of dollars. In Afghanistan, a new AK47 alone can bring $1500. Even an old one will bring $600. He flies out of Algiers on his McDonnell Douglas MD something or other frequently, but I doubt it this time."

"Everyone is looking post 2018," Minnah claimed. "I think this year will be the make or break year for Bakir. Firepower in Afghanistan is going to be critical. As usual, he's playing his double game in the hope to get triple the outlay. He gets his stuff from a variety of sources, and sells the most useful stuff to his supporters in Afghanistan and the inferior stuff to anyone silly enough to buy. He has more quality firearms than anyone else because he buys the rubbish as well. He has markets in several African countries."

"Fabien," said Amadullah, "will move as soon as he has a fix on Bakir's suppliers. That's a problem because it will probably involve exposing significant government officials, a dangerous business for any policeman."

"I'm not sure how I helped tonight."

"Tom, just by being here, you encourage me," Minnah said with the kind of conviction that always encouraged Tom. "Sure, Bakir was having his fun, but you must have got the feel of things, the world Bakir and his friends live in. You've got some idea now how the money is being laundered and manipulated to wherever Bakir wants it to go."

"I'm slowly getting the picture. But why did Bakir talk to me? I must be a minor irritation. Does he really care about me?"

"He likes to keep his options open. He might need you some time. He might even like you. He's a complicated crook. Believe me, I know," said Amadullah. "I'm never sure whether there is some residual faith there or whether he is simply an opportunist. It may well be he doesn't know himself."

"You know he gave me twenty- thousand euros in a very fat brown envelope. Perhaps he thinks that's for services yet to come. I might feel part of his conspiracy if I knew what it was. I'm not sure what to do with the money; I guess he sees it as compensation for loss of dignity or something."

"Just hang onto it. Get it into a bank somewhere and leave it there. He might have plans to use it for some pernicious blackmail scheme."

"I will, Amadullah. I had reservations, but I've lost them on the way. I don't have a bank account here though."

"You can start that tomorrow, Tom; I'll help. It's a bit of a task for a foreigner, who doesn't live here, opening a French bank account," said Minnah. "The Commissaire is coming soon. If you trust me, it would be much easier for you to put it into my account."

"I do trust you." Tom's declared faith in Minnah came easily, almost without reflection."

It was nine o'clock before everyone finally sat down for breakfast. With his deputy Capitaine Grimaud beside him, the Commissaire took control. Tom continued to remain outside his comfort zone. He still worried him why a professional like Bartholdi would be making use of amateurs like him. Minnah and Amadullah he understood, and maybe Kaye. They, at least, had some inside knowledge.

"Thank you, Tom, for going last night. Bakir will think he has tightened up a loose end. It increases his already astounding confidence and that makes mistakes more likely. It might not seem immediately clear to you, but, believe me, you have been a great help. You and Kaye have opened up another front for us, if you get the drift."

"Thank you, I'm pleased to help in any way I can."

"Kaye, by the way, is still on-board Bakir's yacht. They spent the night together. Just what that means I'm not sure, but I'll attempt to keep my imagination under control."

Bartholdi, nevertheless, seemed to be sure of a great deal. Bakir was in some partnership with a Russian, Vasily Ryolovlov. The best information claims he made a killing by siphoning off money intended for the Sochi games. The construction industry in Russia was, and still is, one of the most corrupt in the world. Bakir has access to well over a billion euros. The rest of the Russian's money was a consequence of the breakup of the Soviet Union and being in the right place at the right time. Bakir has money in Algeria, but his team had not been able to trace anything in Switzerland.

All, however, was not well between Bakir and the Russian. Both, especially Ryolovlov, had money invested in Cyprus, but a large chunk of that had been lost. According to ROSSTAT, that's the Russian State Statistical Agency, the last decade saw a capital outflow from Russia to Cyprus equal to one half of the total outflow of the last year. There were thirty-five billion euros of Russian money in Cyprus banks.

Bartholdi claimed that Bakir is accusing the Russian of being incompetent and wants him to accept the loss. Unfortunately, he is in double trouble. He's caught up in a turf war between a Russian gang and a bunch of Georgian thugs. He set up a kidnapping of a Georgian gang leader that went wrong. He's in no mood to accept any accusation from Bakir.

"I met Ryolovlov at the party," exclaimed Tom. "I thought he was a decent enough fellow. He liked Australia. Someone had told him it was a great place to invest; I gave him a friend's contact details. So much for my judgment."

"No Tom, your friendliness is useful and, anyway, we want to talk to him. He's in some financial trouble and he might be willing to negotiate. He has committed no crimes in France as far as we know. The kidnap bungle was in Georgia. He might fancy an Australian contact completely outside his circle, and we can't do anything to raise his suspicions. Bakir will probably have said something about you to him. Hopefully he thinks you're just an innocent Australian bystander."

"Is there such an animal in the world as an innocent Australian bystander?" Amadullah was grinning at Tom.

"Well, we can be fairly sure you won't have Kaye's problem," Minnah joined her brother and smiled at Tom playfully.

"Maybe I could get back to Vasily Ryolovlov and suggest I was seeking more information for my friend in Australia. I might learn something. You know, divide and conquer."

"And secure Bakir's wrath, I suspect," suggested Minnah. "What do you think Commissaire?"

"I think we wait just a little longer. I would like to hear from Kaye, although I'm feeling somewhat uncertain there now."

Two days passed and they heard nothing from Kaye. Tom was worried, he had forgotten his disapproval of Kaye's actions. He was genuinely concerned for her safety.

Meanwhile, with or without Tom's concern, Kaye and Ahmed were impersonating Antony and Cleopatra in a modern luxury yacht kind of way. No 'triple pillar' stuff, but maybe a little of 'herein is my space' with booze and the energizing excitement of erotic hunger. Kaye might just have heard the vexing whisper of responsibility, but it's hard to choose discomfort when one's bed remains sexually exciting and soporific.

Like Cleopatra, Kaye was uncertain whose side she was on. Either she takes advantage of Bakir and his money, get as much as she can while it's there, or eat humble pie and try to get her job back in Brisbane. The alternatives were stark and the decision hardly difficult. Bakir, on the other hand, was quite sure he had another possible mole beside the one already in Bartholdi's office. Kaye was a lot of fun, but better than that, she was useful fun. He would not be surprised should she prove to be more interested in his money than him. He was used to that kind of women. And it had the advantage of liberating his own conscience which, he liked to assume, was not entirely dormant.

"Kaye," said Bakir at breakfast on the third morning. "How would you like to join my team?"

"Team?' Sounds interesting. Maeva has made suggestions that sound similar. Do you mean work for you? What would I do?"

Bakir was relaxed and apparently genuine enough. The method was simple. Offer the right amount of money to your target at the right moment and forget the truth. Have your victim enmeshed in duplicity of her own making. He would tell his divided religious conscience that Kaye was not a believer and what he told her would prove inconsequential at the final judgement. He confronted the world as a true follower of Islam but he was, like all fanatics, selective in his morality. That he was Amadullah's hypocrite was beyond his reach.

Kaye was without money or power, but she was smart enough to know that Bakir was dangerous, and that infatuation could well end in tears. The trick was to get out before the fun became boring and the tears started.

"Not much to start with. We would continue to meet as very good friends." Bakir smiled slyly as he said, "Very good friends."

"But of course," Kaye returned the smile. She knew they were playing a game where the rules would be made up as they went along.

"I think we should keep the status quo."

"Which is?" Kaye asked quickly, before she thought about the context.

"Aha," if Ahmed was annoyed, he didn't show it. "We stay together."

"I think so, but I will have to get back to the others even if it is only for a few days. It could get too messy otherwise."

"Of course, I wouldn't want it any other way."

XXV

It was Kaye's second day back at the hotel when Tom said he had something to tell her.

He had told Minnah he wanted to liberate his conscience. She was amused by his naivety, although she was touched by his simple decency. Kaye, however, was not Minnah.

"Oh Tom, what does it matter now?"

"Just wanted you to know that I wasn't happy with my behaviour during those early days in Brisbane; I treated you badly."

"I can't remember, Tom. We've another life now."

That was not what Tom had expected. He was being dismissed to the fringe of Kaye's memory. That night in the restaurant in Brisbane was reduced to an aberration, a misleading insight.

"How easy it is to make a mistake about a woman," he mumbled to himself. The resolution he had expected from his confession felt more like humiliation; which was what he said to Minnah the next day. She was only partly sympathetic.

"Tom, you were indulging yourself. You wanted absolution. Forget it. You need to remember the difference between guilt you manufacture so you can feel good, and real guilt. Kaye would have thought you pompous. The confession of assumed guilt always seems a trifle vain, absurd in the real world. Kaye was bound to think if you were all that guilty, why wait so long to say so? You wanted sympathy, not forgiveness, and she sensed it."

"Okay, I'll wear it. Young and mindless then, pompous now. Still,

143

it's a relief of some kind. It clears the air. For whatever reason, I've done it and I feel better. There you are."

Overcome by a surge of affection he embraced Minnah. Her body melted in his embrace. It seemed appropriate to kiss her on the cheek.

"That was bold. You haven't forgotten who I am?" Minnah made no immediate attempt to untangle herself from the embrace.'

"Yes, it was, and I haven't forgotten. Should I apologise?"

"I won't send Amadullah around to restore my honour. You can sleep soundly."

"You're laughing at me."

"Just a little, Tom. Just a little. You're worried about the Islam you don't really understand. I'm sure if I was a full blooded Western woman you wouldn't be in anything like a muddle between embarrassment and fear."

"Perhaps not. But you're a recent widow who straddles both cultures, are you full-blooded in either?"

"Ah Tom, that's something you'll have to find out, and when you do, let me know. In my head, I think I know, but in my soul, or is it spirit, I'm not sure."

With that Minnah kissed Tom on the forehead. "I'm off to bed. See you in the morning. *Bonne nuit, mon cher ami.*"

"*Bonne nuit*, Minnah."

Tom walked to his room slowly with the sensation of the kiss moist on his skin. He was tired. Where to from here? He was not due back to his practice for nearly two months, so that pressure was off. The astonishment of it all was he was beginning to enjoy himself and he felt more alive than he had been for years. He had been dragged to France against his will, imprisoned, and given a series of tasks where he was not entirely at ease. He hadn't even thought to protest. Who to? And, anyway, the intense frequency of the changing events was contemplation difficult.

Minnah was… he wasn't quite sure, bewildering would have to do.

She was beautiful, intelligent and off limits for reasons he could only faintly imagine. She didn't wear the burqa, but she was still unapproachable. Sheltered by her inaccessible and disciplined religious will.

Kaye was easier. There had been a time when the lights went on every time she walked into a room but, alas, not anymore it would seem. He was puzzled and disappointed. She was preoccupied with something she wanted to keep to herself. It was hard to admit that she wasn't the old Kaye he had once loved. She'd changed, or maybe it was him, perhaps he'd changed. Someone certainly had.

Minnah transcended her religion and maybe her culture. Tom wasn't sure what he meant by 'transcend'. Perhaps it was something as simple as basic human decency overwhelming religious superstition. There was nothing of the fanatic about her. She was a woman of a dignified and rare maturity. It was impossible not to admire her. Any fear of Islam or prejudice he might have had faded in her company. Minnah was a friend. Against his will, comparison with Kaye was inevitable. Kaye's high cheekbones were threatened by a recent gauntness. What an absurd thought to enter his mind just then. Tom imagined her youth was fading without the consolation of that Rubenesque fleshy ripeness he had admired in his secretary.

Tom, in moments of such indulgence, liked to think he had a literary frame of mind. He was tempted to see Minnah as the Islamic answer to Shakespeare's Prospero. A strange conceit, but not altogether unsatisfactory. The whim intruded, but he was not prepared to cast himself as a latter-day Caliban. More the lightweight Ferdinand, ready to love but just a little too proud. Minnah was giving him a language for the thoughts that were struggling to find life. Getting to know her was proving to be the most pleasing of pilgrimages. With those rather agreeable reflections, Tom slept the sleep of those at ease with the world.

Early, too early, Minnah woke him with a loud knocking on his door.

"Tom, it's Kaye. She's gone walkabout again."

'Walkabout.' What does this woman not know? She even embraces the Australian vernacular.

XXVI

Bartholdi gave himself the morning off to assess the events of the last few weeks. His wife had taken the children out for the day, so he took the rare opportunity to stay home. With something as significant as the Bakir case he needed all the time he could get to think without interruption and, anyway, he enjoyed the solitude in his new home. It had cost him a fortune to find something on the Southside so close to the beaches. His *beau-père*, Alex, had been a great help. He tried not to dwell on it. Nevertheless, he was thankful.

"You've been married six years now, Fabien, so I suppose you're not going to leave my daughter now. I can relax; my money's safe."

Bartholdi's marriage to Alex's daughter had not initially brought his approval. Fabien had two children by his first marriage and Isabelle also had two by a previous marriage. The difference was that he was divorced and Isabelle was a widow, ten years younger. Alex and his wife were of that rare breed in France: practicing Catholics.

It was two years after the marriage before Alex warmed to Fabien. Maybe it was Fabien's background that finally did it. He was an Italian who loved his new wife and her children. He loved his own children, his sisters, and his mother. But it was Fabien's close friendship with his first *belle-mère* that finally overwhelmed Alex. It dawned on him one day that Isabelle had a remarkable husband.

Bartholdi knew that his authority could be threatened quickly, so he didn't have much time. The politics, bureaucracy in Paris, and Bakir with his sympathizers were a volatile mix. If Jean Hollande, the *sous-préfet* of the fifth arrondissement, was really Bakir's lackey, he had to move skilfully and shrewdly. He had enough evidence to get a series of convictions, so why not take the risk? If he waited, Paris could make things too complicated, so he had to move. The Hassads were the only weak spot. Certainly, they were tied up in the whole gun-running deal, but where and how closely involved were they? They had to be the couriers between France and Afghanistan. Both had relatives in Iran. He hoped they would get scooped up in the net of recrimination that always follows when individuals like those around Bakir are arrested. He had seven names of people in the system who were thought sympathetic to Bakir. As soon as he was behind bars he would bring them all in. Some would want only to save their own skin.

Grimaud could lead the team. As soon as they were sure everyone was 'onsite' they would swoop: Bakir and his 'bodyguards', Hollande, and then the Hassads. Simultaneously, the *Sûreté Nationale* would pick up Bakir's suspected contacts in Algiers. And if there could be some consequences in Afghanistan all the better. It was difficult to know how they would spin out, no matter what he did in France. He had to work through Paris on any Afghanistan connection and any action there was always difficult. His mind was made up. Tonight, it was wife and children; tomorrow Bakir.

Isabelle arrived home with the children at seven o'clock. She was exhausted and the children were tired and grumpy. Fabien had anticipated such an eventuality, he was ready. Alex had recently bought him a very expensive barbecue and he was determined to use it. Maybe it was a gift to indicate his final approval of marriage to his beautiful daughter. Fabien noticed that it had been delivered only days after the loan for the house had been wiped from the books. And, of course, it was necessary that Alex and Isabelle's mother, Christina, was there. The children loved her, so life with tired kids was always much easier when she was around. She made better salads than her daughter. Fabien made sure he had her favourite rosé cold and ready. He was everyone's hero.

A revitalised Bartholdi wasted no time in his office the next morning. He was confident. "Right, Robert, it's time to move tonight. You know the drill. We'll have everyone in the bag first thing in the morning. Hollande and Bakir first. They mustn't be allowed to contact each other before we have each one safe in a cell. Bakir's men will be with him. Aazam El Hashem is critical, so we really have to make sure we get him."

"That I do know, he's mad. Sarin Sultan is a gentleman by comparison."

"Take Jean Baeza, Phillipe Amaury, Eric Levy, and Sylvie Carami to detain the Hassads. They've been briefed. The Hassads shouldn't be trouble. Bakir, Sultan, and El Hashem are on 'The Shark' tonight. At 0:300 hours, precisely I close in on the yacht. I'll leave you to collect Hollande as well as the Hassads. The customs and excise fellows will have a fast boat handy with five of ours on board, just to make sure Bakir and his cronies can't escape by sea. He's bound to have something sorted out for emergencies. He could put up a fight if we don't do this right. I'm taking ten men with me with a remodelled 543 each. Let's hope we don't need to use them."

"One thing, Commissaire, where does Bakir store his hardware? And, something I've never worked work out, why does he bring the stuff into France?"

"Now that's the issue. I know I'm rushing things, but I can't afford to wait. The last question is the easier one to answer. He has people in Marseille he can trust. His greatest danger is a loose mouth. There must be a storage centre somewhere, maybe several. I had hoped the doctor could have helped us there. That hospital would be an ideal cover."

"Most of his arms come from Russia or, maybe, Iran." Grimaud spoke in a monotone. "But you know that. It's not unlikely that he has suppliers in this country. You're right, Marseille is an ideal distribution point. He can fly or ship stuff out easily through all his criminal connections here. Marseille might well have been the bright European city of the year. It's still one of the most lawless cities in Europe and will be next year and the year after."

"Yes, yes I know all that." Bartholdi wondered what his colleague was waffling about. What was he trying to prove? He worried him sometimes.

By midnight everyone was in place. The Hassads were home in bed, Bakir and his bodyguards were on his yacht, and the wayward Hollande was watching an adult movie on Canal+.

At exactly 0:300 hours, Bartholdi gave the order to close in. Hollande and the Hassads, as he had predicted, gave no problem. None of them was awake enough to realize what was going on. Maeva's arrest was almost comical. She was quite sure that it was Bakir knocking on her door, so early in the morning she opened it herself.

"Oh," she exclaimed to the four uniformed officers, "I thought it was Ahmed."

Eventually, when Hollande finally realized the game was up, he collapsed like the most ordinary of cardboard boxes put under very little pressure. The Capitaine said he felt sorry for him. The Hassads protested their innocence and, after Bartholdi's instruction, were released on bail for one million euros. They returned immediately to their house in Cassis. Two of Bartholdi's finest kept watch.

Unfortunately, neither good fortune nor the comic muse attended the Commissaire's boarding of 'The Shark'. Bakir was not on board.

"Bakir had been warned," an angry Bartholdi told Amadullah, Minnah, and Tom the following day. "There's a mole somewhere, I dare not think who it might be. That had to be it. What else? Hollande couldn't have known anything about the raids."

"At least we got El Hashem and Sultan with their pants down," interjected the Capitaine. "Both were in bed with women. No idea who they were, one nighters. We've let them go, but we'll keep an eye on them. They might lead us somewhere but I doubt it."

"Why didn't El Hashem and Sultan run if Bakir had been warned?" Amadullah was puzzled. "I know Bakir, and he wouldn't have left them to stew in their own juice. It's more likely that he'd have either got them out of the country or even disposed of them himself. He's fanatical about loose ends."

"It is odd. They were on-board at 0:900 hours and no one saw Bakir leave. No boat went out to 'The Shark' or left it. There was no sign of Bakir anywhere and Kaye Reynolds has disappeared as well. It seems she's a willing team member, probably bed-mate. Bakir will have something up his sleeve as far as our Miss Reynolds is concerned."

"What happens to 'The Shark' now? Do you impound it? I'm curious," said Tom.

"I could, but it's a recent and very expensive addition to the Bakir collection. It has a crew who are employed by him, but you can be sure they will have no idea or even care what their master does. They're all young and foreign: two Australians, a New Zealander, and three Americans."

"So, what will you do?"

"Keep an eye on it and appear magnanimous all at once. Seizing it now could have legal complications we don't need. Bakir will have some 'innocent' to fill in and give the crew instructions. That's the way he works. He maintains a buffer between himself and the front-line. Let's hope he gets careless. The Hassads, for some reason, were an exception. I suspect Bakir has had an affair with Maeva."

"I can't believe Kaye's foolishness." Minnah was genuinely puzzled, "She is such an intelligent and brave woman, I thought. Surely she is not so easily seduced?"

"You're sure she's with Bakir willingly?" asked Tom.

"It looks like it, you'll have to admit."

XXVII

Minnah, as it turned out, was right. Kaye, aroused by her recently discovered passion for risk, accompanied Bakir. They had left 'The Shark' two hours before Bartholdi's raid. Although Bakir had no idea of the impending raid, he guessed his yacht was being watched, so he and Kaye swam to the shore to confuse anyone who might have been watching. So, he told Kaye. He planned to be seen the following morning having breakfast in a waterfront café. The watchers would have no idea how he got there with Kaye. He loved playing his little games. The police, quite sure he was on the boat, would be embarrassed. Eventually they would work it out, but it was still fun.

A phone call to his secure line changed everything. Bakir's informer called him too late to warn those left on the boat. It was 'the will of Allah' that he was not on board. His arrested colleagues might assume they had been left for the dogs to lick, but there was nothing he could do about that. Bartholdi was a fool, he had no hard evidence. What was he up to, acting so prematurely?

Kaye might not have been clear on the issue, but she had changed sides before she quietly slid into the water with Ahmed that evening. Perhaps it was the warm calm of the Mediterranean. The irrevocability of her position seeped into her mind during that critical swim with Ahmed. She experienced the closest thing avarice can have to an epiphany. It was, she convinced herself, a simple matter of common sense and loyalty. That comforted her as she and Bakir drove to Rome the following morning in a borrowed and deliberately nondescript Fiat.

Kaye was dimly aware of a self-inflicted psychological subterfuge. In Afghanistan, she had buried any possibility of regret in a zip-up bag she kept embedded in the deepest recess of her mind. She resolved, just after they entered Italy, never to open it. It was lost baggage.

The Bakir universe was lending her life an impassioned intensity. It reverberated with the throb of those early days with Tom, although she wasn't in love as she had been then. Those days of youthful idealism were gone forever. But, no matter, Ahmed was certainly the most congenial company on offer. Sexual pleasure, she was discovering, didn't depend on love as much as it did on money. But chemistry and money together were, well, intoxicating.

It wasn't only Kaye's myopia that had blinked. So too had Bakir's. Bartholdi, at long last, had made his first move, so he would have to lie low for a while. He thanked Allah again that he had not been on his yacht that night. Now Rome with Kaye would be as good as anywhere for a few days. She would be his consolation while he came to grips with his plans. An observer might have thought his confidence bordered on arrogance, but there was no one to observe except Kaye, and she was not in any mood to be at her most discerning.

Eros, the son of Chaos, had never been the most perceptive of the gods. Love, as they say, is blind. Tom, had Kaye asked, would have told her with definitive clarity, that little aphorism was sentimental codswallop. Love sees more clearly that anything. It's lust that wears the blindfold. Tom knew his Greek from university days. He would never confuse the pagan divine, Eros with unconditional love, agape. Kaye had no wish to be so enlightened. She was aware of the spiritual conflict between the intensity of unrestrained erotic love and the sacrificial nature of agape. She was in no mood to do anything about it.

The battered Fiat was as far as Bakir could manage in the business of anonymity. He had booked in at one of Rome's most expensive hotels, the Grand de la Minerve. He spoke vaguely about having a friend in the trade who knew how to keep his mouth shut. It wouldn't have mattered. The luxury continued to nourish Kaye's hungry failure to separate fantasy from reality.

Rome, for Bakir, was a time for reappraisal; for Kay, it was a mouth-watering stopover on her freshly discovered pilgrimage for grown-ups. Nevertheless, the evolution of their separate desires seemed to be taking each along the same unfamiliar freeway. Eros was happy to share the bed with ambition. And what a lovely little conjugal partnership it was.

Kaye had more than sufficient knowledge to enjoy Rome. She particularly enjoyed walking around the Villa Borghese Gardens above the Spanish Steps. One of Ahmed's friends had arranged an early morning private tour for her. The guide was young, about twenty-two Kaye guessed, but he was amusing and knowledgeable. But so too was Kaye. She knew a great deal of its history. She loved it that the gardens had been developed by the patrician and Consul Lucius Licinius Lucullus from a Persian model. Kaye liked to believe that her time in Iran gave her special insight into the connection.

It was Claudius's Empress, Messalina, who fascinated Kaye the most. She had forced the owner of the garden to commit suicide before it became her favourite playground. Ironically, Messalina was to be eventually murdered in the same garden on the orders of her husband Claudius, after he suspected her of plotting against him. Kaye despised Claudius.

It had been Kaye's last year at school in Iran. She had translated a forbidden passage in her Latin class from Juvenal's Satires about Messalina. She had been mesmerized and embarrassed in that equivocal way so common to adolescent girls.

Then look at those who rival the gods, and hear what Claudius endured. As soon as his wife saw he was asleep. This arrogant whore preferred a common couch to that of the imperial bed. Putting on her nightclothes and with only one maid, she went out, concealing her raven hair under a light coloured wig. She took her place in a brothel smelling of over-used covers. She had a room to herself and went by the name, Lycisca. With nipples bare, and gilded, she exposed the womb that bore you, O noble Britannicus! She invitingly received all comers, asking from each his fee. When the keeper dismissed his girls, she remained to the very last. With passion still raging hot within her she went sorrowfully away. Exhausted by men but unsatisfied, with soiled cheeks, begrimed with the smoke of lamps, she took back to the imperial pillow all the odours of the stews.

Ever since that moment in the classroom, Kaye had mixed feelings for Messalina. Her alleged raw sexual power intrigued her. Juvenal was just a hoary old misogynist so he was bound to have presented Messalina negatively. The much-maligned woman was rather more than just a frustrated wealthy Roman whore; she was an imprisoned woman trying to find her own kind of freedom. She was more heroine than whore.

It was fitting that mosaics, made with gold sandwich glass excavated from a 16th century garden, were owned by a powerful and rich woman, Felice della Rovere, the illegitimate daughter of Pope Julius II. Kaye imagined something new; there was an intrinsic subtle poignancy in being a woman. Her confidence was not groundless. It would have been shallow to claim that Kaye was sexually enthralled by Ahmed. She was not that weak. The magnetism of sexual collusion was there, but she was in control. Consent was the controlling ethic. Messalina, Kaye was certain, had always been in control of her own body. That was her magnificence.

There was no way she could have known or even imagined why Bakir was in Rome. Had she known, fear not confidence, would have been her waking emotion. Bakir's first action had been to send a text to the French mother of a suicide bomber in Syria: 'Your son Pierre is a true martyr. He has died in the arms of Allah in a bombing operation in Damascus.'

Pierre Bonfils was one of twenty young French converts Bakir and his co-religionists trained to participate in Jihad. Without exception, they were young French malcontents, who refused to work, from the impoverished *banlieues* in Paris and Marseilles. Pierre had said before his mission that he wanted justice in the world. No longer did he want to be exploited by the corrupt French State. Kaye could have seen a picture of him holding one of Bakir's Kalashnikovs on YouTube. He was trying to convince other young unemployed seekers of justice to follow him.

Bakir was always amazed how readily so many young Frenchmen were willing to become jihadists. It was a mystery why so many young thugs were attracted by the puritan fanaticism of Islam. There were already over one hundred in Egypt and Syria that he had personally encouraged and helped train. There were at least another five hundred waiting in the wings. The Ministry of the Interior's figure of two hundred made him smile. It was so gratifying to use the enemy's own children to destroy them. The irony was exhilarating.

XXVIII

It was Amadullah who helped calm Fabien's embarrassment after the debacle on Bakir's yacht. His connections had discovered both Bakir and Kaye in Rome. Kaye was a willing, and probably enthusiastic, partner. There was no suggestion that she was being held against her will. The news helped to absolve Tom's guilt over his. fading affection, but he still felt miserable. Kaye might be excused her inconstancy, but he baulked at the discomforting revelation of his own fickleness. Still, there was no denying a kind of relief. Kaye's behaviour was letting him off the hook.

Bartholdi's response was not ambivalent. Bakir's escape made him more determined than ever. He was going to get the terrorist his way, no more half-baked co-operation with Paris.

"Right, Amadullah, I'm going to rely on you for a great deal. Keep Bakir in your line of vision, and let me know as soon as he sets foot in France. I want him. I don't want the Italians or anyone else here to grab him."

"There's no way he'll get away from us." Amadullah was emphatic, "We know what he has for breakfast. We see him, hear him, and smell him."

"Kaye still worries me," said Minnah. "She can't know what kind of game she's playing or what Bakir's world is like. I'm going to Rome with Amadullah, catch up and talk some sense into her. What about you Tom? You must be concerned. Kaye could find herself in a French prison or with her throat cut by one of Bakir's thugs."

"Is it that bad?"

"Believe me, it is."

"Fabien," said Amadullah, "Bakir's going to have to come back to France sooner or later. I doubt that, even if Tom and Minnah do manage to talk to Kaye, Bakir will be influenced one way or the other. I suspect he's already made up his mind about Kaye's future."

"Well, Amadullah, my friend, as far as Rome is concerned, you're in charge. I don't want the Italian police interfering. It will be no surprise but I trust you more than many of my official colleagues. And, just in case, I have a clever lawyer sister working in a rather lovely old building on the Via del Corsa near the Porta del Popola."

"Ah yes, I remember her; charming to say the least."

Bartholdi's admission surprised Tom but not Minnah. She was intimately aware of the bureaucratic muddle in the administration of the Italians and French around the whole issue of Islam. Few officials seemed capable of grasping either the historical or contemporary struggle within the religion. The anti-clerical and secularised French mind is unable to contemplate the working declarations of the Prophet that politics and religion were married in heaven. The Enlightenment obsession with the supremacy of reason still ruled in the profane heart of the French intellectual. They believed that all men could be reasonable, given the right education and presumably the chance. For Minnah, such absolute faith in the reliability of reason was a terrifying blind spot. The only conclusion available to the rationalists was that the essential political problem with Islam was that it was plagued by too many hothead extremists. That it might have some profound error in its core was ignored because of their infatuation with the gospel of diversity. It would take a desperate crisis to change them.

"Well, do we have your blessing to talk to Kaye in Rome, Monsieur Bartholdi? She will have some freedom and I'm sure she will listen to me. I remember what she was like in Afghanistan."

"It's a dangerous game, Minnah. If Bakir discovers you have

spoken to Kaye it could place her in more danger."

"The longer she stays with Bakir, the more dangerous it will become for her."

"Okay, you may talk to her, provided you and Tom accept that Amadullah is in control. That would make me feel better."

"Sure," agreed Minnah, "That would have been the case anyway."

"I'd like a chance to talk to Kaye too, I might have some influence... I did once," said Tom with resignation.

"That's settled then. We'll leave for Rome tomorrow on the train. I'll arrange accommodation," Amadullah was definitely assuming control.

XXIX

It was early evening when the three avengers rose above the Latin chaos of the Stazione di Roma Termini. Tom was thoughtful and uncertain what to expect or do. Amadullah, in his quiet efficiency, had organized a tasteful apartment for them on the Via del Corso.

"It's a good spot. I'm sure you'll want to have a look around the city," he said to Tom and Minnah as he showed them their separate rooms. "Just leave the first few days for me to arrange things. I'll try to find out what Kaye is up to and maybe the real nature of her relationship with Bakir. The more we know, the better, if you'll pardon the obvious."

Tom had always wanted to come to Rome and here he was; not even at his own expense. It was an exercise of duty. He allowed guilt to hover a while as he remembered the French taxpayer. And then there was Amadullah. He remained an enigma. Tom suspected there was a great deal more to him than even his sister knew. Her brother seemed to move in and out of various groups with such confident ease. Bartholdi, while certainly not obsequious, treated Amadullah with a respect that seemed out of proportion.

What Tom didn't know was that Amadullah was a critical player in what was left of the Iranian pro-democracy movement. Indeed, he knew nothing of such a movement. Neither did he know that Amadullah was supported by a small group of wealthy Iranians living in the US and France, nor did he know of Bartholdi's connection to that group.

Fabien and Amadullah had been friends since their student days at the University of Aix-Marseille, previously the University of Provence founded in 1409. Fabien, although brought up in Italy as a child, was proud of the second biggest university in France. With nearly two female students to every male on the Aix campus, he envied the contemporary students. And it was up there with Paris in literature, linguistics, and economics. The weather was a lot better and the girls exposed more of that deliciously smooth Provençale copper skin.

After they had finished their studies, each had gone his own way but kept in touch. Since 2008, Amadullah had been Fabien's informal and confidential adviser on Muslim issues and its theology, although Fabien was not convinced that Islam had a coherent theology. Not that it mattered. The friendship had been reinforced because it had been professionally productive for both men. Minnah too had attended university in Paris, she knew about her brother's longstanding friendship but little about their recent working partnership. Amadullah's silence was practical and protective. He wanted no one to know he was working formally with the Commissaire; he didn't want to put anyone in danger, and most certainly not his sister. But now events were overtaking his brotherly concern. He had not dreamed in those early days with Bartholdi he would be working with his sister and a rather likable Australian unbeliever. He would not go there, but he was finding the Prophet's claim of two distinct and opposing worlds harder to accept. Dar al-islam and dar al-harb were less clear in his mind than they once had been.

Amadullah had no intention of losing his focus. His work with the pro-democracy movement was closely tied up with Minnah's work in Afghanistan. It was an impossible dream, but reform of Islam from within had been their goal. And for a while progress had been encouraging. A sort of democratic Iran looked possible. But the movement was exiled from Iran and several of the leaders imprisoned or murdered. Few people in the West understood what the pro-democracy movement was doing.

And now Bakir was making any kind of reconciliation more difficult. If he and his fanatical 'brothers' took control of Afghanistan after the Americans left, his work would be set back for generations. It was unlikely that Bakir would be concerned with any kind of reform in Islam or anywhere. Kaye was not helping, she was a bitter disappointment. He had always suspected she was motivated by a self-serving liberal idealism. In Afghanistan, he had given her the benefit of the doubt for his sister's sake. Tom, on the other hand, was growing on him. He was modest like a good Muslim and he seemed not to be entirely godless. That was a start.

They had an immediate task; rescue Kaye from corruption and stop Bakir. That would almost certainly mean executing him, but that had become a problem. Amadullah was not at ease because his goal was not in accord with his friend's. Bartholdi wanted Bakir in court with all the attendant publicity. It would be a significant personal and political victory for him. Amadullah knew that, but justice demanded Bakir's death because honour demanded it. In his more fanciful moments, Amadullah saw himself as an avenging angel doing the work of Allah. Any hesitation he felt had nothing to do with Bakir. Rather, he was deceiving his friend and that sat awkwardly on his conscience.

"I suggest," said Amadullah at their second breakfast, "you give yourself another couple of days to see Rome. That will give me time to do what I must. I'll contact Kaye and attempt to convince her to talk to all of us. I'll have to convince her she's in danger. I have a 'friend' in the hotel who has daily access to Kaye, so I can keep things nearly normal."

"I get the picture. You want a clear run."

"I need it, Tom. I have no desire to put either you or Minnah in danger. Relax, I'll keep in touch. I don't want Minnah to be seen anywhere near the hotel."

"I don't doubt your competence. I just hope you won't slit Bakir's throat while he sleeps in that dissolute Italian hotel," Tom was only half joking.

"I'll resist the temptation this time."

Amadullah's friend was housekeeping supervisor at the 'dissolute' hotel, but more important, she was his unbelieving Italian lover. So, it might be observed, even the faithful Amadullah had something of the ordinary man's weakness. Indeed, he had enjoyed the fruit of that sweet weakness for nearly three years. It was the meaning of Alessandra's name, defender of mankind, that had initially attracted Amadullah. They had met one wet April afternoon in the 'Book in Bar', an English bookshop on Rue Joseph Cabassol just off the Cours Mirabeau in Aix.

Both had been looking for novels hoping to improve their English in the least of painful ways. A local writer had just brought out a Provençal mystery that was becoming popular. Alessandra recommended it to Amadullah as he picked it off the shelf. And the rest, as they say, was that kind of history written in the stars. Muhammad's ambiguous disapproval of fornication had not proved potent enough to prevent the confluence of those stars. Amadullah learned to think of Alessandra, with some justified relish, as his passionate pagan.

It would have done neither Alessandra nor Amadullah justice to see their love affair simply as an exercise in forbidden lust. It was much more than that, but not entirely what either wanted. Certainly, they shared a romantic altruism, but Amadullah's religious sensitivities would sometimes leach into their ecstasy. Both experienced the tension, but said nothing. In the heart of their lovemaking there was a space where neither could go.

Minnah knew nothing of Amadullah's passion. Perhaps she was wilfully blind as sisters often are about their brothers' sexual proclivities. It was not easy for either to consider the other a sexual being in a realistic way. It would have embarrassed Amadullah, especially, to think of his sister's sexual life. It wasn't that he deceived his sister, it was just that the topic didn't seem important enough in a world where the throb of politics was more compelling than that of sex.

Alessandra was already at work. On Amadullah's instructions she had made a point of keeping an eye on Kaye. As supervisor of house-keeping she had contacted her to make sure all was to her satisfaction. She had made quite a fuss about Kaye being Australian. Brisbane, Alessandra had said, was one of those cities in the world she would love to live in. Kaye had been missing friendly female conversation.

Alessandra, although Italian, moved easily from English to French, and she was becoming familiar with Amadullah's Islam. Her easy manner eased Kaye's fears somewhat. Despite attempts to convince herself otherwise, intimations of concern about Bakir would some-times intrude into her vision of the future. Ahmed could reveal an implacability that was intimidating. It worried Kaye. She found her-self confiding in Alessandra on their second meeting.

Woven into the chit-chat, she sought advice in the third person.

"What are Muslim men really like? How do they treat women in the West?"

"Really like? That's not easy to answer, Kaye. The truth is that most do see women as weaker, inferior even, but not all. Some are ideologues who will never change. They are not strong on forgive-ness. Even the good ones find it difficult."

"I can see that." Kaye spoke hesitantly.

"Forget about Western notions of equality. It's not on the agenda. A rich Muslim would probably have a mistress but he will look after his wife and children, with money anyway. Honour is important and all that. Family honour is deep rooted and quite outside any Euro-pean concept of the idea. It's not directly related to truth like it is in the West. We're not talking about King Arthur's court here. One day the husband will protect his sister from harm for the sake of family honour and another day kill her for the same reason. If anything, honour is about pride, saving face."

"I know; I saw something of it in Afghanistan. Where does it come from?"

"Not sure, the Qur'an maybe, you'll need to ask your man. He might know."

167

'He might know.' What did Alessandra mean? Ahmed scared her. He was so different from Amadullah. She had no intention of broaching the subject with him; she was not brave enough. Kaye sensed a hard core in Ahmed, she didn't know what else to call it. There was a part of him that was out of bounds and it was that anxiety that made her uneasy when the sexual heat had cooled.

In the hotel bedroom, all was going to plan for Ahmed and Kaye. Or, more precisely, everything was going to plan according to the carnal aspirations of each. Divergence, if it was to come, was nowhere to be seen or felt. Both remained embarrassingly adolescent in their coupling. Each sexual encounter was fun at the time but afterwards there were other things in the world to get excited about. However, it would not be long before Ahmed would need relief and Kaye reassurance. Neither dwelt on the unwelcome reflection, that grief might lie ahead, least of all Ahmed. His tendency to use money and submissive women was so habitual it clouded his vision. He might have ranted about promiscuous Western women, but he remained a hypocrite and passion's slave. Duplicity and his sense of honour made self-examination unwelcome.

With the limitations of male discernment, Ahmed allowed Kaye to ignore any misgivings she might have had about her rejection of self-denial. His vigour and hard sinewy body filled her present. She could smell his warmth long after he left their bed. Kaye, with a little excursion into the ironic, hoped it was not a perversion of some kind, but the smell of his deodorant mixed with fresh sweat was exhilarating. There was a time for everything. This was not the time for restraint.

It was Kaye's fifth day in Rome when she had her longest chat with Alessandra. Bakir had 'some business to attend to' and Kaye was having a late breakfast alone.

"Ah, Kaye, I hope everything is still to your satisfaction."

"Indeed, it is."

"I've just seen the news. The flooding in Brisbane seems terrible.

Is everyone in your family safe?"

"Yes, they are, thank you. They live in an area not in danger of flooding."

"Australia's floods and bush fires frighten me. And then there are the snakes and spiders."

"Oh, it seems worse than it really is. Millions of Australians have never seen a snake except in a zoo and bush fires and floods don't happen everywhere."

The two women continued to talk. Kaye enjoyed the chance to relax without the ebb and flow of sexual tension, so she spoke freely. Alessandra had gained her confidence. That evening she told Amadullah as much when they met for their evening meal.

"Next time I get a chance to speak, I'll suggest that Kaye speaks with you. I'll tell her I know you from university days and that you have asked me for her to contact you."

"Okay but play it by ear. I don't need to tell you to be sensitive."

"No, you don't, and certainly not in that backhanded way." Alessandra was just a little annoyed but her smile concealed it.

"It will be a surprise that I'm attempting the contact rather than Tom. Her curiosity will be stirred, I hope."

"I'll make sure it is."

"Here, would you come down to my level and have a glass of Lambrusco? It's Cleto Chiarli, your favourite hamburger wine."

"But, of course." Alessandra smiled, leaned across the table and kissed Amadullah on his forehead.

"Ah, Alessandra you're such a delight."

"I'm pleased to hear you say so."

"Be careful you might arouse my provincial tastes."

Amadullah had developed a taste for Lambrusco. It was a minor transgression. He was not an expert on Italian Renaissance art, but he did know the Mona Lisa and maybe a few others when pushed. Not that it mattered. He was quite sure Alessandra's smile outshone, by the most picturesque of country miles, that of Francesco del Giocondo's wife.

The discovery of his love for Alessandra had passed through Amadullah's body like a tremor from a moderate earthquake. It was unexpected and, for a while, distressing. It had shaken his centre of gravity. Knowing he loved her came like a thief in the night who had left all his loot behind. He chose to ignore any suggestion of dependency or even mutual need. Such an admission would not be in harmony with a pillar of Islam. Dependency on Allah, perhaps, but a woman?

Alessandra was aware of her lover's ambiguous religious inhibitions. Their failure to protect him was a kind of confidence booster for her. She resolved her dilemma like Tom had with Minnah, by accepting that Amadullah was better than his religion, although she dared not say so to him. It was too complicated and she wasn't sure she was right anyway. It was enough that she understood the man. She knew that she was loved by a good man, and that, she knew, was not common.

Alessandra arranged for Kaye to meet Amadullah and Tom. Kaye didn't want to confront Minnah because she was too strong and a reminder of her failure in Afghanistan. Surprisingly, Kaye insisted that she talk with Tom. It was simple really, she said; she just wanted to see him. Bakir's amatory vigour, Alessandra discovered, had not disconnected Kaye completely from her memory of Tom.

They met in the same restaurant where Alessandra and Amadullah had eaten previously. Kaye had arrived early and had already drunk a glass of vino rosata. Her smile caused Tom's heart to flutter unexpectedly. Unable to help himself he embraced her, with what he was to call later, compromised passion. Images of the St Lucia restaurant were not absent. Kaye sensed his disquiet. She was unnerved by the depth of affection that overtook her. It awakened a new sadness. She exchanged the conventional kisses with Alessandra and Amadullah and just for a moment it was as though nothing had changed.

"Well, I know why we're here," Kaye was the first to speak. "I'm pleased you've found me. We need to clear the air. I've wanted to, but I wasn't sure how to go about it. Alessandra, bless her, solved my problem. I'm sorry. I'm sure you must think I'm either a fool or a traitor."

"Traitor's a bit strong, Kaye," said Tom, trying to be encouraging. "I'm not sure we need to be that dramatic."

"Ah, dear Tom, still forgiving I see."

"Not really Kaye."

Tom had returned to that sometimes miscellaneous mood of his teenage years. Had Kaye said to him that she was sorry and that Bakir was a tyrant. Please forgive me Tom. He would have relented willingly. Had she returned he would have accepted her, but it would have been an act of duty rather than love. Well, maybe, he wasn't sure.

Kaye had no idea what she was going to say. From somewhere she found new strength. She hardly understood what was going on within her. Tom, with more than a trace of heartache, was later to describe it in Old Testament language, she "hardened her heart".

"You need to know I've changed. Ahmed is not the man I expected or the man you said he was, Amadullah. Tom, he has treated me with gentleness and respect. He trusts me."

Tom was disappointed, he had not wanted to hear anything so definitive so quickly.

"Kaye, you're sounding more confident than I hoped, but you seem to have made up your mind. Ahmed Bakir is not the man you think he is," said Amadullah. "Sure, he's a charmer, as many women have discovered. The truth is he's a self-serving killer whose god is money. It is certainly not Allah, praise be his name."

Either Kaye was not listening or Amadullah's impassioned plea sounded too much like religious ranting for Kaye.

"The truth is he's wealthy and he's been kind to me. I enjoy both. I love him in my own way. Oh, I know that sounds crazy to you. I'm sorry Tom, to be so blunt but that does seem to become the tone of our conversation. There it is."

"I see," said Tom quietly, more saddened than deflated. "I only hope that you know what you're doing."

"And please tell Commissaire Bartholdi I will have no information to give him. I suppose you could say I've changed sides. You know, I wasn't sure of that before coming here, but it's true, I have."

If Tom was shaken, Amadullah was angry. Kaye had reinforced what he had always suspected of Western women; they were promiscuous self-seeking whores. They were incapable of loyalty if it demanded sacrifice. He said nothing. Quite suddenly, he rose from the table and left the restaurant, followed by an upset Alessandra. Tom and Kaye were left alone.

"Well, goodbye Tom. There's nothing more for me to say. I feel sorry for Alessandra." For a moment, Kaye was absorbed in some secret musing. Tom imagined he saw a glaze of tears cover her eyes.

"Tom," Kaye was almost whispering. "Please tell Minnah I love her. I'll never forget her."

"She stood up and kissed Tom on his lips. Smiling, as a mother might departing from a teenage son. She left quickly and silently.

Alone, Tom was left to pay the bill; a tedious little reality hardly at the heart of the drama, he observed. Resolution of any kind was still elusive. Minnah might have become a less cloudy image than Kaye. Neither image was satisfying.

Amadullah and Alessandra were waiting outside sipping coffee with Minnah. "Sorry about that, Tom, my friend. Alessandra has rightly chastised me but Kaye made me so angry. She has no idea what she's doing. She is unbelievably stupid. I just can't tolerate such mindlessness. Has the woman no core, no character?"

"She's been seduced by an inescapable fantasy. That's the closest I can get I'm afraid."

Alessandra sighed, "Amadullah, you know, in a way I'm only a little different. I love you and yet we are nearly as different as Kaye is from Ahmed. I have the good fortune to love a good man. Kaye loves a dangerous man. She knows that, but it won't kill the fantasy. She is quite unable to confront his malevolence and, anyway, neither the desire nor the experience to do so is there."

Amadullah smiled and embraced his teacher. He knew she was right. His mood changed from frustrated anger to a simple admiration of Alessandra. He didn't say so aloud, but he was thankful to Allah. This Western woman was a long way from being a whore. He was satisfied with the rebuke.

"Well, we know where we are," said Tom, also impressed by Alessandra's insight. "Kaye has shaped her destiny. We can't save her and, anyway, I suspect she doesn't want to be saved."

"It would seem not." Minnah felt deeply saddened. "When we were working together in Afghanistan I really loved her. She was so enthusiastic. Is it possible to really know someone?"

"The best we can hope for now, Minnah, is that Kaye doesn't get caught in some mindless crossfire between Bakir and his competitors."

"I'm really afraid. I have absolutely no desire to see Kaye hurt."

"Minnah, I need to tell you that Kaye asked me to tell you that you loved you. She meant it, I'm quite sure."

"She will be so much alone in a world that could become so terribly hostile. I pray she will never have to confront that hostility."

Minnah knew what it was like to be alone. She loved her brother and her family but she was drifting away from Islam. For her family, she would already be apostate, and in the minds of some, deserve death. For her brother, she would be the cause of great sadness; she would break his heart and that was hard to bear. Without desiring it Islam had become increasingly unacceptable. The gap between what she had been taught as a child and young adult and what she now believed was unbridgeable. She could speak to no one, except, perhaps, Tom.

The honour-shame ethic embarrassed her and yet it was so embedded in her psyche, she knew her unbelief would dishonour her brother and the memory of her father. Rokhshana would be deeply wounded.

When Kaye returned, Bakir was ready to leave for his underground warehouse in Brignoles. He had made up his mind to take her with him, but she had no idea that her faithfulness was to be tested. Bakir had grown unexpectedly fond of her and in so doing he tended to confuse obsequiousness with faithfulness. Possession was still the compromiser of his unexamined desire. Kaye remained stimulating and sexually exciting, so it was more agreeable to keep her than dispose of her. Of course, Bakir did not think it through with such naked precision. He told Kaye that he loved and needed her; perhaps he meant it. Living on the edge of the law was becoming a way of being for Kaye, and Bakir's endearments sharpened her senses. Each day she felt just a little more alive so she had no difficulty in absorbing her lover's penchant for duplicity. Ahmed instinctively approved the changes in Kaye's character without recognising how she was changing him.

Kaye was not ready for what was waiting for her in Brignoles. Bakir owned three adjoining houses at least six hundred years old. They were right on the wall that had once surrounded the ancient town. By chance or a gift from Allah, he discovered a huge cavern underneath two of the houses. Sometime in the fifteenth century, the area had been a large inn complete with two entries at opposite ends of a maze of various sized chambers, all with arching stone ceilings. Informed local mythology suggested that the two entrances were necessary to allow wealthy clients of the attached brothel to escape their fornication becoming public knowledge.

Bakir had discovered a labyrinth of tunnels. One tunnel, not local knowledge but still intact, ran for two hundred metres to his second property near the river. Here it was easy to load crates quietly during the night or even in daylight. Locals paid no attention to what they thought was a warehouse for refrigerators and washing machines; which, in fact, it was. Bakir did have a legitimate business distributing a variety of household appliances.

In the large underground area of the two houses Bakir had had everything strengthened and cleaned up. Wooden floors were repaired or replaced and the ceilings cleaned. Lighting backed up by his own generators lit up every chamber which were packed with wooden crates of various sizes.

"Arms, my dear, arms. I wanted you to see these. When the Americans finally leave Afghanistan in a few months it's likely to be a bloodbath. I hope to help prevent that. Peace will be short-lived. It's my job to get as many weapons in the right hands as possible."

Bakir had convinced himself that Kaye would accept his view of the world. He knew, of course, that he had to be cost effective with the truth. If she believed he was a liberator of sorts, then she would be helpful when he and his organization took over in Afghanistan. An educated western Pashto speaking woman could be a huge asset. Diplomacy so often failed when language failed. He could not imagine any woman who would be a better fit.

"And what are the right hands?"

Ahmed looked straight at her. Perhaps the question was too direct.

"You must have done a lot of thinking," she prompted.

"Ah, yes, my love. You have no idea how much." Ahmed's smile remained captivating. "I have been preparing for my country's freedom for twenty-five years. The right hands belong to those who love Afghanistan. There are thousands. For years now, we have been stockpiling weapons. Believe me, in my country that's not easy. You need people you can trust. What you see here is just a small portion of what we have. We must be ready when the time comes."

Kaye was the woman who knew too much and that frightened her, but there was no going back. Ahmed had clearly designed this visit to get her more deeply involved. She looked at Ahmed and embraced him.

"Do you really trust me, Ahmed?"

"Yes, I do. I think you understand what all this means."

"I do."

"I won't bore you with an inspection of the weapons. This supply is mostly older Russian stuff with some Chinese." Ahmed looked at Kaye with an expression that seemed almost childlike. "May I tell you something, Kaye? My better judgement tells me to keep silent, but I want to share something with you."

"Oh dear, that frightens me more." A voice somewhere in Kaye's head seemed to echo, '… deeper… deeper. You'll never get out'. Now was the time to get out. But how? Perhaps Ahmed was right and the others just didn't understand. He wasn't a terrorist at all. He was the hope for Afghanistan.

"Ahmed, I'm not stupid. I know what you're doing. You're testing me. You want to see if I have what it takes. I know now what my value is to you. Okay, now it's your turn. You say you love me and that I can trust you. It seems to me that I'm two people, your lover and your employee. Let me test your resolve. Look after me and protect me as a lover and pay me as an employee."

Bakir laughed in such a way that Kaye knew she was on safe territory. She was talking his language. Without trying, she had entered his terrain. He understood exactly what was driving Kaye. He was not a sentimentalist. Even lovers had to act out of self-interest. Personal sacrifice was weakness. That's why the Christians would never win and why the story of the Cross was nonsense. He accepted his spin on the call that went out from every minaret in Islam every day, 'Come to success.'

"Come with me, my love." Bakir took Kaye by the hand with an unusual tenderness. He led her into a room she had not seen. Light poured in from a massive skylight four metres above their heads and a large canopied bed filled one quarter of the room. Around the walls were some old but very beautiful cupboards and two renaissance paintings she didn't recognize. The clay tiled ceiling was curved the full width of the room. A suggestion of the incongruous slipped fleetingly into Kaye's consciousness; the room resembled a modern church attentive to its architectural history.

"Wow, some room, Ahmed. Did you do this?"

"I'm proud to say, I designed the renovation. Some friends of mine from Algeria did the work. And here's the pièce de résistance, I'm fairly sure this room was part of a brothel in the sixteenth century." Ahmed was grinning as he pulled gently Kaye onto the bed and began to unbutton her shirt. Kaye did not resist and, anyway, she had no reason or desire to do so. It was impossible not to wonder though, why Ahmed had been so careful to point out the room's history. Was he trying to tell her something or did he just think that she might find the story stimulating enough to excite her imagination a little?

As it was the story must have had its impact. She was relaxed and responsive. When she woke, the sun had gone and the light from an almost full moon had replaced it. It made Ahmed's naked body look like a corpse. For a moment, the image of two naked corpses being discovered on the bed troubled her. Maybe it was the old room that encouraged a kind of morbid fantasy.

It was five in the morning when she glanced at her Hublot; it was Ahmed's first present and very expensive, but she had no desire to know its value. She had slept for eight hours.

The counterfeit corpse was beginning to stir.

"Ahmed, do you realize we've been asleep for over eight hours?"

"Ah, the sleep of the just after is hard to beat, is it not?" Ahmed smiled with a suggestion of a smirk. Kaye didn't find the feeble attempt at a joke at all funny.

"Time for a shower and then a late breakfast. There's a very pretty village about twenty minutes away. It's market day there and lots of great restaurants. You'll love it. We can drive on to Marseille from there. I want you to meet the couple who look after this part of my work."

The phrase, 'part of my work' was vague. Kaye was tempted to mock Ahmed but thought better of it. He was right about the village though, it was lovely. Dominated by high cliffs, complete with caves once inhabited by troglodytes before the Romans, the village was fascinating. During the Middle Ages, the caves had been used as a refuge by the poor from plague and war. Houses were built into the cliffs, expanding on the caves as places of protection and dwelling, and a few lower ones were still in use.

The market was colourful, bustling and inviting. Along both sides of the wide thoroughfare, restaurants displayed an enticing array of menus. No one seemed in a hurry to eat although it was late morning when Ahmed and Kaye arrived. There was one queue, at the only ATM machine in the village. It had broken down. *'Il ne marche pas. Il doit être fixé rapidement,'* an anxious stall owner suggested to Kaye.

After an enjoyable wander through the narrow paths and between the stalls, Ahmed was willing to climb the steps up to the caves. Kaye, maybe without justification, imagined his willing acquiescence the agreeable consequence of a fine lunch and an excellent Syrah.

It was the first French village market Kaye had seen. The clothes, jewellery, and home-made cheeses, preserved meats, olives, nuts and fruit were stunning. She saw the French phrase, *tout le monde* in a new light. If everyone in the world wasn't there, it seemed like it.

"This is the most beautiful nectarine I've ever tasted," declared Kaye as she savoured the juicy yellow flesh of the fruit in her hand. "Ahmed, it's just lovely to be here with you in the sunshine. Everyone seems so relaxed and friendly."

"It's village life in France, my love, although I must say this one is especially good. I suspect it might have something to do with the tourists. A lot of English speakers live in this area. That boulangerie and patisserie on that corner behind you is owned by a woman from Liverpool."

"Really, what a day this is! It's quite the most enjoyable one I've had in France. I'm beginning to love the country. It's just so, well, civilised."

Bakir smiled indulgently but said nothing. How could he? Of course, France was 'civilized' but his entire life had been given to despising the West. He could not permit ambiguity to weaken his resolve. He ignored the contradiction out of habit. Submission to the possibility of poignancy and, God forbid, anaemic compassion would derail him. He had a job to do and Kaye was sufficient concession and comfort.

Bakir and Kaye walked up a wide, paved path that passed in front of the old oil presses that led up to the old Hospice de la Charité. They followed the narrow paths carved into the cliff face to a view out over the red tiled roofs of the village houses.

The 'stuff' would be out of Brignoles by the end of the week and well on its way to Afghanistan. Ahmed would leave the place empty for at least a month. By that time his client in Rome would have passed everything on. Then the work of siphoning the real stuff the Americans left behind would begin. He would be saving them hundreds of thousands of dollars, millions probably. What more could they want? He had to convince them that the weapons wouldn't fall into the wrong hands. Fortunately, the Americans were seldom clear on the difference between right and wrong hands. That could work both for and against him. Subtle diplomacy was the name of the game. Kaye could be an asset. She was saturated in Western liberal lies and more aware of the critical nuances that could make or break his game. It was worth a try. The timing was perfect and Kaye's minders in Afghanistan would be expecting her back.

XXXII

Amadullah, Minnah, and Tom were subdued the day after their encounter with Kaye. Tom was beginning to understand the risk that she was taking. Although Amadullah's warning had registered with him he was hopeful that things would turn out well. His inherited decency still protected him from realising the cruelty of Bakir's world. If he had been asked he would have said he understood, but he had no personal touchstone to guide him. The only two Muslims he knew were remarkably trustworthy, and in Minnah's case compassionate. And really, Bakir had not treated him all that badly. Personal experience is difficult to overcome.

Tom was becoming enamoured by a conviction that he was not the main player in the theatre of his own life. Even now Amadullah was deciding what they should do. Their stay in Rome was almost over and it was back to Marseille. Kaye, Amadullah had said, might well become 'collateral damage, to use a military euphemism.' It was that remark that particularly upset Tom. The possibility of Kaye being caught up in any fallout undermined his Christianised sense of justice.

Most of his working life as a surgeon and consequent position at centre stage had encouraged an easy and satisfying confidence about life. One got up in the morning expecting to be in control of the day. Perhaps one is never really in control of anything. 'God's in His Heaven and all's right with the world.' Well, perhaps it was for Browning living in Italy with his talented poet-wife. God might well be in His Heaven, but all was certainly not right with the world. The events of each passing day were reinforcing that.

"Amadullah, I'm not a slow learner, well not very, we're going back to France to catch up with Bakir. You still intend killing him, don't you? What do you intend saying to the Commissaire?"

"Tom," intruded Minnah, "there are some things you can leave to us, to Amadullah anyway."

"I can't really, I'm here. I know what you have planned."

"You don't, you know," Minnah spoke quietly and firmly. "I don't even know what Amadullah has going on in that fertile little mind of his. Do I Amadullah?"

"I hope not."

"One more night in Rome, Tom, and I'm taking you out. It's Amadullah's command and money, I should add."

"Is it indeed? Submit then, do I?"

Submission to Minnah was becoming increasingly pleasurable. Her dark Afghan loveliness was cause enough, but her mind was more captivating than ever. He remembered what she had said about loving one's enemies. He'd looked up the context. 'But I tell you, love your enemies and pray for those who persecute you that you may be children of your Father in heaven'. It was a long way from Islam even on his slight knowledge of the religion. He understood how astounding to Minnah it must have been, and she seemed to take it so seriously. But then, she would, because she took her own religion with such unfathomable seriousness.

"Living was a cheek to cheek pilgrimage with death and separation from those you love," she had said one night.

Islam could be so profoundly bleak. He couldn't comprehend the loyalty she had to her brother with such a meaningful understanding of the religious dogma that controlled him. Tom wondered if there was a kind of love he still had to learn about. Much of Minnah's emotional power came from a lifetime given to sacrifice. Because she was a Muslim woman? Perhaps. Sacrifice was her duty to her family and Allah. All that was woven into the cover of her mind. But something new was taking shape. Was she learning that there was a sacrifice motivated by love rather than duty?

Whatever it was, it was compelling stuff. As a child Tom had not quite understood the agreeable union of character with beauty. The moral gap between the fairy tale 'Beauty and the Beast' and the Beatitudes was not all that great. Beauty tamed the Beast with her loveliness and purity of her character. It was a tantalizing fairy tale.

There was, Tom mused with attending puzzlement, something frightening about the purity of beauty. Maybe that's why the sublime could be such a fearful thing. Awe and fear can be so close. 'The fear of the Lord is the beginning of wisdom'. Minnah would probably agree; it wasn't that he was afraid of her, but she just seemed so unattainable.

The last night in Rome was replete with good cheer. They were tourists having an enjoyable night out. They all spoke English for Tom's sake, and they did get a smidgeon loud. Alessandra was tastefully affectionate towards Amadullah, Tom observed with approval. It was pleasing to see his friend have a good time. Minnah shared Tom's sentiment. Amadullah, not given to indulgence or extravagance, seemed to be experiencing something of an exception that evening. Tom was thankful. It was fun to be in Rome with three remarkable foreigners from another world. The wine helped, but it was the warmth from Minnah's closeness that had Tom wondering if it ever got any better.

Minnah and Amadullah chatted about their lives as children, and Alessandra told them about her kindly mother and father who she still loved. Minnah was more curious than usual. She asked Tom about his work in Australia, his family and, most daring of all, how he met Kaye and what their life together had been like. Tom was forthcoming. He spoke to Minnah and the others about his youthful lust and impecuniousness with enthusiasm. Each little revelation squeezed a little more glue of friendship from the bottle. With every squeeze,

Minnah became more desirable and just a little less unattainable. It was Amadullah who brought them back to the task in hand.

"Bakir has gone to the Var with Kaye. He has a house, or rather a series of buildings, there in a town called Brignoles. My man couldn't get inside. It's a fortress. Right now, he's in a trendy little village, Cotignac with his Australian friend," Amadullah smiled slyly at Tom. "Tomorrow, Minnah and I are going to the town where his house is. We need to have a good look at it. I won't be surprised if it's his main weapons storage base."

"Tom, we can't make you come with us, but I would like you to come. You're free to go back to Marseille and report to Bartholdi but what would you say?"

Minnah's voice echoed King Lear's Cordelia, 'soft, gentle and low'. Something had changed, or had he missed the obvious? Tom had assumed they would be going back to Marseille and giving Bartholdi a progress report. But what would he say? 'Those crazy Francophile Afghans have gone off to finish Bakir.' Hardly.

"Tom, don't fret. We'll be back in Marseille in a few days. We just want to make sure we know a great deal more about Bakir than he knows about us. Don't worry, we are not going to desert the Commissaire, he's an old friend, remember?"

"Sure, I know, but you have your own agenda when it comes to the crunch. Minnah has said as much."

"True, but I hope that we can still be on the same pathway as Bartholdi. In the long run, it will prove a matter of timing."

Tom wasn't sure what he thought, hardly new. It perplexed him how easy it was to forget Brisbane and his work. With few reservations, he had come to be part of something he couldn't possibly have ever wanted. The entire situation was crazy. He had to keep telling himself that. He was a surgeon for God's sake and a bloody good one, but here he was still a kind of captive. He wasn't locked up, but he was locked in. The subtle difference might have been significant, but for all practical purposes he was still a prisoner. It was just that the present imprisonment was a lot more fun than the former.

Tom wondered what would happen if he said he was going back to Bartholdi immediately. He wasn't, of course, and the others knew that.

"Okay, I'm up for it. Where're we going?"

"First thing in the morning, we drive to Brignoles where Bakir has his stash. I'm sure we will find arms hidden away somewhere. It'll take us about nine hours if we're lucky with the traffic."

Two of Amadullah's men had followed Bakir and Kaye to Brignoles. Either his men were very good or Bakir was getting careless. They had observed Bakir and Kaye enter and leave the house and had sat only a few tables away from them in the restaurant in Cotignac. Maybe Bakir thought he was in safe territory. He was sure the police had no idea of his place in the Var. They didn't. But Amadullah had resources not available to the police. He was burning with a desire for revenge and a working hatred for anyone who manipulated Islam to his own will. He was a loyal friend but a deadly enemy.

Amadullah would have been happy to hear from Tom such a description of his friendship and nature as an enemy. It would have been as fine a compliment as he could have wanted. Tom was a friend and a friend of his sister. Now Tom was more like a brother. But Tom wouldn't have understood. Kaye hadn't. The tyranny of family need and the contradiction of Amadullah's learned instincts of manliness were outside his experience. His Western faith in reason still ordered his mind. But then, Amadullah could not possibly comprehend Tom's recognition of God's grace and forgiveness.

That was not without irony. Although both men were profoundly different in their spiritual insight, they were not far apart. Both respected truth, honesty, and courage. In short, they were both masculine men. Both believed it was courage that gave goodness its power. They loved strength and hated weakness. The difference was that Tom hated his own hidden weaknesses; Amadullah despised weakness in others. He had no desire to be cruel. It was just that weakness embarrassed him. A man grew up to be strong, otherwise why be a man?

XXXIII

Brignoles, Tom discovered, had once been a town at the core of the bauxite mining industry in the Var. Now, with about twelve thousand inhabitants, it remained historically interesting but certainly not on the tourist beat. It was a working town with a make-do mosque and a sizable Muslim population in the old town. Just off the Nice-Barcelona AutoRoute it was easy for Bakir to transport his cargo from such an unsuspecting little place. One of his companies owned several large camions transporting green beans and cherry tomatoes from Morocco to France and the Netherlands. France, Tom also found out, was Morocco's largest trading partner, so getting stuff across the straits was largely problem free. His company, though small by comparison, was recognized as one of the most efficient and friendly that used the port of Algeciras. Because it was one of the biggest ports in Europe, Bakir could readily change and vary destinations. He sent none of his arms to the usual ports.

"So then, I know I keep asking, but what's next?"

"Well, Tom, the plan is," said Minnah with conviction, "to get Bakir while we have the chance. We can't afford another bureaucratic bungle. We have a few days before we should report back to Commissaire Bartholdi. I would love to tell him we have Bakir in an airtight bag."

"Bakir is in Cotignac, only half an hour from Brignoles. It seems he's really enjoying Kaye for longer than we guessed. He must be planning something. He's certainly spending a lot of time on his mobile. I don't know how he does it, but he seems to have a system that avoids tracing. Even Bartholdi couldn't get him. We do know he employs a couple of geeks permanently. They must be good."

"It wouldn't surprise me if he ran his own phone company, Amadullah, my dear," said Minnah. "He certainly has the money. The rumour is that his geeks have invented an app that transfers the call to another phone, a different one each time. There is, so far at least, no way of getting back to the original caller. And what really must amuse Bakir is that the dummy caller's phone is charged."

"Is that possible?"

"No idea, Tom."

"It's all part of Bakir's ambition when he rules Afghanistan. He wants to be in complete control of the television, phone, and internet systems."

"Of course, he does, dear brother. He's a megalomaniac. How else do you explain him?"

"Does that mean he's ill and demands our sympathy? Sorry, my little joke," said Tom, realizing too late he was being too subtle.

"There're plenty of explanations for the existence of evil, Tom," said Minnah, ignoring Tom's attempt at a joke. "But that doesn't help much. We still have to defeat it."

"Yes, I know, I know. I don't doubt anymore that Bakir is evil. It's just that it's so hard for me; he has such a human face."

XXXIV

Just as Tom, Minnah, and Amadullah arrived in Brignoles, Bakir and Kaye left Cotignac. They moved into the Hostellerie d'Abbaye de la Salle, a ten-minute drive from Brignoles and the arms cache. The Hostellerie dated to the twelfth century, and it pleased Bakir to be staying in a building that echoed the decline of French Christianity. Originally the Abbaye had been the home of Benedictine nuns, but the building had a somewhat scandalous history; something about sex and nuns, Bakir liked to believe.

Allah had determined to smile on his wayward and wilful child. Two of Amadullah's colleagues had been watching Bakir since he left Rome but had lost him coming out of Cotignac. Because it was market day the watchers were caught up behind a truck for about five minutes. Bakir had no idea of his good fortune and Allah was not predisposed to tell him.

Ahmed was in a good mood. Kaye had been creatively accommodating with her body before leaving Cotignac, and his two arms experts were waiting for him at the Abbaye. They had already given their report, but Bakir wanted to hear everything first hand. He received the report while Kaye listened, so she knew what Ahmed was doing. However, had Ahmed been aware of what Kaye was thinking, he might have rethought his strategy.

It wasn't that Kay was having ungrounded second thoughts. It was the slow revelation of reality. Kaye's ambition and avarice were miserly things alongside Ahmed's Titans. The miserly things were

189

slowly being undermined by fear, and Kaye was afraid. It had come to her quite clearly in another of those insightful post-coital moments; she was isolated. Her actions were being controlled. But it wasn't immediately the control of a tyrant. It was the control of her own submission; a submission she had given. It had crept up on her. She imagined she felt as some Muslim women must feel. Submission had been gradual and without any clear danger signs, like the frog in the kettle, it felt normal.

But it couldn't feel normal for Kaye. Fear and a resurgent pride were insisting she act. She had to get some control back. But how, without being misunderstood and arousing Ahmed's anger? She didn't want to leave Ahmed forever, but it was all very difficult. Perhaps it was a cultural thing that she would have to live with. She realized that her idea of normal had kept expanding like it did for a woman in an abusive marriage.

Pierre and George, Kaye was sure that was not their names, had seen the merchandise and had had the final interview with the buyer. Everything could be shipped in three days. Bakir was continuing to allow Kaye more information than necessary. Perhaps she was expected to find that flattering, but it continued to worry her instead. She would resist Ahmed's grooming; the more she knew the more tenuous her life could become.

Trust was becoming a bigger deal than she imagined. Necessity was forcing her to trust Ahmed and that was becoming less and less comfortable. Then, and for no reason she could make sense of, she wanted to talk to Tom again. Those early days in New Farm flat back in Brisbane had been so easy. She had never thought about trusting Tom because she did so without thinking. That's the problem as soon as you start thinking about it, it becomes a problem. But why did she want to see Tom? She had made up her mind and had given a definitive goodbye. Tom was hardly likely to reassure her about the trustworthiness of Ahmed. And she had no idea where he was. She was not just isolated; she was a captive, but she had no idea where the perimeter fences were. She couldn't do anything without Ahmed's permission. Anywhere she wanted to go he would want to know why. Kaye needed some space.

"Ahmed dear, I would love to go into Brignoles this afternoon. It has a museum with one of the first ever concrete boats. When I was a kid my father made a little one out of something like concrete. I would love to see what the museum has."

"Why not? I have some boring stuff to do. Pierre can take you in. He has a final little job for me."

That was not exactly what Kaye had planned. She had hoped to drive herself and enjoy some of the countryside. But still she would get out and have time alone to think.

The museum was fascinating and the concrete boat was not a disappointment. It was nearly another epiphany for Kaye. The boat was much bigger that that attempted by her father but the same shape. It was very odd, but she cried a little when she saw it. Right at that moment she would have loved to see her father just to have the comfort of his uncomplicated and undemanding embrace. She had lost her innocence and there was no way back. She needed a drink.

Kaye found her way through the narrow streets to Place Caramy with its bistros and restaurants. She sat down in the very bright sunlight under a square yellow umbrella and ordered a 'martini blanc' and then two more. She had over an hour before she had to catch up with Pierre. It would, she thought, be very easy to slip into the maudlin. She was feeling more than a little sorry for herself.

But not for long, as it turned out.

"Kaye! What on earth are you doing here?" Minnah tried to sound as surprised as possible.

Kaye was shocked, "Minnah!"

Minnah had observed Kaye arrive and sit under the yellow umbrella. She was going to the Spar supermarché for supplies to get everyone through the night. Minnah was excited to see 'her friend' but initially uncertain whether to speak or not, so she waited. Kaye could warn Bakir that she, and probably Amadullah and Tom, were in Brignoles. But when she saw Kaye drink three martinis too quickly, she decided to speak.

"Oh dear, so you know where we are. Does the Commissaire know? Is Tom here? What are you doing?" The questions came very quickly.

"Yes, Tom's here," Minnah ignored the other questions.

"I know you are going to think me a fickle woman, but I would love to talk to him. I've been very silly."

"I'm sure he would be more than pleased to see you, Kaye. I could take you to him now, if you like."

"Tomorrow, could I meet you here? I must go now. I'm getting a lift back to La Celle."

Minnah was uncertain whether Kaye's revelation of where she and Bakir were staying was a signal of some kind or just plain naivety. The former would have made her more confident.

"Certainly, about this time then."

The women stood and embraced, both hoping the other sincere and really wishing the other well.

Kaye made her way back to the car, relieved that she had met Minnah. It was impossible for her not to remember that at the last meeting she had wanted to have nothing to do with her. But now, fearful of Ahmed, she needed her. She made her way back to the car where Pierre was waiting. She had never liked him and now he seemed more hostile than ever. He grunted and said nothing as they drove the short distance to La Celle. He parked the car in the grounds of the hotel and left Kaye to find her own way into the building.

XXXV

Tom was astonished when Minnah told him and Amadullah she had spoken with Kaye and that she was bold enough to say she would meet her the next day. Initially Amadullah was angry. Minnah had endangered everyone, but he calmed down slowly as Minnah explained her actions. Kaye, she was quite sure, was ready to leave Bakir, and she was certainly afraid. With her out of the way they could close in on him as they had originally planned and rule out the possibility of 'collateral damage'. And there was a bonus. Kaye's information would be more than a little helpful. They just had to be sure that Bakir was not suspicious, and that he didn't find out they were in Brignoles hoping to get a look at his storehouse of firearms.

While Minnah had been talking to Kaye, Amadullah had not been idle. He had watched as Bakir's men went to and from the house. As the day progressed they became careless and he managed to pick up the code of the outside steel door on his new Italian camera, a present from Alessandra. An inside door was still a problem. Nevertheless, they would have to move that night to discover what was there. Even if Bakir was captured, they wouldn't cripple his organization. Close examination of the arms would tell them where they came from and where they were going. Amadullah knew what had gone to Afghanistan and to whom. He knew the kind of stuff everyone wanted and how discerning Bakir was. He had turned down an offer of Russian SA-11 missiles because they were too old. Obviously, he had something newer in mind.

It was after midnight when Amadullah decided to move. There had been no action around Bakir's house for several hours. Using the code picked out by Amadullah's camera, they had no trouble with the outside steel door. Inside, however, an even thicker door blocked the way. They had come prepared with the best C-4 explosive Minnah could find. Sometimes her contacts were better than her brother's. Tom learned something new every day.

But then they had a remarkable stroke of what seemed to be good luck. The internal door had been left unlocked.

"Tom, watch the outside door for a moment. Keep it open. I'm not entirely sure what's going on here. Minnah and I will go in first."

Amadullah pushed the door open slowly. The first room was lit only by the faint street light coming in through the open doors. He found the switch; the room was empty.

"This doesn't look good, Minnah," whispered Amadullah. "Let's try that other room. Those doors must go somewhere."

Both doors yielded to his push. There was one low table in the middle of a very large empty room. Beside the table there was a reading lamp that had been left turned on. The reason was obvious. Kaye, with the light shining full in her face, lay across the table. Minnah was so shocked she failed to comprehend for some moments what she was looking at.

"What has he done? Is not the curse of Allah upon this man?" Minnah shouted to the echoing chamber. Amadullah was silent for a moment and then in a fit of passionate anger, with all the sense of Muslim justice and dignity he could muster, he cursed Bakir.

"Oh, Kaye, my very dear friend. What have we done?" Minnah looked down on the body bathed in light blurred by her weeping. She prayed that her tears falling on the body would bring Kaye back to life. There was no sign of a violent death. "Did it have to come to this?" Instinctively, she called out to Tom.

Tom rushed in, looked at Minnah, and saw the body. His awful cry of angry powerlessness brought an even more terrible grief to

Minnah's weeping body. Amadullah remained grey and silent. Tom found strength from somewhere; from the faith of his youth, he hoped. He looked about the room and rushed to kneel beside Kaye's body. It was, mockingly, still warm. If anything in his life had been like the most feared of dreams this was it. He shut and opened his eyes several times, fully hoping to wake up and find Kaye alive.

Finally, Amadullah could speak. "Well, Bakir has proved himself this time. He must have found out about Minnah's chat yesterday and thought Kaye was betraying him. What a coup! He knows we won't go to the police and he leaves us Kaye's body. He knows we won't leave it. He turns melodrama into the pathetic and sin into poetry."

"Bakir, it would seem, knows far too much," Amadullah spoke so softly it was difficult to hear what he said. "He's completely outwitted us."

No one said what they were all thinking. Had Minnah not spoken to Kaye in Place Caramy she might still be alive. It would have been unhelpful, unkind, and unnecessary.

"Where have all the weapons gone? I was sure they were here. There has to be another way in."

And there was. Tom found the vaulted bedroom and kitchen complete with furniture and Amadullah found a tunnel at least two hundred metres long that lead to a gate onto a vacant lot and a warehouse. All the time they were watching the house, Bakir and his men were loading trucks at the end of the tunnel hundreds of metres away. It had been a dispiriting night and morning.

Kaye's body was the pressing issue. Simple respect and ordinary decency demanded they do something about it. Their loving affection demanded more. And her parents... what could Tom say to them? Kaye was not a creature unconnected from those who loved her. That was what made her death more appalling. It was such a waste, and yet Bakir would have known the pain he caused. It would have been deliberate. Kaye could never have been part of his world in any permanent way. They all knew her end would have been the same tomorrow or the next day. She was unfortunate, a beautiful and foolish woman who had strayed into a winter that seemed, just for a space, like summertime.

"There's only one thing we can do, Tom. I know what you're thinking," Minnah was speaking with that quiet authority again. "We fly Kaye's body back to Afghanistan and a decent burial becomes possible. After all, that's where everyone in Australia thinks she is. It won't be difficult. We could have Kaye in Marseille in a little over three hours and a couple of Amadullah's friend's will be pleased to help. They despise Bakir. If we can arrange the right flights, everything could be over in a few days. I'm sure they can facilitate the process of taking a body home. They do it all the time."

Tom had no idea of what he felt or thought. Numb, he was completely in the hands of his friends. The anguish of the immediate loss was overwhelming. He had seen people die many times and occasionally a death, for a variety of reasons, was profoundly sad. But Kaye's murder was devastating. She was a lovely and unfinished work. He had neither the energy nor the will to disagree with Minnah.

"There's nothing I can do here. Bakir has fooled us again. I'm so tired."

"Look Tom, you go back to the hotel and leave Minnah and me to tidy up here. Have a rest; give us a couple of hours."

Tom remained in no mood to argue. "Okay, I'll walk back." He didn't care what he did. He knew life had purpose but at that moment life was so dreadfully empty and without purpose. It wasn't just Kaye's death, it was the whole deal. The victory was to the strong and even if it wasn't it certainly seemed like it.

"I have seen something else under the sun. The race is not to the swift or the battle to the strong, nor does food come to the wise or wealth to the brilliant or favour to the learned. Time and chance happen to them all."

Living in the Brisbane Hill suburb of Kenmore was like living in a gated subdivision, insulated from the world. Violence and war is the real world. Anguish and pain is simply normal. How easy it was to slip into that victimhood thing, to feel sorry for oneself.

"Bloody hell! What fucking nonsense!" He shouted his deliberate profanity to the empty narrow street. The echo rebuked him. Two windows opened but no one responded. Perhaps they thought he was just an *Anglais fou*. And that, had he known, would have annoyed him too; he was a bloody Australian.

That evening Tom sat on the seat beside his bed and examined his pistol. He looked at it and checked the magazine. He took the hard, black grip in his hand and pointed the muzzle at his image in the mirror. He looked dreadful: pale and unshaven. If the mirror image had been Bakir he would have pulled the trigger with relief and enthusiasm. For a brief intoxicating moment, he relished an imagined change in his character. He had gone from a competent and affable city surgeon to a would-be assassin obsessed by a desire for vengeance. Tom put the pistol down gently on the table beside his bed and lay back with a deep sigh. Providence, he might have thought, was on his side. He was asleep almost immediately.

"Tom… you okay? It's getting late." Minnah was at his door.

Either by habit or instinct, he got up and opened the door without being fully awake.

"Tom, you look dreadful. Did you sleep in those clothes?"

"Well I…"

"And your gun, did you expect to be attacked during the night?"

"No, I…"

"Kaye's gone. Her minders in Afghanistan will be told she was killed in a terrorist attack. That's easy enough to arrange. There are attacks all the time and Kaye is just another mangled body that had to be buried very quickly. In fact, she will be buried in Kabul, in Sherpur Cantonment. It's the old British military cemetery looked after by a local man and his son. Kaye's military connections make burial there possible. At least her parents will be able to grieve with some sense of honour."

"Yes, I need to speak with them; let them know I'm not heartless."

"Of course. You can Skype them tonight. We're off back to Marseille to confront an angry Bartholdi. We gambled and we lost. He'll regret the day he decided to trust us."

XXXVI

Bakir had neither gambled nor lost, but that was no help in understanding Kaye's wasteful death. She had been a promising asset. Bakir hadn't enjoyed her execution; he was not a sadist. His enemies misunderstood, he gained no pleasure from killing, but it was a necessity in the world at war. Some deaths were more regrettable than others, and Kaye's death was the most regrettable of all. But he'd been angry. She had betrayed him and there was no other solution. She had to die. His other enemies could wait until his return from Pyongyang.

One of Bakir's most spectacular deals was, at last, almost done: three hundred million dollars of missiles and communications equipment from the North Koreans. He was also hopeful that at least fifty of his men could be trained in tunnelling. North Korea had one of the most sophisticated attack and defence tunnel systems in the world.

Bakir believed that, at the most, he had two years left to be in on the ground floor at the formation of the new Afghanistan. It was imperative that he have his arms and infrastructure ready. The first few months after the Americans finally left would be critical. He assumed there would be a kind of honeymoon period while everyone caught their breath.

Then would come the struggle for power. The battle would go to the strong and the swift. In the end that was always the case. It was to his continuing benefit that many in the United States administration had forgotten that. The Europeans had lost the language to even think about it. Maybe the British still had a few words left, but not enough to get a good paragraph onto any page.

The safest way to get to Pyongyang was to fly from Shenyang with Air China. At just over an hour, it was shorter than flying from anywhere else. It was one quarter of the flight time from Kuala Lumpur, and anyway the Malaysians no longer flew to North Korea. Neither the Chinese nor North Koreans would be supplying the Americans with passenger lists. Malaysia might be a Muslim nation on paper but it still had a long way to go. He seldom felt he was among friends there.

Not that he was among friends in Pyongyang. He didn't have to love those he traded with. He worked with the Americans to gain their moral and military support, but the Koreans needed hard currency and he wanted the missiles. The US dollar was still the best.

To the American military the real Bakir was an impossibility. Educated in England and France, he had read Adam Smith with relish. He understood self-interest without appreciating the moral tradition that shaped Smith's heart. Instead Islam operated in his mind like one of the old Roman religions. Allah was there to be appeased to receive his blessing. Any connection between his religion and contemporary morality was a coincidence. It wasn't that Bakir could have explained all the contradictory forces driving him. There was no need to. The contradictions were drowned by his necessary and fluid ethic. Allah was happy with that.

Bakir had twenty-four hours in North Korea and that was twenty-five too many. He hated the place and its derivative politics and culture. Where else would you find a triumphal arch bigger that *l'Arc de Triomphe* and intensely ugly? Or a tower deliberately less than a metre taller than the Washington Monument apparently to make an elusive point? Juche, that strange fusion of a political religion with atheism was absurd. The creation of ever changing principles to defend government policy was a joke even to him. It was the ultimate denial of Islam, whose principles could never be changed. Bakir couldn't wait to sign the contract and get out.

It was the 'Great Leader' stuff that annoyed Bakir. It had to be a sham of some kind. He knew about the accusations of racism and xenophobia, but he didn't care about those. The forced abortion of North Korean women impregnated by Chinese men and the attempted lynching of black Cuban diplomats were not an issue for him. He hadn't thought about it much, but, if he had been asked, he probably would have seen in all in the context of North Korean honour.

The irony of Bakir's reaction to the 'Great Leader' doctrine escaped him. His need for power was as urgent as the 'Great Leader's' but he was blind like all Pharisees, ancient and modern. Bakir remained unaware of his most debilitating weaknesses. In nearly everything he had attempted he had been successful, and he was admired and feared by his colleagues. It was that knowledge that gave him the strength to aim for the kind of greatness that would have been daunting to a normal man. Failure and disloyalty were the unforgivable sins.

That was why Kaye had to go. He had trusted her and she had failed to measure up. He had no choice but to have her executed. Hamas had given her a choice: bullet or injection. She chose injection. That didn't surprise Bakir, but he was puzzled by what Hamas had told him about the way she faced death. There were no hysterics just quiet tears as the needle pierced the brown smooth skin of her arm.

"Oh, Dear God, poor Tom, forgive me," was all she said as death carried her across the river to that far country.

That was why Bakir decided to put Kaye's body where Tom would find it. He was impressed by the stoical way she died. He had never given Western women the benefit of any doubt in the past. It might have been all those days and nights enjoying the warm softness of her body. He regretted again the necessity of her death. With limited insight he experienced the nearest thing to the grieving of guilt he had ever experienced. He didn't know, but it was the closest he ever got to the eternal.

XXXVII

The dispirited and tired lame ducks met Bartholdi in his office the day after they got back to Marseille. But the man they met was not the man they expected.

"We've got him."

"Who?" Minnah was confused.

"Ahmed Bakir, who else?"

Bartholdi was buzzing. Ignoring Amadullah's expertise, the amateurs had been just that, amateurs. They had been watched by Bartholdi's men the whole time they were in Rome. For their protection, Bartholdi claimed, and he probably meant it. He was unwilling to take unnecessary chances. Back in Brignoles, Bartholdi's men, four of them, had watched everything including Minnah's chat with Kaye. Not that it did her much good, Tom thought, as he listened to the Commissaire. His men too had failed to discover the tunnel and the emptying out of the armoury. They had been too busy watching Minnah and Amadullah.

Bartholdi had not heard about Kaye's murder. The news affected him deeply. For a moment, when Minnah told him, he went noticeably pale.

"I'm sorry. I'm sorry, Tom. Not something we wanted."

"No, it wasn't," said Tom rather lamely.

"Well, if it's any comfort at all, the day of vengeance is at hand." Bartholdi enlightened his three friends, claiming Bakir's day of reckoning had finally arrived. The trip to Brignoles was the catalyst.

Because the Commissaire's men had been watching the amateur 'trinity', they had discovered Bakir's whereabouts in La Celle quite by accident. Bakir had not helped his men load the trucks. He had stayed in his hotel so Fabien's men didn't lose sight of him this time; they were able to follow him back to Marseille. Had he been working with his men, instead of fornicating with Kaye, they would have missed him.

The unexpected discovery was that Bakir had gone to North Korea, where he had transferred a large sum of money. France, Bartholdi declared, had a new office in Pyongyang going through something of a honeymoon period. The left hand was not quite sure what the right was doing. Nevertheless, they discovered Bakir in Pyongyang and let Paris know. The Brits had been helpful too because the French didn't have an embassy there. With obvious delight Bartholdi pointed out that Paris was embarrassed about the last debacle. The Commissaire had insisted Bakir escaped their attempt to capture him because they had, and still have, a mole. Consequently, they were trying to placate him by keeping him in the loop.

It was this turn of events that amused Bartholdi. They had failed to get Bakir because Paris had not believed him about the mole and now they were putting up conscience money; half a million euros to help Bartholdi rein him in. Now they knew more about Bakir and his net would extend much wider. It was all very satisfying.

"We had no idea he was going to Pyongyang. We had managed only to trace him as far as Kuala Lumpur."

"Where is he now?"

"Here, in Marseille, since early this morning."

The Commissaire had not been idle. He had the names and descriptions of twenty-seven of Bakir's men. All of them were under surveillance.

"Ahmed's North Korean pilgrimage has been a godsend to us. For a start, it got Paris talking to the Brits, and, consequently, Paris taking us seriously. For reasons I have yet to understand, the politics seem less complicated. I don't feel that I'm wading in a swamp this time."

Bartholdi's eyes shone as he explained. The balance of power in Afghanistan and Pakistan was erratic. The radicalization of young French malcontents was increasing. The Americans and NATO were very little help. Proselytizing preachers were coming in from Pakistan, Iran, Saudi Arabia, and who knows elsewhere. Extremist groups were coming out of Afghanistan and Pakistan to launch terrorist attacks in the West.

There was, however, a lot more going on. The Americans and their allies had to know they were leaving a mess. Iran's Shias fear the Sunni extremists who set up camps on the Pakistan border. The Chinese, too, were apparently concerned with terrorist groups coming from Afghanistan and Pakistan. There was little doubt now the Taliban now controlled large areas of Afghanistan in the south and east. Paris was nervous.

"We have very good information that Bakir is in control of much of the terrorist action. He is a very big name, particularly in the south-east. We suspect this is where he will begin his takeover when the US finally pulls out."

"Amazing, but where do we fit in?" asked Tom.

"Well, Tom, there really is a place where you fit in. We know where Bakir is, but now he is surrounded by armed bodyguards, day and night. Sure, we could move in and blow him out of the water, but we want him alive. We need to isolate him."

"Yes, but I don't see…"

"No, I don't suppose you do. But, Tom, you remain unique among us. You have spoken to Bakir and, as much as he likes anyone not in his world, he likes you and respects you in that odd way of his. You have saved his and, he believes, his brother's life. His code of honour is strong; strong enough for him to speak to you again, at least."

"I see; I'm bait, like Kaye once was."

"Not quite. Let me explain. I would like you and Minnah to book into the Hotel Dieu for one week. You and Minnah will act as very visible lovers. How you do that is up to you, just be convincing. I will get the word to Bakir that you are short of money; indeed, that you are in some difficulty and that we have fallen out. Minnah apparently has no idea that you are strapped for cash and you are trying to keep it from her."

"Minnah, this is close to outrageous. You don't agree, do you?"

"Tom, I can't help warming to the entire idea. Fabien has already spoken to me this morning. Only a Frenchman's mind could think like this. It's dangerous, but it just might work. I have no serious objections to being your theoretical lover for a week and, goodness me, perhaps even two weeks, should my duty demand it."

"Two weeks, really? And duty too? How do you 'get the word' to Bakir?"

"Ah, the usual way; we use someone who knows someone who knows someone."

"Of course, why did I ask? But Bakir is not going to contact me. Even I wouldn't be dumb enough to do that."

"No, he will send a lackey and ask you to meet him where he chooses. Doubtless he will give you complicated instructions at the last minute to make sure you are alone when you meet."

It was a hard sell, but Bartholdi managed it. Well, it was not entirely a hard sell. The possibility of being alone with Minnah was not an unpleasant task. Indeed 'task' was hardly the right word. He could see why Minnah was necessary. They had to be by themselves to reinforce the rumour that they were sick of everything to do with Bartholdi. That was the point. Bakir must think that his enemies have fallen out.

"You will have your own mobiles with a special app inserted that will contact us immediately. Take them with you if you finally get a chance to meet Bakir. The tech guys will give you specific instructions on everything in the morning."

XXXVIII

Hotel Dieu, 1-6 Daviel Place, District 02 was an impressive edifice. The Deluxe Twin Bed Suite, with harbour view, was spacious and heavy with curtains. Tom was unclear whether the twin beds were Fabien's concession to modesty or his own little joke. The entire enterprise could easily be an absurd play from the sixties, but it was deadly serious. Tom had little difficulty realising that. He was one of those actors who waited in the wings. He got his instructions, went on stage, delivered his lines, and went off. But this time there would be no refuge in the wings.

Minnah had no illusions as to the risks she was taking but, because this could be her best chance to get close to Bakir to kill him, she ignored the danger. Ever since seeing Kaye's body, she had promised herself again she would kill Bakir. It had been unmistakable for a long time what had to be done; she had gone over it in her mind often enough.

The first night in the hotel was not without an element of farce. Tom was subdued but he was not without a suggestion of a rising and tantalizing nervousness. Minnah's closeness, without a minder, was beguiling, to say the very least. Tom was comforted with the thought that any man would have found the situation mesmerizing. What was Fabien really thinking? Was his desire to get Bakir so great that he couldn't see the flaws in his plan?

They completed their first duty as lovers at dinner. Tom guided Minnah affectionately as they moved across the dining room and they spoke softly at the table, each conscious of the other's eyes. It was the most extraordinary of situations. A man and a woman who found each other attractive pretending to be what they really were. It was a complicated evening. The subterfuge obscured the desire but at the same time made the satisfying outcome of the desire more likely. Minnah and Tom knew that; but neither knew quite how to speak into it. It was the intrigue of the relationship that dominated their thoughts. The danger contributed its own special piquancy. Like actors from a 1950s Hollywood movie both undressed in the bathroom and went to bed in the dark with only a little over a metre between them. Tom thanked God he wasn't eighteen, and hoped he wouldn't snore.

Day two was being seen about town. That, too, hardly proved an imposition. The instructions, after all, were to look as much as pos-sible like a honeymoon couple. It was imperative that any of Bakir's watchers would see they were completely absorbed in each other. If Tom finally did get his chance to tell their story of betrayal Bakir's suspicions would already have been put into the back of his mind. That was the theory.

The peculiar fantasy continued all day and into the evening. Nei-ther Bakir nor one of his lackeys showed. Not that it mattered, be-cause neither Tom nor Minnah would have noticed. Tom wondered if Fabien Bartholdi had placed too much faith in the Muslim sexual ethic that he assumed Minnah had absorbed. Had he permitted his judgement to wander into a wilful fog that made it impossible to see the inevitable? Maybe Bartholdi didn't care what went on in the bed-room if Bakir showed.

That the subterfuge reinforced the real thing amused Tom, but it also made him anxious. One needed to be in control, and fantasy was never the best setting for self-discipline. Their situation had so much potential to turn sour. The entire business of being alive frequently imitated the absurd, but when intensified by sexual desire who knew where it would go? He would not encounter failure.

Neither would Minnah. Islam and its laws were becoming less demanding by the day. For years, she had been adrift in a sea of demands and prohibitions. Tom, without understanding, was helping to place her feet on the beach. It wasn't that Minnah was fully aware of the new forces guiding her, but she knew enough to assent to their power. Tom was an assurance and agreeable bonus.

So, by the third night, and still without any sign of Bakir, the twin beds were pushed together with startling affinity. Minnah and Tom stood on either side of each bed like a couple of uncertain adolescents on heat. The usual little exercises in modesty had taken place, but this time they arrived at the side of their beds at the same time. It had been a very satisfying day. The dinner had been outstanding and Tom, for reasons quite beyond any reason of human understanding, ordered a bottle of champagne. He had mumbled something inane about champagne being necessary on the third night of a honeymoon.

It was difficult to know exactly who started to push the beds together first. Not that it seemed to matter, because they embraced almost immediately with an empathy that was rewarding and hardly unexpected. Their laughter was loud and almost certainly heard in the next room, but a listener would not have understood its relief and thankfulness. Neither would the listener have imagined how the lovers' inhibitions and fears were assuaged by the thankfulness.

Day four started slowly, with the usual anxiety of each lover warily concerned about the other. The gap between them, so small at night, had grown during the morning because neither Tom nor Minnah would acknowledge a gap of any kind. For a while their conversation was awkwardly banal. Such is the inhibition of the religious conscience, even if it is speaking only softly. For Tom, it was just a whisper, almost trivial.

For Minnah it was an unwanted and unacceptable intrusion. For the faithful Muslim, fornication is real. For Minnah, it was an absorbed prohibition hard to forget. As a child, she was taught that there were certain things she must do or not do to please Allah. She had learned to pray five times a day for mercy, guidance, and forgiveness. She had been taught to be obedient and subservient. She had been told how to dress modestly so not to arouse male lust. Failure to comply meant condemnation. Such religious power was foreign to the unbeliever. Even Tom would find it difficult to comprehend.

"Tom, do you still pray?" It was late morning and neither apprehensive lover had left the room since breakfast.

"Sometimes."

"Why do you pray?"

"I'm not sure really. When I'm in trouble. I was taught the Lord's Prayer, and I did learn that prayer was about being thankful and asking for things. Being the kind of woman you are, I guess you know it better than many of my half-hearted Christian contemporaries."

"Perhaps, I can't say I understand what you call the 'Lord's Prayer'. It's the first couple of lines that get me; they're so intimate. The idea of God as Father is astounding. It's heresy to Islam. Allah is an unknowable mystery."

"God unknowable? That hardly makes sense, does it?"

"No, I guess not," Minnah was subdued. She was silent for some time and Tom did not intrude. Minnah was weeping, silently and gently. Tom sat on the bed beside her.

"You know, I've had so much wrong for most of my life. I know it's probably hard for you to understand but I have tried to please Allah, just like Amadullah and every other faithful Muslim. I thought if I did the right things I would please him. Westerners are so secularized they don't seem to understand the power within Islam. They can be so profoundly ignorant and self-righteous all at once."

"I know. We've banished God only to replace him with ideologies that seldom rise above superstition. Mood has replaced mind."

"I have discovered," Minnah almost whispered, "One serves God by loving him, because he loved us first. It's only in the last few months I've understood what the crucifixion is about. Of course,

Christ had to rise from the dead, otherwise the entire Christian faith is nonsense."

Tom was silent. He wasn't out of his depth but to speak would have seemed vulgar. The complexity and emotional power that permeated Minnah's little sermon was evident to both. Tom was still infected by a kind of pride that found much of its life in the secularism that Minnah condemned. Minnah had no such problem. It was hard to tell why, but that morning he felt closer to her than he ever had.

XXXIX

It was early afternoon before the political and religious honeymooners were disturbed by the telephone leaving an automatic message to say a letter had been left at reception for Tom.

"Well, about time. It must be from Bakir; who else?"

But it wasn't from Bakir, it was from Maeva.

"She's on bail, so I guess Bakir has been in touch with her. I didn't quite expect this. I should have. Bakir is going to use an intermediary. He always does. Does Bartholdi not have Maeva's phone tapped?"

"Tom, what does she say?"

"It's remarkable. She is inviting us to her house in Cassis for the evening to meet an Australian she has met. She also says she understands I'm having a hard time and maybe she can help. Fabien's rumours have certainly had an impact."

"You'll… we'll go of course."

"How can we resist it? Tomorrow at eight."

"Why don't we keep up the honeymoon subterfuge and go to Cassis in the morning and make a day of it? I wouldn't mind a little trip around the Calanques."

"Minnah, you astound me. There's no end to your enthusiasm."

"Really? How lovely," Minnah was radiant. "That's because my heart is moving from one world to the other. I'm excited and I'm scared. Right now, Tom, I need you."

The confession nearly overwhelmed Tom. Minnah was stronger than he could ever be. And yet she was declaring weakness and need.

He seized Minnah, besieged by victorious passion, and held her without speaking. The mature womanliness of her body was intoxicating.

"Minnah, I love you. I can't help it. I know that even as I say, 'I can't help it'. I probably sound a bit silly, but there it is."

"I know, Tom. I love you too. I hope you never stop. I'm tempted to say it was all meant to be, but that might be just a little immature, or do I mean premature?"

That was all they said. It was too complicated to go further. They had lunch in Cassis and sailed around the Calanques in calm seas and little wind. It was one of those days that would prove impossible to forget. There was only one other couple on the boat, elderly Americans who smiled knowingly at them and spoke a little from time to time. They wore their faux honeymoon badge like professionals who still enjoyed their sport.

The badge holders arrived at Maeva's a little after eight.

"What a pleasure to see you again, Tom. And this is Minnah. Lovely to meet you, my dear. I've heard so much about you," Maeva spoke to Minnah in French and used the intimate pronoun. The subtlety was lost on Tom and Minnah was not suspicious. Was Maeva trying to say she knew what they were up to?

"Tom, I've a big surprise for you. He's waiting in the dining room."

So Bakir was here after all. Why not? If he was as much up with the play as he seemed to be then there was no reason why he shouldn't be there. They would find out soon enough what the next move was. Maeva guided Tom and Minnah through the double doors of the very large reception room.

"Hello Tom," exclaimed Tom's squash partner Roger, extending his hand. "I bet you didn't expect to see me. I've come for my $100."

"Roger," said Tom, taking his hand. "What on Earth are you doing here? Minnah, this is my good friend from Australia."

Just for a moment, Roger looked puzzled.

"Ah Minnah, delighted to meet you."

"*Enchanté*, Roger."

Tom turned to a broadly smiling Maeva.

"What is going on here? How do you two know each other?"

"It's your fault, Tom. I had a visit from a very charming Russian who knew you. That was my first surprise, the second was finding out you and Kaye were in France."

At the mention of Kaye's name, Tom glanced quickly at Maeva. There was no flicker of unease on her face. She would not know Kaye had been murdered. Bakir was unlikely to tell her.

"Kaye, I understand, has gone back to Afghanistan to finish her assignment, Roger."

"I wondered if that was what had happened."

At that point of the revelation they all went through to dinner to unravel the causes of their meeting. Apparently Maeva's husband was away somewhere on business. Roger had spent the day with Vasily Ryolovlov, the Russian Tom had met at Maeva's party. Ryolovlov had gone to Australia and, during his stay, had sought out Roger with a business proposition. He had wanted to invest in Australian property and had suggested that Roger return the favour and seriously think about the South of France. Roger was intrigued but cautious. Côte d'Azur might sound more romantic than Surfers' Paradise or the Sunshine Coast but he was too astute a businessman to be taken in by a mere name, no matter how good it sounded. Vasily, who had done his homework weeks before meeting Roger, was enthusiastic, and committed himself by purchasing several acres of Roger's land not far north of Noosa. He was more than happy with the price. Out of a spirit of thankfulness at Roger's helpfulness, Vasily Ryolovlov had suggested that Roger should at least consider a purchase in Cassis. He knew just the man who could help.

Roger, of course, had no idea of the dynamic between Ryolovlov and the landowner who 'could help'. Ahmed Bakir meant nothing to him. Neither did he know that Vasily was keen to do Bakir a favour to mend their recent disagreement. Roger could not have known that the proceeds from the sale of the land would go directly towards the purchase of arms. And, if he had, it might not have mattered. Land was land and if the price was right the dynamic between owner and agent was only meaningful if the purchaser could somehow use it to his advantage.

All that, when he met Tom at Maeva's remarkable house, was not an issue. Roger was delighted to catch up with Tom. After the meal, he managed to take Tom aside.

"How long have you been here? I thought those bloody Taliban must have cut your throat. No letters, you bastard. What have you been up to? Have you given up on Kaye?"

"It's a long story, Roger, but I can't tell you now. The truth is, Kaye is dead."

"Dead? That's terrible, but I'm not surprised. It was always on the cards. I really am sorry though. I'm not sure her parents know. Such a waste. How was she killed?"

"After the kidnapping… remember?

"Ah, yes, but she knew the danger; and, anyway, you've clearly had your compensation. That Arab bird is spectacular. You always did have what it took when it came to women."

"That 'Arab bird' is a very sophisticated colleague. We worked together in Afghanistan."

"I'm sure you did."

"Are you really going to buy land here? The owner Ahmed Bakir is a big time villain." Tom had no intention of supplying his friend the unnecessary details. It would have placed them in a compromising position that had too much potential to become a real issue between them.

"You two must be enjoying yourselves." Minnah had left the chatting to Maeva and Vasily. "I think I have given you long enough to yourselves, until tomorrow anyway."

"Tom wants to know if I'm going to buy the land Vasily mentioned at dinner. What do you think Minnah?"

"I'm sure Tom has suggested you be cautious. And if he hasn't, I will."

"Oh, I will, believe me. I'll have plenty of time to talk. Vasily and I are staying here tonight. Maeva's hospitality has been remarkable, but I'm not naïve. They want something and I'm not sure that it's just my money. I suspect that Vasily would like to enter into a partnership in Australia. I'm sure he wants to live there. Sydney prices are still rising faster than anywhere else and he fancies something flash in Double Bay or Rose Bay before the Chinese swamp them."

"Perhaps we can see you tomorrow, Roger?"

"Certainly, here you can get me on this number." Roger gave Minnah his card and looked playfully at Tom.

The drive back to Marseille took longer than it should have. Tom and Minnah were tired and subdued. Minnah was first to break the silence.

"You must have enjoyed meeting your friend tonight even in the odd circumstances. It's frightening how much control Bakir seems to be able to execute. He's almost like a malevolent power pulling strings we can't see."

"There's a mysterious divinity; Roger was certainly a surprise. I couldn't get a chance to warn him about Bakir."

"You'll see him again?"

"As soon as I can… tomorrow, I hope."

XL

The next day began slowly for the no longer faux lovers. Tom knew he had to say something to Roger about Bakir, but he wasn't sure where to start. The whole story might sound ridiculous but anything less was unlikely to be convincing. Any kind of deal with Bakir had the potential to derail Roger's business expectations, in spite of his natural savvy.

"Minnah, it might be a good idea that you talk to Roger about Bakir. He is more likely to believe you and accept what you're talking about. You can introduce a note of realism he'll accept."

"Perhaps, I hope he's not too far advanced. I'll think about it."

A telephone call in the early afternoon sharpened their plans. Roger was enjoying himself so much with Vasily and Maeva he was going to stay another night. Why didn't Tom and Minnah come out again and help with his decision making? Maeva was looking forward to seeing them again.

"He's made up his mind already. He just wants praise and approval. I know Roger."

"I hope not, Tom. We have to go."

"Yes, we do," Tom spoke thoughtfully. Roger's apparent state of progress was a messy complication in the Bakir business. It was astounding how his throwaway line to Ryolovlov could be having such far-reaching consequences.

"Minnah, I haven't seen any of Fabien's men anywhere, have you?"

"No, but that has to be good. If we could, so could Bakir's thugs."

It was late afternoon when Tom and Minnah drove up the white stone driveway of Maeva's villa. Roger met them at the now familiar dark green double doorway.

"Great to see you again," said Roger speaking to Tom and Minnah at once. "I must say I have had the most stimulating time. I've never met anyone like Maeva, she's so... civilised. Vasily isn't a bad bloke either. Do I look a bit antiseptic? I've just had a swim."

Tom and Minnah exchanged anxious glances, both of which asked the same question. Are we too late? Roger was showing the relieved enthusiasm of a man who had just made an important decision.

"Maeva has arranged for me to meet an expert on property this evening. I can't wait. Vasily showed me a lot of compelling stuff today. Maybe you sophisticates can keep me objective. What do you think?"

"Well, we can try," said Tom, not sure what to expect. "We'll continue to encourage caution."

"I'm sure you will."

Maeva walked up behind them with flowers she had picked from her garden.

"Aren't these just divine."

"Lovely," Minnah smiled, attempting to put everyone at ease.

"Let's all go in for an aperitif. We have nearly two hours before we eat. Tom, Minnah, freshen up, perhaps a swim. I'm sure we could find something, if you're modest."

"Yes, a swim would be pleasant," responded Minnah. She wanted some time alone with Tom.

"Good girl," said Roger in a tone that seemed almost patronizing.

"Excellent, come with me and we'll find something appropriate for you to wear. That is, should you want to? I've heard that you and Tom are much closer than you were," Maeva smiled with the satisfaction of the liberated. "And Tom, I'm sure I can find something for you. We won't be long."

Minnah returned ready to go in a white one piece suit that called more than a little attention to her athletic form. Roger and Vasily gave her more than a cursory glance. She was clutching blue striped briefs that Tom would have called his 'speedos' had he been in Australia.

"For you, Tom, with love from Maeva. Don't worry, she won't look when she comes down. We're not in Afghanistan."

Minnah's amusement helped to raise Tom's spirit. But even without that, he would have leapt into the pool naked had she asked.

"Tom, where do you think Roger is up to with Vasily?"

"It's Bakir in the wings that worries me. I can't believe he would be interested in Roger, unless it's all a ploy to get back at us in some way. Roger is rich, but by Bakir's standards he's small beer. Maybe he is genuinely helping Vasily but I would have to be convinced."

"You'll have to get Roger aside this evening and warn him about the company he's keeping."

"Yes, I will."

The lovers whose pretence had been supplanted by their own cloistered truth swam several lengths of the pool, starting from different ends. Tom was a lustful teenager. Every time he passed Minnah he stroked the curve in her back and hoped she found the ritual as reassuring as he did.

After about twenty minutes Tom climbed out of the pool and watched Minnah continue to swim. Her body slid through the water with an easy grace that would have enticed any man. But the astounding thing was she wasn't any man's. She was his. The possibility of losing Minnah was unthinkable, too terrible to contemplate. He marvelled at how quickly his friendship had changed from the unattainable to the indispensable. It was hardly surprising he doubted the wisdom of his assent to the Commissaire's scheming, and yet without that he might never have had the courage to declare his devotion.

His background and Minnah's culture had made it difficult for either to really say what they felt. Both had been awkwardly conscious of a gulf between them. On paper, if that's where you put these kinds of things, they were irrevocably divided. Fabien's crazy scheme that had made intimacy possible had the power to separate them forever.

Either one or both of them could be killed.

And Roger, again he regretted that throwaway line to the Russian. How could one simple little suggestion have such potentially devastating consequences? He had started at the periphery of something and now he was at its centre. So much now depended on his success with Roger, getting Bakir flushed out, and trying to understand Minnah in her lust for revenge. It was still there, he could feel it. And Amadullah... what on earth was he up to?

Minnah climbed out of the pool and sat beside him. The cool wetness of her body increased his delight of having her close. They looked out across the orange tiled roofs to the sea. Neither thought of it, but they were gazing out to where Bakir's yacht had been the night he took Kaye on board.

Tom still felt the junior, if not the inferior, partner. Minnah was so determined and competent. And yet love making, he mused, is always some kind of submission for a woman. In that, nature remained absolute. Feminism, or whatever ideology was presently in control of the popular mind, could not deny that reality. The notion of equality between men and women was a red herring. Their complementarity was more exciting. Working with Minnah and sharing danger with her was the most invigorating thing he had ever done in his life. That's what he found so exhilarating. It was so much more fun with a woman than with a man. Danger gave friendship a boost and his sex life a spiciness, even when it didn't need it. Tom had no idea that Kaye had made a similar discovery weeks earlier but in a very different context.

XLI

The meal began with an understated elegance that Maeva designed to put everyone at ease. Maeva had no permanent staff apart from the gardener. But for special occasions she employed a cook, sometimes two, and always someone to serve and look after drinks. This time she had one cook and one to keep an eye on the needs of the guests; both were young men who Maeva undoubtedly knew very well. They had learned their lesson of blending into the background well. The champagne, with *les hors d'oeuvres et les entrées*, slid down all the throats with consummate ease.

"Tell me, Minnah," asked Maeva, "What are your plans for the next few days?"

"Well, if Tom agrees, very few. Life has been so busy over recent weeks," Minnah wondered just what Maeva knew.

"It certainly has," said Tom.

"Really, what have you naughty people been up to?"

"Oh, travelling about. Tom wants to see as much of this part of the world as possible before he goes home to Australia." Minnah had no intention of giving Maeva any insight into their affairs.

"You're going back soon, Tom?" Roger seemed surprised.

"Well, soonish maybe. I do have to earn a living. I'm not in that decadent league you and Vasily are in."

"Decadent?" Vasily looked a little hurt.

"Don't worry, Vasily. It's Tom idea of a joke. He's jealous, really."

"I am too," Tom grinned at the Russian.

"Have you two 'businessmen' had a successful day? I hope your time together in my house has been of some use to you."

"Oh, it certainly has." Roger's response was just a little too enthusiastic for Tom. "What would you say, Vasily?"

"From my point of view, it's been a satisfying day."

"You bought some property then, Roger?"

"Not quite, Tom. Not quite."

Tom rubbed his eyes. Ahmed Bakir was standing in the open doorway smiling at everyone. He had materialized like a creature from an alien world. His presence very clearly discomforted everyone except Roger. Maeva recovered quickly.

"Ahmed, how lovely to see you. I had no idea you were coming tonight."

"Ah yes, with such important guests." Bakir looked directly at the honeymooners. "Ah Tom, Minnah, don't bother stamping your foot with that silly device in your heel. Both have been neutralized. I have my tech boffins too. Bartholdi's men will not be coming to your rescue. They have no idea I'm here."

It came to Minnah and Tom with disarming precision. Fabien's own man, the Capitaine, had to be the mole. It had to be him. It was the only way Bakir could have such accurate inside knowledge about the 'silly' devices in their shoes.

"Please continue your meal. I'm sure you won't mind if I join you."

"Who's this guy, Tom? What's he talking about?" Roger was beginning to think his land purchase deal was more complicated than Vasily had lead him to believe. He imagined mafia and oligarchs everywhere. There was no way he was going into business with the Russian now. It was far too dicey. He should have known the Frogs were devious bastards, although this guy looked more Arab than French.

Maeva's young man had an extra place at the table almost before Bakir crossed the floor. The rapidity of the change of mood made Roger angry and muddled his thinking. An extended and awkward silence was alarming. He hardly felt Minnah slip something heavy into the pocket of his jacket.

"Now, my friends," Bakir spoke to Minnah and Tom, "Minnah and Tom, you'll be armed I'm sure. I would like you to give your handguns to me. I'm not armed but, as I'm sure you will realize, my men in the entry are."

Tom surrendered his immediately, without thinking. Just briefly, he regretted he would not get the chance to use it.

"I have no weapon, M. Bakir," said Minnah. "Maeva is welcome to search me."

Bakir nodded to Maeva to do just that. She found nothing. It would have been impossible for Minnah to conceal anything under her form fitting dress anyway.

"You surprise me, Minnah. I'll have to search your belongings, I'm afraid. You must have a handbag or case somewhere."

"Welcome again, M. Bakir. I swam earlier today. All my clothes and other things are in a room upstairs. I'm sure Maeva will show you."

"Thank you. Maeva, would you be kind enough to take one of my men and search Minnah's room?"

Maeva left the room but, if Tom's suspicions were at all accurate, she seemed reluctant to follow Bakir's instructions.

"Interesting, Minnah, perhaps romance has softened you. No matter, you won't get a chance to use a weapon, hidden or otherwise. In the meantime, let us enjoy our meal."

Which was what they didn't do.

Roger was the first to ask Bakir the obvious. He spoke directly to Bakir, more motivated by angry frustration than alarm.

"What is going on? I guess you must be a friend of Vasily, but what's all this cloak and dagger stuff? And Tom that handgun... what on earth have you been up to?"

"Ah yes, Monsieur, I'm afraid you have fallen into a situation not of your own making. We may still be able to salvage something. I'm sure you understand that I have some business to conclude with your countryman and his fine lady."

"Well, I don't. I have no idea what's going on. The sooner you and Tom sort things out the better."

"Exactly. We would all agree." Bakir had hardly finished the sentence when Roger felt Minnah's handgun in his pocket. He knew instantly what was happening. Minnah didn't want to give up her weapon and she had slipped it into his jacket pocket as she sat beside him. He was uneasy. The bulk and weight in his pocket would be obvious to anyone who happened to look close enough. Bakir had evidently assumed he was unarmed.

"Let us continue to enjoy this excellent meal and wine. Roger, if you and Vasily would be good enough to chat business in the library when you have finished. Maeva and I will conclude our business and Tom and Minnah may retire when they wish. We will discuss everything tomorrow, when everyone is fresh."

Time is usually an enlightening phenomenon, and for Roger its brief passing had dissolved at least some of the fog. Tom and Minnah were in some kind of trouble and, in spite of the Arab's charm, Roger's instinct was not to trust him. Minnah was sure to want her handgun back. But what did she have one for, and Tom? Anyway, he could hardly hand it over now; it would make Bakir look less than in control. Roger had sufficient savoir-faire to know that would be unwise and that Bakir's politeness was a phony by-product of the over-reacher. There were thousands of men like him in the world of finance, all of them phonies. He would have to be careful and not blow his top. Whatever Tom and Minnah were up to, he had no desire to make their job any harder.

He would stall the Russian. He wanted Bakir to think he was still interested in purchasing land but needed a little more time to think; forty million euros was a lot of money. But Bakir's next move unsteadied him somewhat. He insisted that everyone stay in Maeva's house for the night. He made no mention of any alternative. There was no need. Inside the house there were four armed, mean looking customers as Tom had noted. Roger was given a room to himself while Tom and Minnah had a room to share, and the Russian seemed to fade away.

"We must respect the marital bed," Bakir said to Minnah in a tone that was deliberate and mocking.

The rooms were not locked after everyone had retired, but in every case the windows were securely barred on the outside. Minnah and Tom were too busy trying to work out their next move to consider 'escape'. Roger certainly had no intention of wandering off with the armed heavies in the garden. He went to Tom and Minnah's room and knocked on their door. It was not a surprise to discover they were expecting him.

"Tom, what is going on? And where's my lucky $100? You weren't meant to spend it, you know."

Tom had to tell his friend as well as he could what was going on. There was no option. He began with his arrival in Afghanistan. He told Roger about Bakir and his abduction, and he spent time telling him about Amadullah and Bartholdi and the mole. It took a while for Roger to absorb everything, but he was more than a little impressed.

"Tom, you're crazy. How could someone as bright as you be in such a predicament? Don't answer that. It's Minnah, isn't it? You've fallen for her and you couldn't give her up. What do you think, Minnah? Don't answer that either. I prefer my present level of ignorance. I have a feeling it could be safer."

The silence offered something like a punctuation mark.

"By the way, I have your present. Would you like it back? I don't imagine you intended me to keep it." Roger handed Minnah her handgun.

"Thank you. I was sure Bakir wouldn't search you. The infallible one made a mistake."

"Thank God he did."

"He knows everything about you. Bakir owns the land you were hoping to buy, but I guess you know that now," said Tom.

"Yes, not too difficult. Why is Bakir playing games with you? If you're working with the police and Bakir knows that, why doesn't he either get out of the country or, I know it sounds frightening, slit your throats?"

"He's very confident. He has friends in Paris who protect him. The US is ambivalent about his activities in Afghanistan. Both attempts to bring him in so far have been embarrassing failures. The closest the police got to really damming evidence, that even Paris couldn't ignore, was last week. We found one place where he hid his firearms, but he got rid of them before the police could move."

The situation was not good. Bartholdi's technology had been found wanting. The dear Capitaine Grimaud was in charge of everything, so he would have taken his men off surveillance. Bartholdi would have no idea. But Grimaud couldn't keep up the subterfuge forever. Sooner or later his boss would discover what was going on. And that was the issue; what was going on?

Maybe Bakir still hoped that Roger would buy his land. So, everyone was safe until then. Roger agreed, provided he was still breathing, he would continue to stall the Russian and Bakir for as long as possible. As far as he could make out, Ryolovlov was not intimately involved with Bakir except that he was, in some way, in Bakir's debt. Minnah confirmed Roger's suspicions.

"It's all your bloody fault, Tom. If you hadn't had that rush of blood to the head, or to whatever place your blood rushed to, and chased Kaye to Afghanistan, none of us would be here. And I haven't had a decent game of squash since you left."

"Neither have I, come to think of it."

XLII

The next morning began with a late breakfast. Bakir was waiting. He talked as everyone was eating. He spoke like the man he was, completely in control. There was no need to be secretive. His repertoire ranged from feigned disappointment, particularly in Tom, to anger and preaching. Minnah was the only one who comprehended the nuances of his particular enjoyment. Not only had Bakir managed to outwit Bartholdi again, but he had a captive audience to admire his victory. He had always needed admiration, adulation even. It convinced him that he was on the road to paradise.

"The question is, Tom, what am I going to do with you? I'm inclined to believe that your destiny remains in your hands. We come from two very different places. I suspect you still don't understand the difference between Dar al-Islam and Dar al-Harb, even if I explained it. But I will; it's quite simple. You live in Dar al-Harb and I live in Dar al-Islam. You're not living in submission to Allah. Of course, you could decide to enter Dar al-Islam and that would solve my little quandary. But don't despair, that won't be the condition of your freedom."

"Ah, so we are prisoners," said Roger stating the obvious.

"Yes, you are. That is the will of Allah, praised be his name."

Roger, indignant as he was, went pale. He had an uncomfortable vision of his body lying headless in the sand. It did occur that he might have been watching too much television in Australia. He knew neither what to think nor say. Perhaps if he did buy land off this lunatic all would be well. Dear God, how did he get here? Only two weeks ago, he had been having a barbeque with his wife and children, presumably in Dar al-Harb. He had no idea where the hell he was now, some kind of Frenchifried Disneyland?

Minnah knew the name of Bakir's game precisely because she was the worst kind of infidel. She had left the true path, and maybe Bakir was more of a Muslim than Amadullah had given him credit. Sure, he was an opportunist, but he needed to believe something. In the labyrinth of his mind he believed his religion justified his actions. He thought he was pleasing Allah. Minnah had probably been right. Bakir had lived in France too long; where he had absorbed a kind of secularism by political osmosis. Islam gave him a veneer to protect his conscience.

For Tom, redemption was always possible, but for Minnah's apostasy there was no way out, certainly not in this world. She almost laughed out loud as the irony of her position irrevocably imposed itself on her. In time, it might be quite possible to see her as a martyr. In the meantime, her comfort was the weapon in her handbag. She would make sure that Bakir got the first bullet, the second, and the third. And if she should fail, Amadullah would succeed. At that moment, had she been alone with Bakir, the apprentice martyr would have pumped the three bullets into his body.

Tom could almost discern what Minnah was thinking. His intuitions had been sharpened over the last few weeks. He understood Minnah's disenchantment with Islam and he knew just how difficult it was for her. He loved her. At that moment, had she taken her gun from her bag and shot Bakir dead in cold blood, he would have found an excuse and forgiven her.

"Prisoners!? Good grief, man, what are you talking about? This is France not Afghanistan. What will you do if I was to walk out now? Shoot me in the back?"

Roger's delayed angry response grew out of ignorance, but it was no less real.

"Ah, no. There is no need. I have no argument with you, my friend. You will be free to go very soon. Maeva's housekeepers have left already. And perhaps, should all go well with Tom, we might be able to continue our business."

Roger was shocked into silence. Bakir was on another planet; he had no idea. Did he imagine that everyone else was there for his benefit? He seemed civilised enough and certainly he was very smooth and charming, in a smarmy way with the snake underneath. He had to be a con man. Minnah and Tom's story made increasing sense. It was easy to accept that this guy was a gun runner and terrorist boss. Just what all that might mean for their immediate situation was far from clear.

"Here is what I want," said Bakir, apparently reading Roger's mind. "I want Tom to agree to work for me, and you, Minnah, will stay here with Maeva another night. Roger, you are free to go later this evening. I will be gone but I'm sure Maeva will assist you with whatever you need."

"And what do we do for the rest of today?" Minnah was subdued but precise.

"Well, it all depends on Tom really. He just has to decide what he wants to do: work for me or not. Perhaps you could convince him of the advantages of such an arrangement."

"Hardly, I think."

And with that Bakir was gone, leaving three frustrated 'prisoners' to rage, they were quite sure he would have said, in their own kafir bluster. Minnah tried to clarify things in her mind as well as the tension of the moment would allow. She pointed out again that Bakir was playing his usual game, but with an edge sharper than usual. He was hoping to divide and conquer. He just loved the power play. She was sure Roger was not in any danger, because there was nothing he could do to harm Bakir. Tom, on the other hand, was in real danger because he knew too much. Nevertheless, he had a way out; it was a Hobson's choice certainly, but a choice nevertheless.

Minnah was quite certain that Bakir was numbering her days, hours perhaps. There was no doubt that he would be exceedingly pleased with himself.

"The trouble with Bakir is that he identifies Islam with progress," claimed Minnah. "He thinks he is actually contributing to it. That's what makes him so dreadfully self-righteous. He's in the same rusty old wheelbarrow as the communists and the multiculturalists. They all believe they can create some kind of utopia.

"It's not hard to see why he plays these little games. He wants is nasty little hand on the joystick. The bugger is so sure of himself. He wants us to know just how confident he is. That's how he gets his kicks." Roger was angry.

"The question is what we do now?" asked Tom quietly.

XLIII

Bakir was in no doubt as to what he was going to do. Grimaud could not keep Bartholdi's people chasing the wrong fox for much longer. He would visit his 'friends' early in the morning, and dispose of Minnah and allow the Australian to go. There was no chance of any deal now. Not that it mattered, there were plenty of others willing to launder money in property. Then there was Tom. Ah Tom, my friend, let us hope for your sake you make the right decision. It would have been an exaggeration to say that control over the lives of others was Bakir's aphrodisiac, but it gave him the same kind of intense pleasure that he got from the power he had over women. Indeed, it was better; it lasted longer.

But Bakir was not as pleased with life as he should have been, considering recent events. Everything had gone with such satisfying ease. His largest shipment ever was well on its way to Afghanistan and Grimaud's deception was very slick to say the least. The Americans in Kabul suspected nothing, and if they did they had decided he was valuable to them. It was that woman who was the problem. Her image still haunted him. He kept remembering her body warm and living, and he had snuffed it out. He'd not known a woman like Kaye before.

Bakir, for the first time in his life, was overtaken by an ache he failed to comprehend. In spite of his ambitious confidence, he had neither the spiritual nor sexual vocabulary to interpret his discomfort. The Jewish notion of 'one flesh' was beyond his self-constructed religious vision. But if, in the providence of Allah, anyone had spoken of it to him at that moment, he might have started to understand. The guilt and consequent softness of heart that makes redemption possible might have overtaken him. But no such relief would come his way. The only alternative was for Bakir to revitalise the hardness of his heart; he had a job to do and that meant he couldn't afford to be weak like other men. Grieving for a kafir woman was a kind of sentimental weakness he could do without.

That was how he comforted himself, dismissing the image of either a living or dead Kaye from his mind. Work was his purpose. Allah had put him on the Earth. He was here to cut out the rot, of which there was, he frequently told himself, a great deal indeed. Strong men were given the hard jobs, and strength was of no value unless it got rid of the rubbish. The world would be a tidier place.

In the name of Allah, Minnah would not be a problem; she was worse than an unbeliever. Having tasted the fruit of Islam, she was worthy only of death. Of course, it wasn't that simple. It never was. Again, Minnah had been right. Bakir was a pragmatist and a part-time Muslim fundamentalist. Most would have found that a discomforting union, but Ahmed was not most men. He had little difficulty holding two contradictory ideas at once. Indeed, in his mind they were an agreeable partnership. His fundamentalism reinforced his passion while his pragmatism allowed him the luxury of self-interested behaviour. He was a fanatic sustained by convenient and selective belief. So Minnah enlightened Tom and Roger as they tried to work out what they could do.

They knew there were at least four armed men in the house. Maeva, too, was probably armed. Their bedroom doors were still unlocked but all the windows were barred and the external doors were bound to be locked. Getting out without armed guards would be difficult enough.

"Remember," said Minnah, "Bakir plays games. He'll know what we're talking about. He's left us with just a little hope. I suspect he has told his lackeys to expect us to do something stupid. I'll be target number one. He'll be able to gloat in the morning."

"Ah, but no one will know you still have your handgun, Minnah," said Tom.

"I'm not so sure. Bakir seemed uncharacteristically sloppy by not searching Roger. It could easily be another little trick giving us false hope. In his mind, he would be killing an armed woman."

"But we have to do something." Roger was nervous. "This bastard can't keep us hopping all the time."

The lovers sat on their bed, across from Roger on a yellow and blue striped linen couch. Minnah hated the stripes and shape. Anyone who has yellow and blue linen at any time was seriously lacking in taste. It made Roger's brown Australian angularity look incongruous, and it drained the colour from his face. Tom, she was quite sure, would not allow such tackiness.

Maeva was such a contradiction. Her house reflected a tasteful affluence. The décor was elegantly understated. The couch was so obviously out of place. There was something pretentious about Maeva, something of the snob. Maybe it was inevitable when you were rich. She certainly knew how to dress with style.

It was exactly one thirty when the noise began. There was a great deal of shouting and at least two shots. There was silence for a period, and then more shouts and running on the marble stairs. Without warning, the bedroom door flew open and one of the guards rushed in with a handgun pointed straight at Tom. He was the closest to the door. For a reason that no one would ever learn, he hesitated. Two bullets from Minnah's handgun struck him in the chest. He looked so astonished that Tom felt sorry for him.

Before the astonished one slid to the floor, Amadullah rushed in with two other men armed with automatic rifles of some sort. Tom and Roger had no idea what they were, but Minnah knew. They were Israeli manufactured IMI Taver Tar-21s. So, if there was any justice in their use, it was lost on Tom and Roger.

The rescuers were dressed entirely in black. Only Amadullah had removed his mask.

"Oh, Amadullah, are we pleased to see you!' stating the obvious, Minnah rushed to embrace her brother, waving her own weapon in the air.

"Right, let's go before Bakir has time to get reinforcements; two of the guards have fled and Maeva is hiding upstairs. Leave her there."

"We're right behind you," said Tom, catching hold of Minnah as they rushed out into the hallway. Roger stumbled over one of two bodies lying on the floor just by the open front door. One appeared to be in a French policeman's uniform. It was probably that incident more than any other that determined him to get back to Brisbane as fast as possible. His family became more important than ever. It was as though the desire to buy property on the Côte d'Azur had never entered his mind. They were in a car speeding away from 'their imprisonment' before Tom realized that Amadullah was not the driver.

"Where's Amadullah?"

"He had some tidying up to do," said Minnah. "I'm not entirely sure what he meant. He's behind us, in another car."

The trip back to the hotel in Marseille took much less time than the previous trips Minnah and Tom had experienced, and a great deal more chatter. Roger's relief was easy to see. He was off back home as soon as he could catch a plane out of the crazy place. He hoped Tom and Minnah would be safe. As it was, he still wasn't sure why they were in Marseille. The whole thing was an interlude he could have done without.

They were met by a very unhappy Commissaire.

"Paris insists we leave Bakir alone. The crazy Americans claim he is too important to their cause in Afghanistan. So he gets a free ride."

"You know Grimaud was Bakir's man?"

"I do now, Amadullah, but I can't find him. I haven't seen him for two days."

"You won't either. He was with Bakir's men who were guarding the prisoners. Unfortunately, he was killed in our rescue. One of my men shot him. I'm sorry."

"Don't be, you've saved me doing something worse."

Tom was astonished, "I can't believe it. Bakir gets police protection. The world's gone mad. Do those idiotic bureaucrats in Paris know about Bakir's attempt to hold us?"

"No, not yet, but it won't make any difference. They know he's a mad dog but international 'diplomacy' rules, whatever that is."

"So what are you going to do?"

"Minnah, I'm going to do what I'm told to do. I've already pushed the boundaries. I have no choice."

"So that's it then," Minnah was angry.

Slowly it become evident to everyone that Amadullah had said very little. They all looked in his direction but he said nothing as he unhurriedly rose from his seat and quietly left the room. The others were at a loss; no one had any idea how to respond. Even Minnah was troubled by her brother's action.

"I can hardly blame Amadullah," said Bartholdi. "He must be extraordinarily angry. God knows what he'll do now. I certainly don't want to know."

"The truth is we all know," said Minnah quietly. "If we are going to appeal to God, I think it should be a prayer that Amadullah remains rational and that he is not consumed by hatred."

"I wouldn't blame the man if he blew Bakir's brains out."

But, as it happened, there was little chance of that. Bakir had gone to ground. Even Amadullah, as everyone would discover, had no idea where he was.

XLIV

Having received no instructions to do otherwise, Tom and Minnah returned to their hotel. But that was hardly an imposition. Their continuing physical closeness and the intensity of events had not been without effect. Both Afghanistan and Australia seemed a world away, and a long time ago. The immediacy of their growing dependence on each other was agreeably addictive. Bakir's triumph had brought them closer together.

"Minnah, I have a suggestion," Tom sounded seriously awkward or awkwardly serious. One or the other, he was uncertain.

"Have you, Tom?" Minnah wore such a lovely, mocking smile.

"Yes, I have."

"Well, let me hear it."

"Why don't we get married? After all, we've had a honeymoon and, in the interests of good order, shouldn't we balance things out?"

"Tom, do you really understand what you're asking?"

"No, but does that matter?"

"It might be a bit tricky." Tom was unsure whether Minnah was serious or teasing. "I'm not sure you would qualify for a *Jusificatif de Domicile*."

"What's that?"

"Something to prove you live in France. And you will need a medical certificate and a *Certificat de Celibrat*. We French Afghans have to be careful, we just can't go off and marry any old person."

Tom laughed. He knew the absurdity of their position was

relieved by growing affection and the emerging certainty of love. In spite of the beginning, they were now in a world that had been designed for them. Tom found it difficult to speak with the kind of confidence he would have liked, but he was becoming sensitive to the possibility of being guided by a greater power. The explosion of crazy action that had consumed him since his arrival in France had changed so much. Of course, in a way that was a banal observation to make, but that made it no less true. He struggled to find a satisfactory word. Was it perspective or something else? Vision, maybe that was better. His vision had widened, without losing any of his hope. It was kind of redemptive, really. That's what it was.

"Tom, I'm a Muslim fornicator and, according to Islam, already bound to an unbeliever. Maybe you're right, we should get the French government to give us its blessing because Islam will not, and, even worse, Amadullah may not."

It was a new day. Tom didn't reply immediately to Minnah's confession and suggestion. They understood, without a reply. It was not at all modern, and in a way impossible. Both were dependent mortal creatures in need of God's help. It was that oneness of spirit, which they understood perfectly well, that would make marriage inevitable.

"Minnah, I'm not sure whether you've said 'yes' or 'no'. The truth is I know what you'll say. But, before you answer, let me say, in case you've missed it, I've never met a woman I respect and love as much as you. We've grown up in hostile worlds, and yet here we are closer than I would have ever believed possible."

"Tom, my darling man, yes, I will marry you. I would have wanted to live with you even if you had not asked me to marry you. Can you imagine that? But you have asked, and that makes me very happy. Marriage is profoundly significant for me. I'm not, just in case you were misled, a modern woman."

"I know, Minnah, I know. It's no small deal for me either. I guess it's the promises that one makes. Love promises readily and rashly, I think. But here is the amazing thing... you're the first woman since my mother that I have really trusted and respected all at once. Trusting you is actually exciting."

"Tom, I don't know what to say. Not many women have heard their lover say what you've just said to me. I hope, with all that is within me, your trust will never be deceived."

Something unusual was going on, and so soon after Kaye's death. Tom couldn't make complete sense of it, but he felt favoured in some way. Sure, Minnah was a magnificent creature and her sexual power was beguiling. That, by itself, was enough to gain his devotion. But he was conscious of much more. Minnah gave birth to a peace that was at once, spiritual and physical. Just thinking about her made him feel better; even his digestion seemed to improve. But that was hardly a surprise. He had always been sympathetic to the claim that contact with the sublime had a positive influence on bodily functions. Prayer was not a vain exercise. Unless he misunderstood Islam completely, Minnah was better than her religion and yet it was her religion that had initially shaped her.

XLV

Nothing in either Tom's or Minnah's mind would have been of interest to Bakir. Amadullah had been a complete surprise, and that angered him. And now that woman had slipped from his grasp; an eventually particularly galling. The temptation was to permit the desire for revenge to side-track him. It was critical that he didn't lose the confidence of the Americans. He had to reassure them that leaving arms in his care was to the benefit of both. The US hierarchy in Afghanistan needed reminding that he was saving them millions of dollars; that he was trustworthy and influential. Without a doubt, he could contribute greatly to stability, especially around Kabul.

This time he would fly out of Algiers to Afghanistan. The trick was to convince the French and Amadullah he was not going there. He would send the 'Shark' to Alexandria and get the word out he was on board. And there had to be a convincing reason for his visit to Alexandria. The French police had always suspected that Bakir had been responsible for recruiting the suicide bomber who blew himself up outside a church in the Sidi Bechr district, killing twenty people and injuring nearly seventy. He had been careful not to go to Alexandria, but now an apparent visit would set the Commissaire thinking.

Bakir was right, the Commissaire did think there was something going on in Egypt, but he was hamstrung. Bakir was now a protected thug and Fabien's relationships with Alexandria were not good, so there was little he could do except watch. Amadullah was either unable or unwilling to help, and that was annoying. But then, he could hardly blame him. Every attempt that had been made by his office to get Bakir had been a humiliating failure. There was no justice in the world but it had not always seemed that way. In his undergraduate days with Amadullah, both had been quite certain that justice would prevail and the tyrant, whoever it was at the time, would be brought down. But now appeasement with the tyrant was making work impossible in a county rapidly losing its way. To whom could he appeal? The self-righteous bureaucrats in Paris were lost in their ideological flimsiness and need to placate the enemy.

Fabien leaned back on his chair with both hands behind his head and looked out across the bay to Notre Dame de la Garde; he wondered what Mary made of it all. He remained Catholic enough to feel something of the anguish that he imagined God might feel for his hard-hearted creation. Something caught in his throat and he nearly wept. He had not wept since his first and lovely love Sophie, rejected him. Misery was a slow flowing river through his chest and then the tears. He found a strange and unexpected solace in his tears when they came, although he wasn't sure whether he wept for himself and his own failure or for France.

It was tempting for years of toil to be reduced to a hopeless bleakness. Idealism and law enforcement in a complicated world were unhappy collaborators. That was hardly news, but knowing something and experiencing it were very different. There was no inflammation until after the injury. For a brief period, Fabien flirted with a raging bitterness, but then it dawned on him the heartening truth: hope is what keeps us alive. Lose hope and Bakir had won, not just a few battles, but the whole war. That was the point. France was fighting for its life and so few understood. He had a wife and children he loved and, better still, they loved him.

XLVI

Bakir knew he was safe for a while. His intelligence had suffered a big hit when his inside man in Marseille had been shot by Amadullah; that was certainly a serious setback. Nevertheless, he still had friends in Paris and in the Afghan military, so a few days in Marseille attending to lose ends would be no problem. Indeed, the more normal his life appeared, the less likely he would be to lose the support of his sympathisers. He would spend time on his fruit importing business and then get the arms off to the respective purchasers.

By the end of the week, Bakir took the overnight ferry from Marseille to Algiers using his clean-shaven passport of Ahmed Tabari. It was convenient and safer to keep his first name and his beard would be reasonably presentable by the time he got to Kabul. He assumed he would be at least a week in Algiers. It was over a month since he had visited his ailing mother; that was too long.

When his father left Ahmed and his sisters alone with their mother, Ahmed was quite sure that Allah was a middle-aged woman worn down by work and concern for her children. As he grew older Allah became a kind of phantom who made unreasonable demands on his adolescent conscience. But, like most young men, he changed, and, driven by a confusing jumble of guilt and affection, became his mother's protector.

Yasmin Bakir was seventy-six and heart-broken. Ahmed had provided her with a 'lovely' apartment in Garidi, for which she was thankful. There was a serious housing shortage in Algiers and mortgages were almost impossible to get. Cash was the winner and her son had plenty of that. Indeed, she was a major beneficiary of his largesse. But Yasmin knew that Ahmed was an arms dealer and responsible for the deaths of many. A faithful Muslim, she prayed for her son but the anguish of her grieving never left her. Neither she nor her son could talk about what was troubling both their minds; a great and terrible chasm had opened up between them. And yet, Yasmin was always pleased to see her benefactor son; not because he was her provider, but because he was her son.

Bakir would spend a couple of hours with his mother every day he was in Algiers. And each day he would wander around the Kasbah, remembering his childhood in the old house on Said Kadi. But neither the visits to his mother nor the nostalgic ramblings in the decaying Kasbah were comforting. Amadullah and Minnah interfered with everything he tried to think about. Even the thought of his next meeting with his friends in the US military could not dampen his frustration. Amadullah had made him look like a fool. They were worse than dhimmis, much worse. Muhammad was the supreme master at war and neither of the apostates understood that. The Prophet's great insight was that he understood that the waging of war was about control over the mind, heart, politics, religion as well as over the body. Jihad was complete and total war; a war that began with the revelation of Islam. The use of force was as sophisticated as it was subtle.

Bakir had convinced himself that all nations of the world must eventually submit to Islam because Allah had declared it so. Islam must rule the world. If the unbelievers do not submit, then violence is the necessary self-inflicted consequence. They have no one to blame but themselves. Refusal to submit is an offence against Allah therefore the unbelievers are guilty initiators and the real perpetrators of violence. All Jihad is defensive. It was that insight into Jihad that came to Ahmed with such clarity for the first time when he was in his mid-twenties. Jihad was a 'holy war', but he had to struggle within himself to bring that war to a victorious end. And that was what he was trying to do. 'The man who fights to make Islam dominant is the man who fights for Allah's cause'.

There was no way people in the West could understand him. The fools didn't even understand their own history. Muhammad was the greatest military conqueror ever. He didn't establish an empire that lasted a mere one thousand years. He began a process of war that was still going on after nearly fifteen hundred years. The Gates of Vienna would swing open again, and soon.

In spite of that glorious vision, it was impossible for Bakir to even contemplate the shallowness of his judgement of Minnah. He would never understand Amadullah's human decency. Minnah, however, did understand the totality of Islam, and that's what frightened her. She was a woman and second class. But that was not why she was finally a self-declared apostate. The real reason was that Islam had no coherent theology of forgiveness or grace. God had put all men and women in the same needy world. They were all sinners who needed to be saved from themselves. She was one of those women. That was the 'Aha' moment that ushered her into new life. Either Muhammad or Jesus is Lord; she had chosen Jesus. For Minnah, there was no middle way.

XLVII

The third day Bakir was in Algiers, he drove to the Grand Mosque for sunrise prayer at 5:53 am. It was the first time for months he had entered a mosque to pray. With hundreds of other men, he turned towards Mecca, bowed down, and prayed. He raised his hands and began Selah. His duty was clearer than ever. Amadullah and Minnah had to be punished because they were the enemies of Muhammad, so Kabul would have to wait. He wanted the apostates dead and he wanted to be Allah's instrument in dispensing that special justice.

Ahmed was relishing a change in his character without understanding its nature. It had been such a short step from pragmatic self-interest to purveyor of Allah's justice. It was thrilling to have one's desires approved by the Holy Prophet and Allah. It made one bold and vigilant. He said an awkward goodbye to his mother and caught the ferry back to Marseille. He needed an uninterrupted time alone to plan his strategy. This time there would be no slipup.

Bakir was delighted with his own thoughts on the trip back to Marseille. Things were falling into place rather nicely. Minnah was still in the hotel with the Australian, who would not be the most satisfying of collateral damage. That was somewhat unfortunate but compromise was not part of Bakir's philosophy, he lived in an either/or world. Amadullah was the problem, because he had disappeared. Bakir's minions had failed to find him anywhere, and that murkiness was unsettling. He liked his enemies in his clear line of vision at all times because it leads to assurance and a certain coolness in delivering the *coup de grâce.* So, the first decision had to be made. Did he go ahead and abduct Minnah and her Australian paramour and use her to flush Amadullah out of the shadows, or did he wait? There was no question. If he waited too long Amadullah could get the upper hand because there was every chance his quarry would discover where he was. Bakir, for the first time ever, made every attempt to conceal his return to Marseille.

The first move had to be made. Success was almost certain. As it turned out, it was more certain than he had imagined. With the help of two of his protectors, he had Minnah and Tom tucked away safely in one of his 'safe houses' a few kilometres from the centre of Aix less than a day after his arrival. It was all ridiculously easy. They had been 'captured' in their bedroom after a late breakfast. One of Bakir's underlings had simply managed to obtain a key card from reception. Minnah was taken down to a waiting car first, having been threatened with Tom's death should she 'misbehave'. Tom was given the same story, so, like Minnah, he went quietly. They travelled to Aix in different cars while no attempt was made to conceal the route they were taking. If Tom didn't understand the significance of that, Minnah did. This was their last ride.

Bakir was jubilant at the simplicity of the turn of events in his favour. Everyone had underestimated him again. Amadullah would almost certainly turn up somewhere in some kind of mindless attempt to rescue his apostate sister and her loving unbeliever. He would not be thinking clearly and would make silly mistakes. In the meantime, however, Minnah and Tom had to be kept alive for as long as necessary and there was to be no final reprieve for Tom. They were locked into one room in a house somewhere in the old town. Fortunately, some civilised behaviour was possible; they had basic toilet facilities.

"This resembles a women's prison more than anything else I can think of. I wonder who else has been here; Kaye, perhaps?"

Minnah instantly doubted the wisdom of mentioning Kaye. But she needn't have worried. Tom's response was even, almost relaxed.

"I doubt it. Bakir doesn't suffer fools or unfaithful women with anything like compassion. Kaye's death in Brignoles was the consequence of her first and only betrayal. Something must have happened that caused her to see Bakir as he really is. Perhaps she understood that any sexual liaison with him was likely to be a one-way street. It's more than likely she simply became afraid."

"You know what he's up to now, of course."

"I do. He's using us to flush out Amadullah."

"And, Tom, that's exactly what will happen. There is no way he will leave us here. I just hope he doesn't get angry and do something silly."

They had been in the room for less than an hour when Bakir came to visit them. He was smiling like a poker player with a full house after he had collected his winnings. This was, in fact, not too far from the truth.

"Well, my friends, I suspect this could well be the last time we meet. It's been a great game, has it not?"

"Has?" Minnah was not intimidated by the smugness only partially masked by Bakir's jollity. "I know why we're here. It's so obvious a child could guess it. You expect Amadullah to come charging into this room, on a white horse no doubt."

"Ah yes, I expect him to come, but not charging. I suspect he will be *sans cheval*."

"Monsieur Bakir, as this is to be the last time we meet, may I ask you a question?" Tom tried very hard to sound civil.

"Tom, by all means. I would be disappointed if you didn't."

"What do you gain by our death?"

"Ah, not quite the question I expected. But I will tell you."

Bakir's sense of superiority appalled Minnah. The man was the worst kind of human being: handsome, charming, and conceited, entirely without compassion. His lust for power was intensely ugly.

"It's all too simple. You're an unbeliever who stands in my way. Minnah is an apostate who must die. She will know that."

Bakir meant what he said. Tom imagined, or maybe it was wishful thinking, a suggestion of sham regret in Bakir's voice. Something like a veterinarian might parrot as he put down the family pooch. It was something to be regretted, but necessary to improve the world and easily forgotten tomorrow.

"It's inevitable. There will be no peace in the world until every knee bows to Allah."

Bakir smiled slightly, but Tom could not work out what such a contrived facial action might mean. Was Kaye's killer pretending to live out an enculturated fantasy, or did he really believe what he had said? Somebody was going to be disappointed. He remembered what he had been taught as a child. 'At the name of Jesus every knee will bow, in heaven, on earth and under the earth.' Minnah, the apostate, was clearer than he was on that outcome.

"The days of the Kafir are numbered," Bakir was preaching again. "You've had your day of over-reaching. Europe is submitting in its own blustering way to the Prophet. Democracy and loss of vision will always end in tears."

"Perhaps, but I hope not."

"Hope by all means, my friend, but your hope is vain. Europe will be ours in a generation."

Tom was mute in the face of such unashamed arrogance. He had no idea how to respond to such a risible claim from a man he had learned to despise. And yet, if he was honest and forced to describe Western Europe, ennui was the first word that came to mind. That was not encouraging. Even Minnah, certainly with a different set of motivations, claimed that France was like a museum living off borrowed time and hollowed-out beliefs.

More than any other time in his life, Tom wanted to live. He wanted to live to make amends and declare his thankfulness. He had lived such a privileged life. He had been taught that the human heart is a devious beast and even now he was uncertain how honest he was being with himself. He wasn't even sure that it was possible to be intellectually honest. He'd never been in the business of finding himself; it was too much like touchy-feely nonsense.

It came, not as a flash of insight from heaven but rather it just simply came. Tom realised why Minnah had been so overwhelmed by the command to love your enemies. For her it must have been like a whack on the back of the head. Forgiving one's enemies must have seemed like a declaration of folly. And yet, she now claimed that forgiveness. She had shed the tears that made love possible. She forgave because she had been forgiven. It was like being healed of a deadly cancer and then wanting every other sufferer to be healed as well. Minnah understood better than he did. It was not language he could ever bring himself to use in public. But how would it be possible to explain her any other way?

"Ah, I see you have no answer, Tom."

"I do, but I would be wasting my time because you wouldn't understand."

"No, try me. I might surprise you."

"I suspect, even although a mere unbeliever speaks, you will still get angry."

"I doubt it. The winner does not need to humiliate himself before the vanquished."

"You would have control of our minds and hearts by first enslaving our bodies. Power is your sport. I'm not entirely qualified to say so, but you have to be Islam at its very worst. I know it can be better because I know and love Minnah and Amadullah."

It was Bakir's turn to be silent. His eyes mocked both his captives. He turned quickly and left the room. The lock clicked into place as he shut the door.

XLVIII

It was difficult for Amadullah to accept the desperate nature of the situation he found himself in. Bakir had his sister and Tom. He was expected to rush in and rescue them. Bakir's cronies would be waiting in the house salivating with anticipation. It had been easy, too easy, to find out where they were, and the place was not too difficult to get into. Bakir was challenging Amadullah to come and play the rescuer. So why not go to Fabien? The police could get into the house as easily as he could and Bakir was in no position to resist them. Laissez-faire had its limitations even if it was sponsored by the Americans and Paris. They could be rescued and Bakir might still be able to keep his nose clean. But this this was his final opportunity. Amadullah had an account to settle and he was going to do it his way.

But how? That was the issue. Somehow a diversionary tactic was needed. The minders in the house had to be distracted in some way. Bakir would probably not be there, which was unfortunate; he would have to wait for another day.

Task number one was for Amadullah was to find out how many minders were in the house and get some idea of the layout. He didn't have the comfort of time so he gave himself five days to watch the house and assess what action to take. Bakir could become impatient.

The weather was getting colder and that gave him his first idea. He could wrap up and spend time in a little café across the road. And for the first time in his life he would make use of some elementary disguise. Each morning he would dress a little differently. It was tedious but they would be watching out for him and he had to surprise them somehow. He could not afford to be recognised, so he would watch the house irregularly, a couple of hours here and an hour there. During the night, he would have his two friends, Mahad and Hassan, watch from their car until the early hours of the morning. It was important that everyone got plenty of sleep.

The irregularity had its weaknesses but it had the significant advantage of making it harder for Bakir or the minders to discover either him or his friends. Over the period of five days he should have a reasonable idea of how many were in the house. It was a risk, but necessary. To blend in he would take his computer and look like any local business man. Mahad and Hassan would visit him from time to time to apparently discuss whatever it was a businessman would discuss. It was important that he was inconspicuous to the rest of the café's clientele.

On the first day, Amadullah watched for seven hours with a two-hour break to change his clothes. Two men he didn't recognize left the house during the morning but he saw only one return. No one entered or left during the afternoon or on the second day. A pity he thought, because, at great sacrifice, he had shaved his beard completely. On the third day, a woman he recognized entered the house; it was Maeva.

She didn't leave the house either that day or the next. Consequently, Amadullah worked on the assumption that he had two men and Maeva to contend with. But where was Bakir? Whatever the case, he would have to act soon. Minnah was in mounting danger as the hours passed. Bakir would be convinced that her death was a justified execution. He knew that Bakir would not be able to resist the temptation to impose justice if he thought his prey was not going to show.

For three days, Mahad had been working out of the Mairie to get the plans of Bakir's 'safe house'. The task was not made easy because the house was not in Bakir's name, and the final plans for renovation in 2008 had either not been filed or lost. Eventually, after much persuasion and a 'fee' of fifty euros, an interim plan was discovered. It had to do, even though they could not be sure of its accuracy. Amadullah wasn't sure how relevant it was, but the house plans bore Maeva's signature.

Amadullah and Mahad planned to enter the house at 0:300 hours, the next morning, when everyone, they hoped, would be sleeping most deeply. That was the theory. Hassan would remain at the front door in case reinforcements of some kind were called for. The point of entry for Amadullah and Mahad would be a door on the west side that looked out onto a narrow street, Rue des Magnans. They would just have to neutralise any cameras as they went.

If Mahad had done his homework properly, they had the right keys for that particular door. The interim plan had the locks and latches itemised. But they were unsure if there were any bolts or latches on the inside that could not be opened from the outside. It was another unknown they would have to attend to at the time. If there were locks on the inside, it would make silent entry impossible.

Amadullah was not happy with their plans. There were too many chances for things to go wrong, but he did have one big card up his sleeve. He was forced to keep it there, and not reveal it to either Mahad or Hassan, until the last moment. Indeed, without the card he would not have acted.

The avenging liberators met on Rue des Magnans at 0:300 hours. Each man was carrying a Smith and Wesson 9mm with Liberty Infiniti suppressors and one extra clip. Amadullah was convinced that if they had to use more the cause would be lost. Hassan walked back to the main door and Mahad inserted and turned both keys in each lock of the door on the alleyway. A nearby orange street light made it unnecessary for them to use their flashlights. There was no click, but both locks yielded to the keys.

Entering the house was far too easy. Amadullah was apprehensive. There were no inside locks. He was sweating in spite of the cool night air. He entered first and the two men walked quietly for six or seven metres to an unlocked door. They could see no surveillance cameras.

Forced to use their flashlights, they entered a square internal room with no windows, but there was a door on two sides of the room. Light shone from under one of them. Ever since Amadullah managed to get the plans of the house, he knew that discovering the room where Tom and Minnah were held could be his greatest problem. He had no idea which door they were behind.

"Let's try the door with the light," whispered Amadullah.

"Right."

Mahad slowly pressed down on the handle of the unlocked door and opened it. Inside they were met with a glaring light shining directly into their eyes. It was impossible to see anything. The glaring light faded, the room was flooded with a soft white glow that might have existed for the commencement of a stage play; which is what it was for Bakir. He was sitting on a large black leather chair like a film director, smiling benignly at his visitors.

"Welcome, Amadullah and Mahad. Welcome to our little house. I can't believe how easy you have made everything for me. I knew you would come but, dear me, you've been remarkably amateurish. I'm very sorry but we've had to dispose of your friend waiting at the front door. He was quite vulgar, failing to knock."

"Where's Minnah?" Amadullah couldn't help himself. He pointed his Smith and Wesson straight at Bakir's chest.

"Put your guns down, both of you. There're two armed men behind you. By all means, have a look."

Amadullah recognized two of the men he had seen entering the house over the previous days. Both were armed, pointing their weapons directly at him and Mahad.

"You could shoot now and perhaps kill me, but you too would die and, more important, so would your sister and her lover. Did you know that the good doctor was her loving Kafir?" Bakir was mocking Amadullah, and certainly enjoying himself.

"Put your weapons down and I'll take you to see my prisoners.

I took the liberty to tell them you would be here soon. I discovered you had been to the Mairie making enquiries about this house. You should have looked at the back of the door where you entered. You would have noticed the locks had been removed. I didn't want to make it all too hard for you."

Amadullah could scarcely suppress his fury at Bakir's gloating. He had gone against his better judgement and rushed things. Although, right at that moment, he had no idea what else he could have done. A surge of bitter hatred rose in his gorge. He imagined he could taste the bile of loathing. He placed his weapon on an adjacent table; Mahad followed his lead.

"I have been looking forward for some time now to having you and Minnah together in the same room, Amadullah. So, let's go and see her and Tom; they should be wide awake by now. They are being looked after by a mutual friend. I'm sure you will recognize her."

"I already know, it's Maeva," said Amadullah gently.

"Oh, that is most interesting. How so?"

"Ah, I have my helpers too. I'm not alone."

"I suppose not, but no matter now. Your helpers will be no use to you."

Bakir led his two captives down another corridor into a large bedroom. His two defenders followed in the rear. Minnah and Tom were looking very tired, sitting on wooden chairs opposite each other. Bakir had obviously told them to expect visitors. Both were in bathrobes, no doubt, assumed Amadullah, supplied by the generosity of the management. Minnah rose quickly and embraced her brother. If she spoke only Amadullah heard her. Maeva was standing by a door on the far side of the room. She remained silent and, if Amadullah's instinct was right, looking unusually serious.

It was clear now what Bakir had planned. He had his enemies in one room at his mercy; although in this case 'mercy' was quite the wrong word.

"This room is triple glazed and insulated for sound. The windows are small anyway." He took the weapon from one of his minders and attached a silencer. He looked first at Amadullah, demanding that he kneel. "This time, Tom, I'm afraid, your enterprise will not help."

Bakir was so unfazed, so lacking in any emotion, that Tom couldn't quite grasp the sense of what he was actually experiencing. Minnah knew exactly what was going on. Bakir would 'execute' her brother first and then Tom. She would be last because she had to see what her apostasy had caused. Justice demanded she watch the execution of her brother and 'husband'. Tom was the first to speak because his knowledge of the immediate dynamic was the least developed. Unlike the others, he had no experience to prepare for such a finale.

"What are you doing? For God's sake! Killing a man in cold blood?!" 'Cold blood' sounded so hackneyed, but what else could he say? He thought of vicious, but couldn't quite get it out.

"Yes, you are right. It is for God's sake. I am doing the work of Allah."

Then, without a glance even in Tom's direction, he pointed the weapon so close to Amadullah's head the barrel was almost touching. He looked directly at Minnah, who seemed to stare back at him like someone hypnotized. Tom shut his eyes before he heard two shots and then another. It took him a moment to register that the sound came from close to his left ear. He opened his eyes to see a look of surprised amazement on Bakir's face. The gun slid from his hand as he very slowly collapsed forward onto the floor.

The bad dream dissolved and everything went crazy. Amadullah was fighting the astonished unarmed guard. Then another shot exploded right beside Tom, and a wounded armed guard staggered forward and fell against Minnah. She pushed him aside quickly as his blood stained her robe. It took her exactly three steps to pounce on Amadullah's adversary and drag him to the floor. Hassan, at last, caught up with the action and snatched Bakir's weapon from the floor and fired one bullet into the upper leg of Amadullah's assailant. Silence and then the moaning of the wounded guard was the only remaining sound.

Slowly, everyone absorbed what had happened. Maeva had shot Bakir. Minnah's first thoughts were what an ignominious and just end for such a brute. Killed by a woman he had degraded, misunderstood, and underrated. He would have had no idea why she had learned to hate him. But she did. Bakir had used her just like he had used so many other women. Silently, and just for a moment, Minnah revelled in the just deliciousness of Bakir's death at the hand of a woman.

Only Amadullah had known the detail of the affair that Minnah had suspected, and that it had lasted seven intense weeks. During that time, Bakir had given Maeva many thousands of euros and promised more. In return she had acted as lover and hostess to his comrades in arms. Indeed, he had called them that thinking the ambiguity amusing. Maeva, at the time, had found it equally amusing. That Bakir was an arms dealer of some kind didn't seem to matter.

But he had dumped her. There was no explanation, although Maeva knew he had found another woman. Several weeks passed before she discovered she had been thrown over for Kaye. She was furious. In the heat of their so-called affair he had used her to help undermine Kaye's defences. Maeva found it too challenging to confront Bakir immediately. Instead she seethed daily and planned her revenge like a latter-day Medea.

There was a certain satisfaction in being the jilted lover of an international arms dealer. Her first thought was to offer herself to the police as an informer and, as she was on bail, that was an easy option. She wanted to be the direct cause of Bakir's punishment. Right up to the time she saw Bakir put the barrel of his minder's pistol on Amadullah's temple, she had wondered how she would act.

Maeva's reaction was inevitable. The bullets from her Beretta blasted a bloody hole in Bakir's chest. It was the consummation of all her plans. In that mood of vague abstraction, she had dreamed of killing her sometime lover. But up to that moment she had always believed it too difficult, either to gain the courage or to have the necessary skill. But now the immediate imposed its own ultimatum and dissolved her fear. She didn't consider any other possibility as she squeezed the trigger twice and then once again as Bakir tried to speak. She gazed transfixed as the blood seeped from Bakir's wounds onto his shirt. It would be some time before she would admit it, but she found it exhilarating to watch Bakir slide slowly onto the floor. It was like being miraculously healed from a terminal disease.

XLIX

It wasn't until early the following morning that Amadullah, Minnah, Maeva, and Tom found themselves in the Commissaire's office. Fabien was caught between his anger and his relief that Bakir was dead.

This wasn't the first time he had worked with civilians at the expense of some of his colleagues. The progress and result had been similar. There had been the inevitable frustration and disappointment, but he had made new friends. There had been that remarkable funeral at the chateau near Carcassonne. Günter Zeimer, the ex-Stasi convert, had been shot by his crazy Marxist half-brother. Fabien had found himself engrossed in the funeral's consequences for months afterwards. Günter was dead but avenged by his lover and ex-Stasi colleague, the beautiful Hannah who had shot dead Günter's assassin. He could still remember the terrible cry from Hannah as she knelt over her dying lover. How easily could that mad drama have been repeated by Minnah?

Fabien had continued to visit Bernard Lemercier, the owner of the chateau and his wife, until his promotion to Marseille. For a while he had fancied Lemercier's daughter, Sylvie. He thought he was in with a chance, but he was too slow. She went off to Chicago with her American friend. Bartholdi remembered them all with an affection that gave him a pleasure that was almost spiritual. The friendships had sneaked up on him and the death of the ex-Stasi Christian was profoundly challenging. He had never really managed to disconnect himself from the Catholicism of his mother and her emotional landscape.

It was his experience in Carcassonne that gave him the nerve to continue working with Kaye even when she seemed to have sold out to Bakir. He had not found her death easy to bear. He blamed himself for not being sharp enough. And now Minnah and Tom very nearly suffered the same fate, and would have had it not been for Maeva. What was it with all these women in his life?

"Okay, Bakir was Hydra-headed and his coterie is still out there."

Maeva warmed to the image with renewed confidence. "Yes, but we can scorch the stump. The heads won't regrow. I know many of his friends and how he kept in contact with them. Commissaire you're the new Heracles to scorch the stumps."

Fabien ignored the straining allusion, but he could not believe his luck in spite of a potential mess on his hands. Bakir was high profile, so Paris would have to be informed quickly. The legal bureaucrats would be swarming all over the place only hours after he sent in his report. He was certainly not going to tell them immediately; he needed twelve hours. He must act before the Islamophobes and the Islamophiles fought it out to put their own spin on the news. Fabien needed to act before he was thwarted once again. There must be no more frustrating failures, and no more moles.

"Right, tell me everything you have learned, Maeva. I'll do all I can for you, although I suspect you're going to come out of this smelling sweeter than any of us if your information is as good as I hope."

The new Tom entered the conversation. Relief gave him confidence. "Wherever Bakir is now, sans virgins for sure, he must be indulging in the worst kind of self-flagellation. Brought down by a woman he cast aside, there's an irony there somewhere; a kind of justice. And his gang brought down too; amazing. I'm beginning to understand, and even enjoy, the wide new landscape I've been dropped into. It's satisfying, but that it was so unexpected is the real delight."

For the next two hours, Tom had plenty of time to think because he had the least to say. Only occasionally could he offer some piece of information or insight. Maeva and Amadullah were the stars;

Minnah the perceptive analyst. Mahad was not without his own surprise. Amadullah had known that Maeva was disenchanted with Bakir. That had been his wild card. They had met before Mahad and Amadullah had started to watch the house. Indeed, it was from Maeva that Amadullah learned where Tom and Minnah were being held. Unsurprisingly, she had insisted that Amadullah say nothing to anyone, not even Minnah, about his source. She was playing an unfamiliar and dangerous game.

The range and depth of Bakir's activities astounded Tom; that one man could have so much influence was hard to catch hold of. He had distributed arms and drugs worth billions of euros and had been either directly or indirectly responsible for the deaths of thousands of people. In theory, he knew that men like Bakir existed, but to be intimately involved in their lives and to learn everything first hand raised so many questions in his mind he felt overwhelmed.

Minnah's reactions were very different. She observed, with mounting satisfaction, that Maeva was savouring each of her revelations about Bakir and his minions. It would seem that revenge was indeed sweet. There had been a time when she would have envied Maeva, but now it was just as well the prize of revenge had fallen to her friend.

Maeva revealed where Bakir's largest training camp was and she was able to name four wealthy French citizens in Marseille and Menton who were involved in illegal arms distributions. Fabien moved rapidly. It took fewer than twelve hours from Maeva's first revelations to the arrests of the suspected terrorists in Menton and Marseille. But her gem was information relating to a planned bombing of the Pigalle Metro.

It was a crazy mix of avenging fundamentalism at its most murderous. In the usual doctrinaire fit of self-righteousness, the Pigalle had been chosen for its history of debauchery and because a local theatre was running a mild musical satire on Islam. It took the Paris police only two days to find and arrest the would-be bombers as they came out of a back-street sex shop on rue Victor Masse. The arrest outside the sex shop was deliberate. The police wanted to make the would-be bombers look like what they were: hypocrites.

It was the sex-shop arrest that sealed it for Fabien. He was a hero. Past frustration was forgotten as he bathed in more glory than he had ever imagined. There was even chatter about the Légion d'Honneur. Fabien joked he would be happy with the Ordre National du Mérite. The ribbon was blue; a colour he suited more than the red and green of the Légion d'Honneur. He was happy to be patient.

In the midst of all the adulatory tumult Fabien with his wife, Isabelle, Amadullah, Alessandra, Tom, and Minnah managed an exquisite meal at l'Epuisette. Tom could just understand some of the blurb…

Juste après le pont, perché sur son rocher, l'Epuisette offre une vue imprenable sur l'anse de Marseille. Tout autour, la mer Méditerranée d'un bleu profond, propose un spectacle sans cesse renouvelé.

They sat at a right angle to a large window, where everyone could see the bridge and the city.

"It really is an *imprenable vue*", declared Tom trying to impress, "and the sea really does have that Tyrian Hue."

'C'est parfait,' said Alessandra to Amadullah, as she smiled in the way that always hypnotised him. Tom sat between Minnah and Isabelle and across the table from Amadullah with Alessandra beside him. Fabien looked directly across the table to his wife. It was, Tom mused, a kind of last supper. 'A sweet sorrow and all that,' he thought.

Everyone, except Amadullah, drank champagne and consumed aperitifs for almost an hour before ordering any food or wine. They talked about Bakir, terrorism in France, Afghanistan, and everyone's future. They remembered Maeva and wondered how things would spin out for her. They captured a camaraderie that evening they all knew they would never have again.

"Tom, you order the first white, and I'll suggest a red," said Fabien.

"I'm flattered you trust a mere Australian with such a delicate task. I accept the challenge," he said a little too loudly. "Amazing, and in France too. The world is falling apart. I see a New Zealand Sauvignon at an absurd price."

"By all means, order it. Tonight, my expense account can go through the roof. I can't imagine it will last. I've got a lovely red from the Bourgogne in mind."

Although an uncertain future might have imposed itself on everyone around the table, they ignored its weight. The evening lapsed into a fog of agreeable and lubricated story telling. Minnah and Tom were in no doubt that they were in love in a very special way. Alessandra, given the opportunity, would have been quite prepared to declare she felt the same. She had no need; Amadullah whispered it in, as he said, her very lovely ear.

It was Fabien who remained most conscious of the evening's pathos. 'There was always something about the human condition,' he thought. Even now, in the midst of success and celebration, the seeds of leaving his friends were being planted. He loved Isabelle, but his children, at the times he didn't really want to remember, prompted in him something of the woman who had left him and her children. He could never speak about it; it just seemed, well, kind of sad. But the night was to be enjoyed, and he was determined to do just that.

"Tell me, Tom, where do you and Minnah go from here?" Fabien glanced at Minnah with a teasing smile.

"Well, that is some question. Afghanistan, Australia, or France maybe, but I can say we're going to get married," and then, with a quick glance in Amadullah's direction, "I hope we will." The moment she dreaded had come.

Minnah reached across the table and placed her hand over her brother's. She was going to ask him for something that he would find painfully difficult to answer. She had hoped to have found a more fitting time but here it was.

"Amadullah, my dearest brother," Minnah managed to fuse a

respectful formality with loving sincerity. And then her tone changed. Everyone at the table could see and approve the mystery, not unique to Islam, of respectful familial deference and sisterly love. "Please may Tom and I have your blessing? It's a lot to ask but it's just so important for me. You know that. I'm sorry to ask in such a public way, but it has just happened, believe me there's no deviousness here. It wasn't planned."

Everyone looked in Amadullah's direction. For a moment, he was nearly angry. He had expected Minnah's plea would come sooner or later, but he had not expected it to come with such emotional power. He looked at Alessandra. Her eyes told him exactly what she wanted. Tom, too, was looking straight at him. He remembered his friendship with Fabien. He loved his sister. She knew she was asking for some- thing that, he had been taught, was contrary to the will of Allah.

Only Minnah could have understood the distress that Amadul- lah would feel. It was beyond the wit of the others. They could only guess at the complexity and implications of Amadullah's battle. They could not understand that he was being asked to enter and question the heart of Islam.

It came to him from somewhere, perhaps from Minnah's new God, he was caught between the love of law and love's need of no law. His response would reveal, at least to Minnah, the difference between them in this world, and heaven too perhaps.

For the first time in his life, he struggled to embrace that differ- ence. There had to be something wrong with a faith that put rules before love and forgiveness. Rules would save neither him nor the sister he loved.

Amadullah smiled and put his hand on his sister's.

"Minnah, you have my blessing. Tom's a good man."

Everyone was silent. They all watched with relief and unabashed reverence. The salty tears flowed down Minnah's cheeks on to the white tablecloth. Tom knew he was watching something that some- day he just might comprehend.

For the moment, that understanding wasn't necessary. Minnah looked directly at him and gently squeezed his hand. He knew the sweet sign of victory in her smile and the love shining from her eyes.

Two Women: Two Worlds

by Alexander Logan

Sylvie Lemercier is an intelligent, attractive, and "sportive" forty-year-old whose husband, Nicholas, has just been murdered.

Born in rural New Zealand, she retains something of an appealing naïveté distilled by a discerning mind. But after his death, Sylvie discovers, with reluctant fascination, more about Nicholas than she ever could have imagined.

Nicholas and Sylvie meet the day the Berlin Wall came down when Sylvie was only twenty-one. "Her mind coveted the new politics as much as her body yearned for sexual adventure. Sylvie's optimistic sense of history had not yet ripened into any kind of caution. A sense of longing that she couldn't quite comprehend conspired with the moment. She welcomed the caresses that seduced her. Submission had never been so pleasurable." Nicolas turns out to be a womanizer who participated in art theft with ex-members of the infamous Stasi, the East German Secret Police.

He managed to stay just one step ahead of the law, but years later his past finally catches up. Sylvie receives an unexpected visit from a friend of Nicholas, revealing more unpalatable truths of her dead husband's past. She travels to France and Berlin, to discover yet even more secrets, ex-lovers and, ultimately, her husband's killer.

This explosive novel takes unexpected turns as it reaches its hopeful and poignant climax.